ZANOUBA

ZANOUBA

OUT EL KOULOUB

Translated and with an Introduction by
NAYRA ATIYA

SYRACUSE UNIVERSITY PRESS

I dedicate this translation to my daughter Katrina,
with love and admiration
and in appreciation of her courage and independence.

First Edition 1996
96 97 98 99 00 01   6 5 4 3 2 1

Zanouba was originally published in French in 1947 by Éditions Galli-mard, Paris.

The paper used in this publication meets the minimum requirements of American National Standard for Information Sciences—Permanence of Paper for Printed Library Materials, ANSI Z39.48-1984. ⊗™

Library of Congress Cataloging-in-Publication Data
Out el Kouloub.
    [Zanouba. English]
    Zanouba / Out el Kouloub ; translated and with an introduction by Nayra Atiya. — 1st ed.
      p.   cm.
    Translated from the French.
    ISBN 0-8156-2718-1 (alk. paper). — ISBN 0-8156-0408-4 (pbk. : alk. paper)
    I. Atiya, Nayra. II. Title.
PQ3989.2.O86Z3613   1996
843—dc20   96-21142

Manufactured in the United States of America

CONTENTS

TRANSLATOR'S
ACKNOWLEDGMENTS

I would like to extend belated but profound thanks to Eglal Ererra for facilitating negotiations with Gallimard in Paris, and to express my sincere appreciation to the following friends: Janet Abu Lughod for her guidance and unfailing support; Donette Atiyah, Karlan and Gary Sick and Mary Megalli for their steady encouragement; Amina Megalli for cheering me on with her creative electronic messages ("Zanouba, I once knew a girl called Zanouba . . ."); Deena Abu Lughod, for her willingness to help on the spur of the moment; Liliane Dammond for her ever present interest; Laila Abu Lughod for her generous suggestions of useful resource readings; Tim Mitchell for inviting me to share my work at New York University; Terry Williams for asking all of the questions which sharpen the writer's focus; and Melissa Solomon for tenderly and skillfully nurturing the writer in me. Also, very special thanks to Margaret Kornfeld. And heartfelt thanks to Mary Frank for the cover art.

I owe a very special debt of gratitude to Ragai Makar, director of the Middle East Library at the University of Utah, for bringing to my attention Sonia Ghattas's dissertation and much more. Also to Robert Alford for reviewing the entire final draft of *Zanouba* and for his editorial help, a generous gift of time, energy, and good cheer.

I am, as ever, eternally grateful to my mother, Lola, for her loving support in every way, moral and material. And, to my son, Adam, for discovering a place to write far from the madding crowd.

Last, but not least, very special thanks to my editor, Cynthia Maude-Gembler and, once again, to Asma el Bakri.

TRANSLATOR'S
INTRODUCTION

O ut el Kouloub el Demerdashiyya was descended from a prominent family who founded a Sufi order in Egypt bearing their name: El Tarika el Demerdashiyya. There is a paucity of information about Out el Kouloub herself, however, and available biographical details are at times conflicting. Her final years and death specifically appear shrouded in some mystery.

Still, Sonia Rezk Ghattas, in her 1979 doctoral dissertation for the University of California at Irvine entitled *Visages de Femmes Egyptiènnes: Etude Socio-Linguistique de L'Oeuvre de Out-el-Kouloub* does offer a valuable short chapter about some aspects of the author's life and lineage.

In four brief paragraphs in *Le Français en Egypte* (Beyrout, 1981), J.J. Luthi gives Out el Kouloub's dates as 1892 to 1968 and states that she died in Austria. In addition, a list of her writings and a superficial summary of who she was are included in this sketch.

In "Littérature romanèsque et éspace habité, un exemple d'analyse," an article looking at architecture in Out el Kouloub's novels (*Nouvelle Revue du CEDEJ,* Egypte/Monde Arabe no.6—2ieme trimestre 1991), Jean-Charles Depaule and Sawsan Noweir concur with Luthi's dates but hint at biographical "blanks and inaccuracies" in the synopsis.

Furthermore, they maintain that Out el Kouloub died in Italy.

Dr. Ghattas informs us that Out el Kouloub was born April 18, 1899, but mentions nothing about her death. The life history given in her dissertation is, nonetheless, the most comprehensive I have found. It has been my principal source for biographical notes on Out el Kouloub presented in this introduction.

Out el Kouloub's ancestor and the founder of the Tarika el Demerdashiyya, Abd el Elah el Demerdash el Moham-madi, was a member of the Turkish court of Sultan Kaed Bey. Abd el Elah is said to have died around the year 1517 and been buried in El Mohammad mosque in Cairo. One of his descendents, Abd el Rehim, born in 1853, was Out el Kouloub's father. He was head, Sheikh of the Tarika, until his death in 1930. Dr. Ghattas suggests that Abd el Rehim's first wife, Naima, a fifteen-year-old bride given him by Sul-tan Tewfik, became the prototype for Ramza's Circassian slave mother, Indje, in Out el Kouloub's novel *Ramza.*

Out el Kouloub was the only child of Abd el Rehim and his second wife, Zeynab Tawdeya, a woman of Morrocan-French heritage and a native of the city of Fez. It would seem that Zeynab was her husband's favorite and that their daughter was singularly dear to him. This might explain the unusual and exquisitely rendered bond between father and daughter described in *Ramza* as well as the sense of comfort that Out el Kouloub is said to have had in the company of men. It is interesting to note also that Zanouba, the female protagonist in *Zanouba,* is the diminutive for Zeynab, an affectionate appellation.

In discussing the orgins of the name el Demerdash, Dr. Ghattas proposes a derivation from the Turkish *Taymour Tach, fer et pierre,* (iron and stone). Also, *Taymour Lang, chef mongol qui boite,* (the Mongolian chief who limps). She also cites an Iranian legend which proclaims that Abd el Elah, after descending into the tomb of the Prophet, was struck dumb. She intimates that this event may have given rise to his designation, *Amir Tach, prince devenu fou et qui ne peut plus parler* (Prince grown mad and mute), and ultimately its recasting into Demerdash.

Out el Kouloub was educated at home from 1911 until she became a bride. In 1922 she was given in marriage by her father to Mustapha Mukhtar, a man of stature, an attorney to the king of Egypt, and a judge in the mixed tribunals. He was years her senior. Their conjugal home in Alexandria was located in the elite district of San Stephano, immortalized in Out el Kouloub's novel *Ramza*. It was demolished in 1947, coinciding with *Zanouba*'s publication, and sixteen years after the couple's divorce.

Five children were born to Mustapha Mukhtar and Out el Kouloub: Abd el Rehim, Mustapha, Ahmad, Zeynab, and Mohsen. When the couple divorced in 1931, the mother was awarded custody of their children, a remarkable decision which diverged from Muslim law and custom whereby the father would have been favored.

After her divorce Out el Kouloub diligently set out to further her children's education as well as her own. She is said to have studied privately with such distinguished personages as Larousse as well as other members of the Mission Française who were in Egypt at the time.

According to Dr. Ghattas the author was not only interested in literature but in the sciences and social sciences. Her personal library comprised some 10,000 volumes, a testament to her enlightenment. In 1935 she engaged Kamil Mohammad Ali Bey as her personal librarian, and in 1948 endowed her books to the University of Cairo where the library is said to be currently housed. Kamil Bey continued to administer her collection at the university until the 1960's.

Out el Kouloub possessed vast agricultural land holdings which she herself managed, including 1200 feddans of orchards. In *Zanouba* she describes Abd el Meguid's estate, the fruit trees he planted and lovingly nurtured himself in Matariyya, then outside Cairo city limits. Also, in the novel, a discussion of new varieties of fruit introduced into Egypt and planted on prosperous estates at the turn of the century suggests her personal experience as an agriculturalist.

Furthermore, Out el Kouloub owned considerable real estate in Cairo and Alexandria. The only one of her homes still standing is located in a Cairo quarter named after her family. It has been the dwelling of her son Ahmad who manages what remains of the estate of the Demerdashiyya while attempting to recover their sequestered properties. Additionally, in that same neighborhood, a faculty of medicine and hospital, the Demerdash Hospital, had been endowed by Out el Kouloub's father. Another of the author's palatial homes stood in the Kasr el Nil district of the capital. Some years after the 1952 Revolution it was seized by the government, razed to the ground, and replaced with a municipal building.

The author was often referred to in her day as "the richest woman in Egypt."

Dr. Ghattas writes that Out el Kouloub visited France, her preferred European country, on a regular basis between 1933 and 1939. In Paris she resided at the Hotel Continental where rooms 104 and 105 were yearly reserved for her use. During the time of the Second World War, when Europe was no longer accessible, she traveled to the Holy Lands and neighboring Arab countries where she was received by royalty and notables.

Basing themselves on P. J. Luizard's article "Le soufisme égyptien contemporain," (*Egypte/Monde arabe* 2-1990), Depaule and Noweir inform us that Out el Kouloub went into exile along with some members of her family when their extensive properties were confiscated by the revolutionary government of Gamal Abd el Nasser in 1961. They add that these family members resolved not to return home as long as President Nasser was in power. It would seem that Out el Kouloub died without ever seeing Egypt again.

Out el Kouloub considered herself a traditionalist and a devout Muslim, despite her Francophone orientation and her affinity for European culture (which was shared by contemporaries of her class sometimes to the exclusion of their own culture). Ramza reads an Arabic translation of the Iliad to her father and attends a performance of *Romeo and Juliet* in Arabic. She is also taught the Qur'an. The writings of John Stuart Mill, Richardson, Molière, and La Fontaine are devoured by the budding heroine, possibly Out el Kouloub herself. And, she is affected by the work of enlightened Egyptian thinkers. One night, hidden behind a curtain, the sixteen-year-old Ramza hears a young Kassem Amin condemn the nation's neglect to educate its women and endorse the pressing need to give them equal rights. The next morning she is thrilled to discover his treatise, *The Emancipation of Women* (1899), in her father's library. She and her friends commit parts of it to memory.

Out el Kouloub was most certainly inspired by the pronouncements of the nineteenth century Islamic modernist cleric, Sheikh Muhammad Abdu and the writings of the Coptic lawyer Murqus Fahmy. Sheikh Muhammad Abdu, who is also mentioned in *Ramza,* argued that the development of Egypt as a nation was impeded because Muslims failed to apply the true spirit of Islam to women's lives. And Murqus Fahmy stressed that Egypt would remain a backward nation so long as its womenfolk were not liberated.

It is clear that Out el Kouloub fully agreed with these remarkable men without losing sight of the importance of certain conventions. In her own life she demonstrated the possibilities of a happy marriage between liberal ideals and traditional moral values. While Ramza struggles for emancipation and develops a sense of fierce independence, Zanouba is cloaked in ignorance and is content and submissive.

Ramza, however, is also an example of how education and freedom in a repressive environment can lead to personal rebellion carried to harmful extremes. It is surely Out el Kouloub's conviction that is conveyed by Sheikh Abd el Moutei to Ramza when he says: "Our customs contain more wisdom than you think."

In *Zanouba* and in *Ramza* both Out el Kouloub depicts how ignorance breeds fears and misconceptions and perpetuates mindless superstition. Sitt Shafika, the trained physician who saves Zanouba's life after a miscarriage provoked by one of Abd el Meguid's jealous wives, is an upright Muslim who provides an image of educated and enlightened Egyptian womanhood. Perhaps it is she who is Out el Kouloub's ideal.

Out el Kouloub is a voice for moderation. While she acknowledges being nurtured by western culture and the broadminded ideals of some fellow Egyptians, she emphasizes her profound allegiance to her faith and her steadfast reliance on its values for guidance. In *La Nuit de la Destinée,* published in 1954 and dedicated to her father, she prefaces the novel with an exceptional autobiographical note:

> I was born [in a house] at the foot of a minaret . . . As soon as I was able to listen discerningly I heard the name of Allah pronounced by the Muezzin who called the faithful to prayer five times daily . . . In time, I traveled the world over and tasted of the most brilliant civilizations, but I never lost sight of my religious beliefs. Rather, these became ever more rooted in my heart as I matured. Every aspect of my life is marked by my unwavering attachment to Islam and my dedication to its teachings [my translation].

Keenly interested in literature and the theater, Out el Kouloub frequently held receptions attended by Egyptian and European intellectuals and artists of her time. Dr. Ghattas mentions among others the feminist Mary Kahil, Aziz

Sedki Pasha who became Prime Minister of Egypt, Ibrahim Madkour, and the beloved, blind author Taha Hussein as well as the Quranic scholar Sheikh el Maghrabi, who was her intimate friend. European men of letters such as Jean Cocteau, Georges Duhamel, Pierre Fresnay, and Jean Marais of the Comedie Française, to name a few, also attended her literary salons. However, even when Europeans were present at these gatherings, no alcoholic beverages were ever served in accordance with the precepts of Islam.

Although Out el Kouloub herself was said to be proficient in Arabic, she wrote in French, the language of preference of upper-class Egyptians of her time, and most of her novels are prefaced by French men of letters. For example, *Zanouba* is introduced by Jerome and Jean Tharaud of the Academie Française, *Ramza* by Henri Guillemin, *Harem* by Paul Morand, *Le Coffret Hindou* by Jean Cocteau, and *La Nuit de la Destinée* by Emile Dermenghem, to name a few. In most cases these prefaces are florid and somewhat superficial, imbued with a spirit of voyeurism typical of "orientalist" works. In the preface to *Zanouba,* for example, the first few lines hint at this:

> Who has not experienced the disappointment of being invited to an 'oriental' home [but of being excluded from even a glimpse at the intimacy of its workings] . . . You know that you will be received in the most gracious manner, yet . . . you enter the vestibule . . . you hear voices, the laughter of women and children . . . you are genuinely touched by the playful babble of this graceful little group which instantly evaporates the minute you are announced. . . . You spend a charming couple of hours with your host . . . when you take your leave you are overcome with a profound feeling of regret at having seen nothing of the intricacies of the family's life [my translation].

I sincerely felt that such prefaces, although not without some charm, were dated and added little to Out el Kou-

loub's novels. For this reason, I took the liberty of omitting
them from my renditions both of *Ramza* and of *Zanouba*.

Zanouba was published in Paris by the Librairie Galli-
mard in 1947 and circulated in French and Francophone circles. In "Cairo Memories," an article published in *East and
West,* the late Professor Magdi Wahba offers a textured over-
view of the Cairo of Out el Kouloub's adult life. He explains that to be French-speaking in Egypt before the 1952
Revolution was to belong to a group of people who thought
of Cairo as home but believed that "Paris was the navel of
the world." He explains:

> For some of the more gifted, the lights of Paris shone
> brightly, and their work rolled off the presses of the *Mer-
> cure de France* or the Librairies Stock and Flammarion.
> Few attained the glory of a Gallimard imprint, but there
> was certainly enough coming out of Egypt to engage the
> pens of literary critics from Jules Lemaitre and Anatole
> France onwards. . . . Yet there was a strange malaise in all
> this literature, written with an eye to a Parisian audience,
> often prefaced by a successful French writer, sometimes
> noticed in Parisian literary journals, lavishly praised in the
> Cairene French-language press, but sadly limited to a first
> edition and a number of presentation copies. The second-
> hand bookshops of Cairo are full of them.

Depaule and Noweir mention that Out el Kouloub was
"la plus importante cliente de la librairie de la rue Qasr al-
Nil, 'Les livres de France'" (the best client of the bookstore
on Kasr el Nil Street named Livres de France). Interestingly,
it was in that same bookstore, specializing in French pub-
lications, owned and operated by Ms. Yvette Farazli, that I
became acquainted with the work of Out el Kouloub, in the
late 1970's. Her novels had been remaindered. I purchased
them all.

I was encouraged to undertake translating Out el Kouloub's books by Ms. Asma el Bakri, an Egyptian writer and

film maker, and a dear friend. In fact, I began work on *Ramza* while sitting at the vast dining room table of Asma's Alexandria apartment. Ramza's moving story will always remind me of the Mediterranean sea breezes which gently accompanied me that summer spent in the heart of a family of women who could still evoke the memory of an Egypt long vanished.

As for *Zanouba,* her story is inextricably linked in my mind with my mother's house in Salt Lake City, the canyon winds sweeping down upon the old-fashioned screened-in sleeping porch where I read and re-read the novel, and my late father's room where I set up a card table to begin work; also, the briny bouquet of the Atlantic crashing against fragile dunes across from a daffodil yellow cottage belonging to Ms. Olith Epps and Ms. Gussie Mae Batts, on Topsail Island, North Carolina, where I finished the translation.

My editor at Syracuse University Press, Ms. Cynthia Maude-Gembler, championed the idea of a series of translations of Out el Kouloub's novels, hence this second one: *Zanouba.*

This early novel, about two middle class Egyptian families living in and around Cairo, takes place at the turn of the century. With the skill of a born storyteller and the observant eye of an ethnographer, Out el Kouloub spins a tale where tradition and folklore intertwine and where a sense of place is prominent. The plot centers around Abd el Meguid of Matariyya and Zanouba of Darb el Magharba, their marriage, and their efforts to beget a son.

I chose to translate *Zanouba* for a number of reasons. The first was to offer the English/American speaking reader another of Out el Kouloub's novels. Although written in French, her novels represent Egyptian works by an Egyptian. It is my hope that such translations might contribute to a need for more literature from the Middle East, by women.

My choice of *Zanouba* was also based on contrast. The novel offers us a glimpse at Egyptian middle class life starting in the 1900s as compared with that of the upper classes in *Ramza,* starting around the mid-nineteenth century and concluding in the early part of the twentieth.

Abundant in traditional poems, songs, sayings, and rituals, which endure in folk culture to this day, the story of Zanouba enhances our understanding of certain deeply seated aspects of Egyptian life. The celebration of the Seboo, the seventh day of a newborn's life, is a case in point. Some customs, such as hiring professional weepers to lament the dead at funerals, go back in history to ancient Egypt. Thus, in some pivotal way, Out el Kouloub's lush documentation bridges past and present while telling a tale that is both believable and touching.

In my role as translator I have experienced the dilemma of the ardent traveler going back and forth between two cultures, attempting to make the one accessible to the other while making sense of both. And, in translating Out el Kouloub's work it has been imperative, of course, to grapple with the vehicle, French. This predicament provided a perplexing challenge, particularly when rendering popular poems, songs and sayings, twice removing them from their original. Yet, I never felt a stranger in so doing. Perhaps because of my personal background, I was able to quite naturally enter into dialogue with the characters in the novel, to intuit their feelings, their joys and their dilemmas while remaining focused on Out el Kouloub's intent. Growing up exposed to popular lore in Egypt, speaking French and Arabic at home, and becoming immersed in American language and culture from the age of ten helped me negotiate intricate transitions and allusions with a sense of familiarity.

At times, in working with *Zanouba,* when I considered a passage in need of elaboration in order to become more vividly available to the reader, I added some detail; in cooking or baking scenes, for example, where the preparation of food is mentioned with only a hint of description. Where explanatory footnotes were added by the author, awkward in a work of fiction, I wove them into the fabric of the text.

Also, I chose to preserve certain terms, titles, greetings, and exclamations in the original Arabic where in their integrity they flavored the text: *Sitti,* for example or *Sidi,* terms of respect for an older woman or man, also meaning grandmother or grandfather, mistress or master. Where meaning was not self-evident, I incorporated a twist of definition within the text. And I retained the author's use of "el," as in Out el Kouloub, rather than adopt the present-day convention "Al."

Additionally, where I found certain chapters too long and unwieldy, I divided them. I contributed titles which I hoped would suggest the author's own.

Also, before translating songs and poems, I tried to feel their heartbeat, to dance them through, as it were. In this way, I teased out their meaning and endeavored to retain their spontaneity. I sincerely hope that their essence, particularly, has not been "lost in translation."

In this rendition of *Zanouba,* I have aspired to fulfill my role as translator by imparting the warmth of my response to Out el Kouloub's original work on the one hand, and on the other by maintaining the integrity of the text while attempting to keep the prose fluid, the meaning clear, and the story engaging.

Finally, in this novel in translation, I hope to have come close to realizing what Professor Vincent Crapanzano so succinctly describes as the translator's goal: to render the foreign familiar while preserving its foreignness in one and the same breath.

OUT EL KOULOUB (1899–1968) was an Egyptian author who wrote in French. A member of the Muslim aristocracy, she fled Cairo in the early 1960s after Nasser came to power.

NAYRA ATIYA was born in Egypt, educated in the United States, and lives in New York City. Her oral histories of five Egyptian women, *Khul-Khaal* (Syracuse University Press), won the 1990 UNICEF Prize for the best book on women, children, and development. Atiya's translation of another novel by Out el Kouloub, *Ramza,* was published by Syracuse University Press in 1994.

Part One ▪ *The Seventh Wife of Abd el Meguid*

1 · FUNERAL

Cairo at the turn of the century.

"You-you-you-you! . . ."

Women's piercing cries emerge from number 47 Mohammad Ali Street filling the neighborhood with their mournful sound. In and out of narrow alleys, ambulatory merchants ply their trade. Some pushcarts are low to the ground, stacked with baskets of fruit. Others are covered in alfalfa, a brilliant bed of green, on which vegetables settle in mounds. Holding up hand scales, yellow brass trays glinting in the sun, they place fruits and vegetables on one side, weighted irons on the other. Women call out to them from behind their *mashrabiyya* windows.

Students from Al Azhar University stroll by in pairs reciting verses from the Qur'an. Time hangs heavy on the hands of old men, idle on their doorsteps. Civil servants rush home to lunch and rest, dreaming of retirement.

Veiled women in dark, bustling clusters return to their families after morning visits and errands in the neighborhood. All pause before number 47, the building where Badran Effendi has lived for years on the ground floor with his wife and mother. When his father died, his mother, a widow without daughters to take her in, moved in with her son and daughter-in-law.

Although Badran Effendi is only a modest civil servant, his wife has organized a costly funeral, intent on silencing those who would accuse her of welcoming her mother-in-law's demise. She has hired the best people in the neighborhood's funerary business, including professional mourners to weep. With their repertoire of laments, these women are said to extract tears from stone, even the parched boulders of the Mokkattam hills!

"You-you-you-you! . . ."

Their measured wails are echoed by the company gathered to offer sympathy. It would be unthinkable to refrain from this high-pitched form of grieving. Thus, female voices heave and pitch, overriding even the clatter of newly installed streetcars, on route to and from the Citadel and Ezbekeyya.

Dark, veiled figures flow in and out of Badran Effendi's apartment. The parlor which is modest but spacious juts out a few feet above the pavement, supported by square columns. The space beneath it, acting as an echo chamber, magnifies the voices of the mourners. Family and neighbors, phantomlike figures, women in all shapes and sizes crouch in every corner of the room. Many sit cross-legged on rugs. Some perch on the few wooden chairs available, a leg tucked under a thigh. Others, finding no place to sit, squat where they can or stand leaning against a wall.

For days the professionals have extolled the virtues of the deceased, lamenting her loss on behalf of the family. However, when all that can be said about Badran Effendi's mother has been said, they begin a general litany. With heartrending eloquence, they pity mankind for manifold miseries. Each complaint, whispered at first, crescendos to a chorus of sobs in which everyone joins.

"Oh wretched is the man who has not fathered a son! Silence will meet those who come to pay him their final respects! No son will be there to receive them! Oh, disconsolate is he! No little boy's hand will ever have tugged at the sleeve of his *kaftan*! Oh, wretched, one hundred times wretched is he! Oh, Oh, a thousand and three thousand times wretched is such a man! Pity him! Pity him! His coffin will be carried by strangers! Oh, pity such a man! Oh, pity him!"

All heads turn to a tall, stately woman, eyes brimming with tears which trickle down her wrinkled face. They know her story. Om Mahmood sits on a special gilt and velvet armchair, which clashes with the family's modest furniture, a mark of respect for her superior rank. The armchair had been placed at the far end of the parlor, carried in from the brilliantly colored funerary tent erected in the alley. There, in this temporary room, under the canvas panels appliquéd with intricate geometric patterns and attached to a framework of four by fours, Badran Effendi receives the men's condolences.

Om Mahmood, like the rest of the women in attendance, is all in black. Her gown, unlike the others, however, is cut from the softest Egyptian silk. The satin of her *habara* cloak shimmers. The exquisite crepe of her veil and headdress further attest to her wealth. Although she is wearing no more jewelry than the others, hers is crafted from pure gold. Her bracelets are wide and braided. Her earrings hang heavy in the form of crescent moons. And her imposing necklace, like a breastplate, is richly ornamented with gold coins.

This honored guest, a cousin of the deceased, is the widow of Abd el Hamid of Matariyya and mother of Mahmood Abd el Meguid. In fact, anyone who knows her son, Abd el Meguid, reports that sand turns to gold at his fingertips. Yet, his life is incomplete. Although he is rich and pious, neither his wealth nor his piety have provided him with his heart's desire: a son and heir.

"God refuses to grace his home," the mourners whisper to one another.

His knees rubbed smooth countless prayer rugs in mosque after mosque, in an effort to strike a bargain with God. His endowments have enriched the sanctuaries of Islam in vain. Despite his four wives and two concubines, his house is filled only with daughters.

Om Mahmood, hearing the laments, weeps over her son's misfortune, also her own. Noting her grief, the professionals amplify their weeping, eliciting a heartfelt response from all. Every woman in the room knows there can be no greater sorrow for a good Muslim than to be without a son!

These skilled performers know their business. They manipulate even the hardest heart with the knowledge that the greater the catharsis, the greater will be their reward.

"Oh, sad is a house deprived of a son," begins one.

"Friends can only pity and pray," continues another.

"Daughters who keep the home are a blessing, but what is a home without a son?" asks a third.

"Who will take the father's place when the patriarch expires?" inquires another.

"Shall the ancestral patrimony be lost for lack of a son?"

"Oh, women, must you suffer a stranger in the beloved father's chair? Must your hearts twist in torment to see another smoking his pipe? A stranger on his prayer rug, holding his Holy Qur'an?"

"Oh, woe is me! Oh, woe is me!" intones the company.

"Must a mercenary slaughter the sheep at feast time?"

"Who will distribute two-thirds of the meat to the poor? Who will give alms to those who beg at the door? And, on Ramadan, who will assure them a meal? Who will alleviate their hunger?"

"When they knock, they will be met with silence."

"Oh, pathetic plight!"

"Oh poor, poor ones!"

"Yes, poor, poor wretches, you will go hungry into the night!"

"All for the lack of a son!"

"All for the lack of an heir!"

The list of human afflictions is boundless. The professionals give their most polished performance when their client is rich. But, each woman, rich or not, has her own sorrows and disappointments. One is a widow, another is a mother grieving a lost child, a third has borne a family member's infirmity, a fourth is cursed with an avaricious husband, and a fifth ruined by a prodigal one . . . The list is infinite!

When the weepers intone the litany of unhappily married daughters, a fat woman sitting on a low stool beside Om Mahmood plunges her face into her hands and sobs. The professionals wonder if she is worth their efforts. Wife of a modest shopkeeper in the Mousky, Om Hassan is distantly related to Badran Effendi. They hesitate for a moment. Then, deciding they might strike a chord in a more prosperous heart, they renew their list of indignities.

"Hell is kinder than the home of an indifferent man, my sisters!"

"Kinder by far, oh kinder by far, oh kinder!"

"What use is beauty to the bride who does not win her husband's heart?"

"What use her creamy skin if he will not touch her cheek?

"What use her silky hair if he will not deign to undo a single braid of it?"

"Happier by far the negress with black skin and kinky hair!"

"Oh! poor, poor little bride!"

"Happier by far the negress in the arms of a loving spouse!"

"Oh, wretched little bride!"

"Oh, pitiful one!"

"What good is golden hair and azure eyes if your lord and master turns away from you?"

"Oh, far better to be blind, my sisters!"

"Oh, far better to be blind and loved!"

"Oh, twice and thrice dejected is the wife of an indifferent man!"

"Oh, better by far to have remained unseen, my sisters!"
"Oh, better unseen than rejected!"
"Oh, woe is her!"
"Woe is her!"
Despite the efforts of the chorus, the company falls silent.

Om Hassan wipes her eyes, and blows her nose conspicuously, asking for attention.

"Why are you crying, Om Hassan? I don't remember you having any married daughters," says her neighbor.

"The plight of my Zanouba is what's breaking my heart," Om Hassan responds for all to hear.

She sighs, "So young, so beautiful! A gazelle of sixteen! Dear God, why do you allow unhappiness to batter an innocent child!"

The mourners prick up their ears. Their hostess quickly seizes the opportunity to call for lunch to be served. Soon copper trays heaped with rice, roasted meats, stuffed eggplant, and falafel are brought around. No salads or appetizers are served as these are inappropriate on a day of mourning.

Badran Effendi's parlor is filled to capacity and yet more mourners arrive. No one makes room for them. Even the women who had planned to leave change their minds as the food trays appear. The most abundant ones are first passed to Om Hassan to comfort her aching heart. She eats with pleasure and relishes the thought of telling her tale of woe to such a willing and captive audience.

When she has satisfied her ravenous appetite, she begins.

"One morning, my husband, El Said Abd el Fattah, was in a street in the *mousky* buying slippers. The slippers were hanging in clusters, like grapes: Yellow ones, red ones, white ones, blue ones, green ones, every color imaginable. My husband never takes even the smallest decision in haste. He would not buy a single pair until he had examined the lot to make sure that the stitching was sound. Two hours later, he was still hesitating when Hagg Ali Khalil, the cotton wholesaler, tapped him on the shoulder. My husband had not seen him for a long time."

Om Hassan accepts another bite from a passing tray and continues.

"After greeting Hagg Ali and after all the polite compliments and expressions of friendship, they began to talk about one thing and another, accepting the tea that the shopkeeper was offering them. Since my husband is a cloth merchant they discussed the price of cotton and silk as well as every other subject under the sun."

Om Hassan looks around her, raises her eyes to the sky, and comments, "And they say that women are chatter boxes!"

Seeing that she has captured the attention of the gathering, she goes on with her story.

"As he chatted with Hagg Ali, my husband continued to examine the slippers lined up before him, rejecting any pair with even the slightest imperfection, finally picking three pairs of pink slippers and one green pair."

"Ali Khalil, it would seem, then turned to him in surprise and said, 'How can it be that you are buying three pairs of slippers all of the same color?'"

"'Well, I have three grown daughters at home, the oldest being sixteen and the youngest twelve. If I buy them slippers of different colors, I can be sure that two out of three will quarrel over who gets which. So, I buy the same for all three and save myself the headache. The green pair is for my wife.' They continued until several hours later my husband got up to leave with the bundle of slippers under his arm. Ali Khalil then said to him, 'I am very happy to have run into you. If I may, I would like to call on you at home, tonight after sunset.'"

Om Hassan stops for a moment to observe the effects of her story.

"My husband, of course, thanked him for honoring him

with a visit. True to his word, Ali Khalil came that very same night. He arrived at dusk. The four Sudanese torch bearers lighting his way let it be known that he was a person of some rank. We were still in the dead of winter and so we served him hot cinnamon tea and roasted chestnuts to warm him. The men talked late into the night.

"I had been asleep for hours when Abd el Fattah came into the bedroom, lighted the lamp and called my name insistently. Before my eyes were even open, he handed me a heavy purse as well as a jewel case. The weight of these woke me up instantly. I emptied the purse on the bed, and counted 300 gold Napoleons. The jewel case contained a beautiful necklace of pink diamonds."

"'Have you unearthed a treasure?' I asked my husband with surprise. 'Yes, you could say that and I've agreed to give our daughter Zanouba in marriage to him,' Abd el Fattah answered. He was beaming when he told me that the money and necklace were the first of Hagg Ali Khalil's gifts to his betrothed: the *shabka*. I had heard of Ali Khalil and I was apprehensive. 'He's a very rich man, a big cotton and wheat merchant. He owns 2,000 feddans of fertile land near Simbellawain,' Abd el Fattah then said trying to convince me."

"I protested: 'But he's old! And he's from the South, a Saeedy! How can I give my daughter to a coarse southerner!'"

"'Are you crazy, woman!' Abd el Fattah cried. 'Didn't you hear me say 2,000 feddans! Does one refuse a man with 2,000 feddans?' Before I could say another word Abd el Fattah yells: 'You fool! Are you going to be like the man who owns one cow and thinks he's master of a herd? Did you ever even dream of such a bridegroom for your Zanouba? Hagg Ali is a man who has silos full of wheat in Road el Farag. In Mahmoodiyya, he has bales of cotton bursting out of the warehouses he himself has built. I'm told he has no less than ten secretaries scribbling away day and night!'

"I began to say something, but Abd el Fattah cut me off. 'Besides, our daughter is a city girl; she's well spoken and well bred. This Saeedy, as you call him, will appreciate her a hundred times more than his other wives. He'll make her happy. He'll shower her with gifts!' I had to agree. Abd el Fattah had even agreed on the day when signing the marriage contract—*Katb el Kitab*—would take place."

Om Hassan pauses. She takes a sip of coffee from a miniscule cup, unsweetened since this is a day of mourning. She goes on with her story.

"A week later my Zanouba was married. Everything seemed fine. But, alas! That was far from the truth. Snakes under my own roof were ready to keep my daughter from the happiness she deserves: my two sisters-in-law. They hate me. They resorted to magic to make sure that my poor Zanouba's marriage would never be consummated. The vipers! One of them hid in a room adjacent to where the *Kadi* performing the *Katb el Kitab* was reading the stipulations on the marriage contract. Each time he said a word, one of them wrapped another length of string around a pair of scissors, until there was no way that you could separate one blade from the other. She tied a knot that could not be undone, and tossed the scissors into the Nile, never to be recovered. She had worked a spell on my poor Zanouba. No one knew what had happened.

"A week later the wedding took place and we thought everything was fine. We escorted Zanouba through the streets to the sound of drums and flutes to her husband's house and left her there. When my daughter removed her veil Hagg Ali was overcome with disgust. He should have been delighted because Zanouba is very pretty and well proportioned. But, instead, he was plunged into a somber mood which lasted all night. My sisters-in-law had made sure that on her wedding night her husband's heart would stay closed to her. Imagine my surprise when I took in the basket of candies the next morning and found the bridal bed untouched and my daughter, fully clothed, asleep in an armchair. When she saw me she burst into tears and told me that her husband had not said a word to her. He had gone to sleep on the sofa, turning his face to the wall. She had dozed off in a chair. In the morning he divorced her, returned her dowry, plus money enough for Zanouba's keep for the legally alloted three months. Everything was over."

Om Hassan has concluded her story. Everyone is moved to tears. Everyone is silent. Even the professional weepers are stunned and forget to take up their laments.

Slowly, one after the other, the mourners go home. Only some shiny scraps of eggplant and a few grains of rice remain on the food trays.

2 · PROSPECTS

On the train taking her back to her son's home in Matariyya, Om Mahmood reflects on the day. Her thoughts turn to Om Hassan and her daughter Zanouba.

She ponders: Here is an excellent opportunity, a bride for Abd el Meguid. She is young and still a virgin. Her trousseau is ready. Her parents are eager to see her married. They cannot expect a large dowry from a prospective bridegroom since she has divorced. For the same reason, Om Mahmood would not be expected to shower her with gifts . . .

When Om Mahmood reaches the station in Matariyya, she breathes a sigh of relief. She stops, inhales the fresh air of the country, then climbs into the carriage waiting to take her home, to Abd el Meguid's estate outside of the village of Matariyya. She relishes the thought of going back to her daily activities. Had it not been necessary to attend her cousin's funeral, she would certainly have remained in her familiar surroundings. As it was, she stayed away only the three days that convention required. In the carriage, rocking from side to side, listening to the clip-clop of the horse's hooves, her mind turns back to Zanouba. She is determined to ask for her hand in marriage for her son.

Eager to tell Abd el Meguid about Zanouba, Om Mahmood directs the coachman to take her through the back gate to the men's quarters—the *salamlek*—located at one end of her son's vast property. Her own apartments are in the *haramlek,* at the other end. When she discovers that he is not there, Om Mahmood walks down the wide alley, shaded by the grape trellis she so loves. On either side, she admires the trees laden with ripe oranges and tangerines. Her son is very proud of his gardens. He lovingly maintains the orchard he himself has planted and watched grow. Her heart brims with affection for him. How like a good parent Abd el Meguid is, attending to the exotic Qishtas, the passion fruit, and the delicate mangoes which have been recently imported to Egypt! Despite the admiration she lavishes upon her son, Om Mahmood could not be persuaded to taste these new fruits, regarding them with a certain sense of suspicion tempered with respect. Had Abd el Meguid not told her that a single mango, even unripe, was worth five piasters? She shakes her head in wonder, and mutters one of her favorite phrases, "The world has gone mad!"

She glances in passing at the gazebo. Abd el Meguid sometimes relaxes there, sipping a cup of tea or coffee with a friend, or quietly smoking his water pipe. But the wooden benches with their comfortable cushions are deserted. A rustling sound behind her turns out to be only the breeze blowing through the leaves of a berry bush reflected in a little pond. She picks a few of the berries, peels them and pops them into her mouth, one by one. They are nicknamed "hidden ladies" because of the lanternlike envelope in which they are enclosed. She relishes the perfumes of this vast garden and delights in all of the useful plants which it produces. She inhales deeply the pungent fragrance of the decorative Indian Jasmin. A little further along, she notes with pleasure that the Tamrehenna bushes are in full bloom.

"Last year's sachets have started to lose their fragrance," she thinks. She will dry the blooming sprigs and replace the old ones in the linen chests, between the folds of her dresses and Abd el Meguid's caftans.

As she passes the rose bushes, she thinks that tomorrow she will make the exquisite rose petal jam which her son so much appreciates. She will send the women to pick roses at dawn, when the dew is still on the blooms and before the heat of the day has sucked away the perfume locked into their fleshy petals. How beautifully they have blossomed in the three days she has been away! These are her bushes. This part of the garden is her prized domain. She sighs with satisfaction. Tomorrow the household will be set to work on jam-making.

She stops to rub a leaf of the rose geranium between her fingers, planning to make geranium water, the essence of which is so good in sweets.

"There is always work to be done in a house!" Om Mahmood sighs. In one and the same breath she muses with some pride that her daughters-in-law are not as clever as she is. "It's good that I'm still around to run things!"

What has happened in her absence? She hurries to find out. From a distance, she sees the upper orchard, usually off limits to the women of the household. To go there requires all sorts of precautions, such as making sure no men are around. Despite her advanced age, which excuses her from following the rules to the letter, she rarely crosses the hedge which separates the women's gardens from the great orchard.

Just beyond the hedge, toward the far end of the garden, she glimpses a water buffalo blindfolded and harnessed to the water wheel—*sakia*—turning, turning. She lingers to listen to the rhythmic squealing, the two note refrain, a sound which often had lulled her to sleep, when the insomnia of old age befalls her. She savors its familiar song all the more because she has been away.

When the gardener spies Om Mahmood in the distance, he makes a show of diligence by brandishing his stick, cut from a young eucalyptus tree. The animal steps up its pace, making the *sakia* go faster. "Hon-Hon-Hin-Hin, Hon-Hon-Hin-Hin," it sings as it fills the narrow irrigation ditches, soaking the garden. From neighboring fields other wheels respond.

When she reaches the vegetable patch just outside the kitchen, her heart soars. This part of Abd el Meguid's domain is her world: the kitchen, the store rooms, the baking room with its sturdy adobe oven, the water wells, the dairy, and the shed where ten water buffaloes supply milk for the household. She glances at her little kingdom with a deep sense of satisfaction. When she enters the kitchen, she is met by servants, daughters, and granddaughters. She sees her son's two concubines, purchased as nubile girls on the slave market years ago. Narguiss and Gaulisar run to embrace her.

"Welcome, mother! Ahlan wa Sahlan! The house is ablaze with the light of your return!" they both exclaim with affection.

"Peace be upon you, my daughters," Om Mahmood responds. Seeing an unusual volume of activity, she asks "Is there a dinner party planned for tonight?"

"Yes," says Narguiss, "Abd el Meguid has had guests in the *salamlek* since you left. We have cooked special dinners for them every night."

"I suppose Abd el Meguid has to turn to his friends for companionship since he has no son," says Om Mahmood, sighing. She then adds, "Oh, to think that my son's house will one day fall silent for want of a son!"

Gaulisar, stung by her mother-in-law's words, knits her brows and turns her gaze away. Narguiss, however, who is not known to keep her thoughts to herself, replies, "Why do you always blame us for having daughters, mother? Do you know any women who can have sons on demand? Abd el Meguid has been married four times! Have we ever begrudged him all the wives he wants? He can marry again! He can have another ten wives if he wishes!"

Om Mahmood seizes upon this opportunity and replies, "That may not be a bad idea, my daughter." Narguiss interrupts: "I hope they'll each give him twins yearly!" "God willing," answers Om Mahmood, disregarding the barb.

A few ruffled feathers later, they regain their usual good humor, bantering and laughing. The long years together preoccupied with one man's well-being, the endless chores shared, have woven their lives into one intimate tapestry. These women have true bonds of affection between them.

Narguiss, despite her habit of never mincing words, has a heart of gold. She is frank and lively. Everyone loves this dark Ethiopian with sizzling eyes and fine features, whose demeanor is almost always aglow.

Gaulisar, on the other hand, is slower and more guarded than Narguiss. She is corpulent, with a milky Circassian complexion. Her face is a little flat, moonlike. Her blue eyes are at times elusive or languorous.

Although physically more imposing, Gaulisar always defers to Narguiss. She consults her on everything, finding it easier to follow rather than to take her own initiative. In this way the two women complement each other. With age, they have lost their need to compete for the affections of the man they share. No longer rivals, they have become sisters, allies.

Om Mahmood takes off her *habara* and goes to her apartment to change her clothes. She removes the shoes she is obliged to wear when she goes out, but hates with a passion. Returning to the steamy and busy kitchen in slippers and a housedress she is ready to oversee the food preparation. A pot of rice bubbles on the stove. Squatting in one corner of the kitchen, a servant pounds meat in a special white marble mortar, while another forms it into fingers on a baking sheet. Two women sitting at a low table stuff blanched grape leaves with savory ground lamb, rice and minced onion, rolling them into tight little cylinders. Another arranges them carefully in a large cooking pot. Three girls, sitting cross-legged in a circle, pluck at the leggy stems of the *molokhia* plant and toss the leaves on a clean cloth, making the beloved green soup which heralds summer in every Egyptian household. Gaulisar and Narguiss take turns shredding the leaves, enjoying the fragrance of rich chicken broth, flavored with *misteka*—gum Arabic—in which the leaves will cook briefly. A servant fries garlic in clarified butter, to be added just before serving. All of these mouth-watering perfumes permeate the harem.

"What are you making for dessert?" asks Om Mahmood.

"Come and see, mother," answers Gaulisar, taking her by the hand and pulling her into the next room. There, in the fuel cavity beneath the mudbrick stove, a wood fire burns. Wood is a luxury reserved for baking pastries. Ordinarily, the women light buffalo dung, round, thin patties kneaded with straw and dried hard in the sun. They ignite quickly, burn hot, and give off the sweet odor which heralds baking days.

Gaulisar smiles at her mother-in-law and points to a huge, copper tray brimming with the paper thin dough for baklava.

"I've prepared everything—the almonds are ground and mixed with sugar for the filling, and the syrup is warm. All I need to do now is fill the dough, cut the squares, and bake it. It'll be ready before you can blink an eye," she announces, proudly.

Two little girls have followed Om Mahmood and Gaulisar into the baking room. Their grandmother strokes their heads tenderly. Naima and Aliya are the youngest of the children. They have lost their mother, Nabiha, which is why Om Mahmood spoils them a little. Narguiss and Gaulisar have five daughters. Fathiyya, the oldest is married to a jeweler in the *sagha*—the gold and silver district in the Mousky neighborhood. Khadra, is married to a Sheikh, a teacher at Al Azhar University. Three other daughters died as children.

Although she loves every one of these little girls, Om Mahmood knows that they cannot take the place of the grandson she so desperately longs for. She remembers the weepers' lament and mutters: "Daughters! Daughters! Always daughters! A house full of little heads wrapped in pretty silk kerchiefs! Not a single turban! Not one son!" She wonders if Abd el Meguid has fallen victim to a curse. Here he has had six wives and not a whisper of a son on the horizon, except for the unfortunate incident with Faika . . . Om Mahmood has tried to forget her. Sometimes, however, she cannot help wondering if this cunning young woman had not, after all, tried to please Abd el Meguid. Or was she just attempting to secure her own future?

She also remembers Abd el Meguid's first wife, Nafissa, Fathiyya's mother, who died in childbirth. And his sweet, second wife, Nabiha, who expired a few years later. Om Mahmood's eyes glisten with tears. How heartrendingly Nabiha had commended her little daughters into her care! Om Mahmood pushes the painful memories from her mind.

Noticing that Gaulisar and Narguiss are looking at her quizzically, she asks: "By the way, what's become of Mashalla?" Narguiss and Gaulisar exchange glances and say nothing. Om Mahmood smiles knowingly. Mashalla, Abd el Meguid's wife of eight years, is a thorn at her side. Neither Narguiss nor Gaulisar like her because of her haughty ways. She never fails to remind them that they are slaves and that, unlike herself, they are wives in name only. This arrogant woman treats them like servants and continually humiliates them. Moreover, she is inconsiderate to her mother-in-law. Even if she had wanted to, Om Mahmood could not have defended her on the grounds that she was also a mother to Abd el Meguid's children. Mashalla is barren.

Om Mahmood sympathizes with Narguiss and Gaulisar. She also knows that they are neither jealous nor envious of Mashalla's superb apartment (the most beautiful in the harem) where she receives her visitors like a queen in the spacious living room jutting out over the courtyard. But then, she muses, all the women of the household have enjoyed gathering there.

Nor, come to think of it, muses Om Mahmood, have they ever coveted Mashalla's ample, turreted balcony enclosed by exquisite fruitwood *mashrabiyya* screens; these are so intricately worked with cross and lozenge patterns they resemble filigree. How often have they all gossiped behind them, seeing but unseen, devouring every detail of Abd el Meguid's receptions in the beautiful *mandara* across the way! Here, Sheikhs and rich merchants in sumptuous caftans have mingled with majestic looking pashas as the fine meals prepared by these cloistered onlookers are served.

In fact, Om Mahmood is certain that Gaulisar and Narguiss consider it perfectly natural for Mashalla to have richly textured carpets, silver trays worked with gold, and even a modern bedroom set imported from Paris. Everyone admires the armoire, with its triple, full-length mirrors, yet she has never heard an envious word from Gaulisar or Narguiss. That Mashalla has three personal servants is her right since she comes from a rich family. That she possesses chests full of the master's clothing, linens and undergarments is a source of jealousy, however. Yet, they always acknowledged her right as Abd el Meguid's official wife.

Om Mahmood knows all of this. She is also fully aware that Narguiss and Gaulisar even overlook Mashalla's neglect of her housewifely duties. She never sets foot in the kitchen, the bakery, nor anywhere else the women work. This skinny woman, with her turned up nose, does nothing to endear herself to her companions and is, as a result, detested by the entire harem. "The entire time you were away Mashalla stayed barricaded in her apartment, mother!" proclaims Narguiss. "Not once did she join us for dinner, nor did she lend a hand in making even one pot of jam," Gaulisar adds.

"Did she have a lot of visitors?" Om Mahmood asks. "Every day, mother," answers Narguiss. "From morning until night we heard footsteps on the stairs—light steps, pounding steps, feet dragging, slippers clackety-clacking, voices gossiping, whispers, laughter!"

"When you are gone, mother, her relatives descend on the house like grasshoppers!" chimes in Gaulisar.

"May God give us long life so that we can continue to be two thorns at her side!" adds Narguiss, raising her hands heavenward, eyes twinkling.

"Last night Narguiss told her just what we think of her, mother . . ." reports Gaulisar gleefully.

Narguiss interrupts: "Imagine her gall! Not only did she complain about the service she was getting, but also about the food. She actually threatened to tell Abd el Meguid! Finally, I confronted her. We had a real fight. I told her that if she didn't like our cooking, she could do her own. I accused her of primping all day, grimacing in front of her mirror as she applied *kohl* to her eyes and color to her cheeks! Imagine, she called me a filthy slave, among other abuses. I will spare you the insults I heaped upon her."

They all giggle. Narguiss did not keep a civil tongue in her mouth in the best of times. Still, Om Mahmood advises her to be conciliatory and to avoid quarrels with Mashalla. Abd el Meguid would be upset.

Om Mahmood's apartment, just above the kitchen and store rooms, can be reached by a small, private staircase. She has access to the three harems also located on the top floor of the house. She ponders the question of where to lodge Zanouba if she marries Abd el Meguid. Narguiss and

Gaulisar have no room in their harems for another person. Only Mashalla has an extra room. Om Mahmood is nearly certain, however, that she would never accept sharing her harem with another wife, particularly a young, pretty one. A new wing would surely have to be added. In the meantime, should the marriage come to pass, Fatma, Abd el Meguid's widowed sister, would certainly welcome the young bride. Fatma, who was married to a cavalry officer, lives with her two children in the new quarter of Abbasiyya. "I'm quite sure she would be happy to have some company," she thinks, pleased with her solution.

Om Mahmood, full of her matchmaking thoughts, is eager to break the news to her son. Minutes later, she receives word that Abd el Meguid is on his way up to welcome her home. She greets him enthusiastically. "I have found a bride for you," she tells him right off. Abd el Meguid chuckles. "I have three at home, mother. Don't you think that's enough?"

"None has given you a son, Abd el Meguid," she says emphatically.

"I'm nearly sixty years old, mother, or have you forgotten? I've had six wives and they've given me a dozen children, all girls. I've done all I can, mother. I must submit to God's will."

"You are more handsome and stronger than any young man," says Om Mahmood, looking at him with loving admiration. It is quite true that, at sixty, Abd el Meguid is a good looking man, tall, of noble carriage. He dresses with natural elegance, wearing his *gebba* like a king. This floor length overcoat, with ample sleeves, is well cut from good brown wool. Underneath it his lighter brown caftan, with yellow pin stripes, is comfortably cinched at the waist with a cummerbund, discreetly embroidered with black flowers. On his head Abd el Meguid wears a Sheikh's scarlet cap, masterfully wrapped with a white silk shawl to form an imposing turban. His face is tan and his beard has long been grey. His forehead is high, his nose strongly defined. A hint of sadness plays about his mouth with its full lips. His black eyes, sometimes piercing, sometimes lost in dream or in prayer, are his most striking feature. They are always kind, however, truly mirrors of his soul.

Seeing the tenderness with which his mother looks at him Abd el Meguid's heart melts. "May I know why you want me to marry again, dear heart?" he cannot help asking.

"My son," she exclaims passionately, "I have discovered that the daughter of Said Abd el Fattah, of Darb el Magharba, who is only sixteen years old, is divorced, yet still a virgin . . ."

Om Mahmood then recounts Zanouba's story. She speaks of the advantages of such a union with such eloquence that her son's resistance weakens, and he agrees to let her visit the young woman and, if she is favorably impressed, she will take steps to secure a seventh wife for him.

Om Mahmood smiles. She is certain that the marriage will take place. God will at last smile upon Abd el Meguid and reward him with his heart's desire.

3 · MARRIAGE

With curtains carefully drawn, three harem carriages travel along the shores of the Nile, near Bulac. The women within can glimpse stevedores loading and unloading the huge *ayassas,* wooden cargo boats—their sails gathered snugly around sturdy masts. The men are bent in half under heavy loads. They go up and down the steep banks of the river, crossing and recrossing the narrow dirt road. The boats carry timber from Lebanon, charcoal from England, and bales of cotton from Egypt's Delta region.

The antlike procession stops momentarily, allowing the

carriages to pass. The stevedores, dressed in colorless rags, look up rapidly, their eyes flash in their blackened faces, then flicker away as they resume their backbreaking work. Those who have unloaded their burdens stand immobile for a moment, resting. Their heads and shoulders are covered with hemp sacking to protect them from the fierce summer sun. Their faces stream with sweat. Despite their arduous work, they display smiling countenances. They look on as the convoy of black, shiny carriages, conveying Zanouba and her family from Darb el Magharba, her home, proceeds further down to a houseboat on the Nile, where her wedding will take place.

The carriages stop along the steep embankment. A large, white *dahabiyya* is moored just below, surrounded with *fel-ukas*—smaller boats—their long, slender masts sway rhythmically, bobbing up and down in the dark water.

Zanouba looks out, fascinated. The blue-green water of the river laps lazily at the shiny sides of the two story houseboat. Against the little windows of the staterooms red velvet curtains are tightly drawn. On both sides of the gangway, and on both sides of the path leading to the boat from a tent put up along the side of the road, colorful Persian carpet runners have been set on the ground. Canvas walls have been erected to protect the women from the eyes of curious onlookers. Two of Abd el Meguid's male servants, with eyes averted, push aside a cluster of children who have gathered to watch. Om Mahmoud and her daughter, Fatma, tall like herself, enter first to welcome the others. Early that morning they had left Fatma's house, in Abbassiyya, picked up Zanouba and her family in Darb el Magharba and arrived leisurely at their destination that afternoon.

A gaggle of laughing girls emerges from the second carriage: Zanouba and her two sisters, Faika and Aziza, accompanied by Zohra, Fatma's daughter. A few little cousins are dressed in bright green dresses. All are wrapped from head to toe in black *melayas,* except the little girls. Zanouba too is in black except for her white face veil, indicating she is the bride. The white veil and green dresses add a touch of gaiety to otherwise somber garb.

Om Hassan, the mother of the bride, has come in the third carriage. She is accompanied by her old mother, Sitt Habiba, and a neighbor who somehow strong-armed an invitation to the wedding. All the women follow Om Mahmood and Zanouba to a place on the deck where a calf lies bound. A servant cuts the animal's throat, allowing the blood to cover the deck. Om Hassan then instructs Zanouba to anoint her hands and feet with the sticky, red liquid. The animal is then butchered—the meat is distributed among the poor. Thus, the first wedding ritual is concluded amidst outbursts of joy cries, *zaghareet*—rapid warbles of the tongue.

The group proceeds to the second floor of the *dahabiyya.* The deck has been covered with screens so opaque that only by pressing against the scattered air holes can the women see the Nile water, the mass of green palm trees on Gezira and, for a brief moment, the full sail of a passing *feluka.* With relief, in the shelter of this temporary harem, they finally unwind their long *melayas* and cast aside their face veils, attached with the cylindrical gold or silver *asabas* which leave little teeth marks on every nose.

The littlest girls gather around to admire the bride's costume. Zanouba's long, crimson dress is intricately embroidered with gold thread by an Armenian artisan known for his fine work. They finger the silk and the black velvet bolero she wears on top. They look wonderingly at Zanouba's beautiful hair, snugly caught up in a silk headband decorated with shiny egret feathers. Her shoes are made of fine red leather.

The wedding outfit is all new. Om Hassan would not let Zanouba wear the clothes she had prepared for the first one, thinking that they would surely bring her bad luck.

She proudly displays her first gifts from Abd el Meguid—a gold watch and chain worn around her neck, four gold bracelets, two on either wrist, and a gold brooch in the form of a peacock fanning its tail. Its feathers glint with tiny pink diamonds.

Zanouba wonders what her husband will be like.

The women soon hear heavy footsteps and men's voices. Zanouba recognizes only her father's voice. She wonders if the other belongs to the *kadi,* the officiating judge, or to Abd el Meguid, whom she will see for the first time tonight. Although she knows almost nothing about him, this seems quite natural. She imagines him to be like her father—a master and protector—and herself like her mother. She remembers with pride performing her mother's household duties when Om Hassan was ill last year and feels she can assume her role as Abd el Meguid's wife with confidence. She will carry out the same duties in her husband's home as she did in her father's and, like her mother, she will have children. This is a woman's destiny.

Zanouba remembers having heard that Abd el Meguid is handsome, although he is old. What more could she ask for? She has never dreamed of being married to a man her own age, anyway!

As the *dahabiyya* begins to move, Om Hassan, assisted by her little nieces, prepares to ward off the evil eye. She fills a bucket with water. Her nieces dig into the pockets of her velvet dress for pebbles. She splashes water around the deck and the little girls toss the pebbles overboard, in all directions to frighten away any envious spirits lurking about. Om Hassan is extremely superstitious. She has proposed moving the wedding to the *dahabiyya,* away from the neighborhood where another mean spell might be cast on Zanouba. She has insisted on the ceremony taking place on the sacred day, Friday, at noon, the prayer hour. She has kept secret the day of the wedding, fearing her diabolical sister-in-law.

As the boat rocks gently, Om Mahmood engages Zanouba in conversation. Zanouba responds with becoming modesty, eyes slightly averted. Sitting here with this old woman, almost a stranger, she remembers the first time she saw Om Mahmood in the little parlor of her mother's house. Could it have been only two weeks ago? It seems an eternity. She had been innocently chatting with her sisters when her mother asked her to serve coffee. It had not crossed her mind that she was being observed by her future mother-in-law. She only understood when Om Mahmood kissed her and pinned a large gold brooch on her dress. The pin, in the form of a gazelle, was so beautiful that she had blushed with pleasure. She would never take it off.

Om Hassan, however, insisted on quickly putting it away to avoid any gossip, ordering Zanouba to say nothing to anyone. Om Hassan added, "People might start saying that there is something about you that repels men and that this time will be no different than the last. You have to be careful, particularly of your aunts."

Zanouba had smiled. She could not really see anything displeasing about herself. Om Mahmood had found her pretty. Her only criticism had been that Zanouba was a little thin, upon which Om Hassan fed her every hour of the day.

The fifteen days preceding the marriage had been days of celebration. Zanouba, the center of attention, rejoiced at being allowed to eat as many cakes and candies as she wished. Gifts of food and jewelry arrived almost daily. The seamstress worked feverishly on a new wedding outfit to be sent out for embroidering. Zanouba loved the endless discussions with her sisters about her future life.

During that week, Om Mahmood and Om Hassan had consulted a *fiky*—a holy man—about the marriage. He had examined their talismans—Zanouba's headscarf and Abd el Meguid's skull cap—and had predicted not only that the union would be blessed with a son, but that his name would be Abd el Karim.

A neighbor had warned that this *fiky* always told people what they wanted to hear in order to be generously rewarded. Om Hassan had replied, "Whatever will be will be. We have to submit to God's will." She really wanted to believe him, and did.

Zanouba, without seeing the outcome of her first wedding as a tragedy, was nevertheless a little wary. She had experienced only that one night of sadness four months ago. That was all. It was really Om Hassan who had taken the matter to heart. Zanouba herself could hardly even remember what her husband looked like. She had barely had a glimpse of him when he walked into the bedroom on their wedding night. He had looked at her and had seemed afraid of touching her. He had not said a word to her. Having lain down, fully clothed on the divan, he had turned his back to her and promptly gone to sleep. She had remained awake, waiting, but nothing happened. Finally, overcome with fatigue, she had fallen asleep on her chair. Now, she cannot help smiling when she recalls the scene, particularly in the light of Om Hassan's advice to the young bride. That night it had been useless. She would surely say it again: Don't fidget in bed. Try to hold your breath. Let your husband do what he wants. Above all don't kick him.

The morning after, her mother had come with the customary basket of candies only to find her daughter in tears and the bridegroom gone. She had been furious, and all the more so when the divorce paper was handed to her instantly. Zanouba, however, despite a fleeting moment of embarrassment had not been unhappy to return home.

This second time, standing expectantly on the threshold of happiness, taking her place among women, Zanouba feels a peculiar little tightness in her chest. Her eyes fill with tears. She is apprehensive about leaving her mother and sisters for the unknown. She looks at her little cousins, at her mother-in-law. "What will this night be like? What will tomorrow bring?" Her musings are abruptly interrupted. Her uncle calls her name from the bridge. He is one of the two witnesses who has come to ask for her consent. In an unwavering voice Zanouba answers, "Yes."

The wedding is over. The marriage will be consummated later. The men leave. Their deep voices rise from the gangway. Zanouba and her sisters rush to lift a corner of the curtains to peek at Abd el Meguid. One glance from Om Hassan immobilizes them. Once the men's voices have faded and the way is clear they are let out. Zanouba returns to Darb el Magharba with her mother and sisters.

"How weird!" she thinks, upon entering the courtyard. "I have pronounced the word 'yes,' I belong to a man I have yet to see, and suddenly I feel like a stranger in my own father's house!"

She follows the women to the harem, going into the familiar room she has shared for her entire life. She feels like a visitor. She undresses, wanders aimlessly through the rooms and corridors of the harem, then back to her room. She looks at the spot where the chest containing her clothing had been, the nail where her mirror had hung, the denuded space where her loom had stood . . . She is no longer there. Tears run down her face. Zanouba had been born in this house, tucked at the end of a narrow, dead end street. The peaceful days of her childhood were spent here. A memory is associated with every inch of wall. In every corner of every room, in every ray of sunshine which peeps through the *mashrabiyya,* a scene from her childhood dances before her eyes. She thinks of the courtyard below, retreating in shadow as night falls. She visualizes the four windows overlooking the *mandara,* and remembers the countless times she has looked through the protective screens and run her fingers along the interlacing patterns of the delicate wood work.

She remembers her father's voice rising gently as he walks upstairs accompanied by her younger brother, Ibrahim, proud to be living in the men's quarters now that he is ten years old.

Below, she can see the water well tucked into a niche in the north wall of the old house. Nearby is the kitchen with its big, domed, mud brick oven. Here, every Wednesday at dawn a neighbor who hires herself out as a baker arrives to help to bake the week's supply of bread for the family. Zanouba remembers with a shiver the cold winter mornings when, having braved the dark, narrow stairs, she sat next to the oven for warmth. A delicious feeling of well-being would come over her as she watched the baker start the fire, stoke it, and as she and her sisters helped prepare the dough. She could almost smell the mouth-watering fragrance of baking bread and hear their good humored chatter as they worked. In summer, in the cool hours of dawn, she particularly liked these Wednesdays. The baker was a source of the latest gossip since she baked in every house in the neighborhood. No harem could keep secrets from her. Zanouba smiles remembering the slow drawl of this village jack-of-all-trades. She not only baked but knew all the best artisans and shops. She also did errands, taking a dress to be embroidered one place, bringing back a package of needles from another, picking the best quality thread or colored pearls to decorate a blouse. She always brought sugar candy and penny knickknacks to the little girls, waiting in anticipation.

These are vestiges of another life now, a life she is leaving.

A sadness washes over her as she thinks of her childhood bedroom. She wonders: "Will I be able to sleep in my high bridal bed without falling off the edge?"

She glances at the narrow mat rolled up against a wall, which for sixteen years she had spread nightly on the floor to serve as a bed. She remembers squeezing in close to her sisters, whispering secrets late into the night. In winter with the door closed and the windows secured, the bedroom was snug and cozy. The sisters tucked their sleepy heads deep into the covers.

She remembers summer nights. Mats were spread in the hall to catch the cool breezes, the stars glinting through the holes of the *mashrabiyya* screens on the lightwell—the *manwar*. This skylight was always opened at night, catching the cool breezes blowing off the desert, sweeping the house fresh before the sudden descent of the day's heat.

Zanouba thinks of her little sisters continuing this snug and peaceful life while she goes to live among strangers. With a tender glance around the room, she bids it a silent farewell. "I'll never again be this happy!"

The girls embrace her, tears running down their faces, consoling her—and themselves. "You will return."

"Of course I will," Zanouba responds, ashamed of her instant thought. For a moment, she wishes that this marriage would end like the last one and that her mother would have to take her home tomorrow.

Last night her new furniture and personal belongings had been moved. Two donkey carts had carried a brass bed painted with black enamel, decorated with little pink, green and blue flowers. Also a closet with a mirrored door and a dressing table. Three divans were covered in blue and red percale, two in yellow silk with matching curtains. And three Persian rugs, two gilt candelabras, an oval mirror, a white porcelain table service with pink flowers. Finally, a large red silk bedspread which Zanouba herself had embroidered.

Although it is customary for a young bride to wait eight days after the marriage contract has been signed before going to the harem of her husband, Abd el Meguid is so eager to see her that he pleads with Om Mahmood to persuade Om Hassan to let Zanouba move in right away. Om Hassan agrees Zanouba does not need the extra time. Her trousseau is ready.

It is time to leave for the home of Abd el Meguid's widowed sister, Fatma, where Zanouba will live until rooms have been built for her in Matariyya.

One last hug. One last glance to tuck away in her memories for safekeeping.

Zanouba goes down the stairs slowly, following her mother and her grandmother. She glances at an ancient niche carved out of the wall in the shape of a cloverleaf where doves sometimes nested. As a little girl, she kept a secret cache of candies there.

In the courtyard the servants are gathered to bid her farewell. She also receives the fond goodbyes of her father and brother before continuing along the dark, angular hallway. Two elbow turns had been perfect hiding places for childhood games of hide and seek.

Muhammad, the old porter, says goodbye to her for the last time, tears streaming into his white beard. Neighbors watch from their windows as she boards the carriage taking her to Abbasiyya.

Zanouba has begun her new life as a married woman.

Although she is crying when the carriage clatters away and crosses under the immense archway of Bab el Foutouh, laughter is not far behind. She sees a baboon dressed in a scarlet velvet vest, performing on the back of a white goat, and bursts into laughter. At sixteen, sadness is so short-lived!

Meanwhile, her mother and grandmother casually talk about Abd el Meguid, trying to allay the fears trembling in every young bride's heart.

"Oh, he is as handsome as a young man!"

"He is so rich, he could buy up half of Cairo."

"And you know he is as generous as he is rich; he never goes past a beggar without giving alms. No poor man is ever turned away from his door."

"He is so fair and wise that even the governor of Cairo comes to seek his counsel."

Zanouba looks out the window, ignoring them, but relishing every word about her new husband's many virtues and assets.

"Do you know how glad I am, my daughter," Om Hassan finally says, "that you will be living in Abbasiyya? It's such a short distance from our house. I'll come to see you often."

After a pause, she adds, "Your sister-in-law's house is like the house of a European. I could never live in such a house, but you are young and will probably like it."

They arrive.

Zanouba looks out curiously. Sitt Fatma's house is near the army barracks of the Khedive Abbas. How new it looks. The vegetation is still sparse. Newly planted sunflowers and date palms are still too young to make it seem like a real garden. A one-story house surrounded with balconies stands squarely on this arid plot of land. The property is entirely enclosed by a green trellissed fence on which new climbers are being trained.

Sitt Fatma welcomes them. She lives with her two children in the house built by her husband. The land had been given him by the Khedive just prior to his departure for a mission to the Sudan where he died.

The night is balmy. A cool desert breeze sweeps the summer streets and nearby one can see the Red Mountain. The reception rooms in the house have high ceilings. They are spacious and comfortably furnished. Om Hassan whispers that it is not organized like a pious Muslim home. Men and women would have to live together in such a house because *haramlek* and *salamlek* are not separated. "It is a good thing that Sitt Fatma is a widow," Sitt Habiba replies.

Despite their reservations, Om Hassan and Sitt Habiba loudly admire everything they see, complimenting Sitt Fatma on her comfortable home, thanking her profusely for her hospitality.

Sitt Fatma has prepared two pretty rooms for her sister-in-law. Zanouba's furniture and belongings are already in place. One of the rooms will serve as a parlor. The other is the bedroom, in the middle of which looms Zanouba's huge brass bed.

When Abd el Meguid arrives, Zanouba is inexplicably moved to tears. She casts a furtive glance at her husband.

"How handsome he is," she thinks. She kisses his hand as is customary. Because her head is inclined she misses the expression of tenderness which radiates from Abd el Meguid's eyes upon seeing his young bride for the first time. Om Hassan, ever vigilant, has not missed it. She sighs with relief. All will be well.

Once the introductions are made, Sitt Fatma brings out a prayer rug. Abd el Meguid kneels, touching his forehead to the ground twice before saying a first word to his bride.

Sitt Habiba prompts Zanouba to serve the ceremonial orange syrup drink. Beside her is a tray on which a blue and a red glass have been placed. "The blue one is for your husband," whispers her grandmother. Zanouba is suddenly dumbstruck. As the prayer comes to an end, Sitt Habiba presents the tray to Abd el Meguid herself. He smiles. He knows that the water used in making the drink has been trickled over Zanouba's feet, sweetened with sugar cubes briefly held in her mouth. He tips his glass and drinks it all in one swallow. Then, smiling he says: "Here then is the potion to bind a husband to his wife with bonds of love, lasting as long as life itself. My eyes tell me that I have married the most beautiful and charming of women. God bless and keep you, my child! I pray that in my home you may live all the days of your life in peace and in happiness."

When Om Hassan and Sitt Habiba depart at last, Zanouba's tears flow once again, but they are tears of happiness. Her husband's show of kindness has won her heart. No longer apprehensive, she embarks confidently on her new life.

4 · DAWN

Day breaks. In some respects it is a day like all others. Standing on the wooden balcony off the bedroom, Abd el Meguid looks over the city as it slowly emerges from slumber. The calls to prayer rise with the sun. They ascend like a hum from hundreds of mosque minarets jutting heavenward across the city: an offering, a chant beseeching Allah to bless the labors and joys of the day.

For Abd el Meguid, however, this day feels different from all others. He stretches, inhaling deeply. The early morning air is fresher, purer, newer somehow. Joy fills his heart. Glancing through the half open door, he sees Zanouba, still asleep, her head turned away from the light, long, black hair flowing against the brilliantly white bedding. He raises his eyes and thanks heaven for the blessings bestowed upon him and for this night of bliss.

He whispers, "Praise be to Allah for this young life that has been joined with mine, for this gift I have been given, for the sweetness of this body, for the purity of this heart. Allah be praised for his bountiful goodness, which has renewed my lost hopes. Allah be praised for the piety he has inspired in me and for the privilege of raising my voice in prayer."

Suddenly, Abd el Meguid remembers a song, an old Mawwal he used to sing in his twenties. He hums and hesitates. Slowly the words come back to him:

"Oh! night, draw closed your curtain. Oh! night, nudge dawn's vermillion away. Oh! night, cradle my beloved's cherished head against your dusky shoulder. Oh! night, shelter her brow from the ardent kisses of the sun . . ."

No one has heard Abd el Meguid sing for many years, nor seen his eyes glowing with such happiness and newfound youth. He contemplates Zanouba, breathing softly, lips parted. What grace! Her hair, loosened from its braid, flutters in the early morning breeze, downy and dark against her sweet face. Abd el Meguid is moved to tears. He drinks in her image, taking her with him as he faces the day's burdens.

He must go two hours away, to his farm. He will negotiate with wheat merchants who buy his crop yearly, discussing quality and prices. All the while he will be thinking of the exquisite night beside his new bride. All the gold he earns today he will transform into gifts for Zanouba. He can think of nothing else.

As he departs the garden, Abd el Meguid raises his eyes to a flawless blue sky. His heart swells with joy and hope.

Part Two · *Mashalla*

5 · ZANOUBA IN MATARIYYA

Zanouba, things cannot continue in this way! Have you spoken to your husband?" asks Om Hassan one morning, months after her daughter's wedding.

"Not yet, mother. But I've talked with Fatma. She says there's no room for me yet in Matariyya."

"What happened to the new wing Abd el Meguid promised to build?"

"It's not ready, mother. Besides, a jealous wife lives in that house. She doesn't know that Abd el Meguid has married again. It's really better for me to stay here until he's smoothed the way . . ."

"Those are poor excuses, daughter. It's not right that after ten months of marriage you've not yet been welcomed into your own husband's home! Is he ashamed of you? Or of us? Is this his way of saying we're not good enough for him?"

Om Hassan flushes as she feeds the fires of her indignation.

"Oh, mother! Abd el Meguid is the kindest of men and doesn't think that way. I'm very happy here!"

"It's not a matter of happiness or unhappiness, my girl. There are more important considerations. It's just not right for a wife to be treated like a concubine and kept hidden from her husband's family. What about your family's honor? Does that mean nothing to you? I have to tell you

39

that your father's not pleased either. We can't go on hiding this way, living in fear that Mashalla's family will find out!"

"Mother, please . . ." whispers Zanouba, trying to avoid creating a scene in Fatma's house.

Om Hassan will not be stopped, however. She wants to be heard. She exclaims, "I just can't stand this any longer, Zanouba! I mean, even when I visit Om Mahmood, I have to pretend. I can't speak freely. I have to wait until we're alone to even mention your name . . . This must stop! Abd el Meguid is not the first man to have four wives! You have to prevail upon him! Is he master in his own home or not?"

"Mother . . ."

"And when you give birth will he have to hide the baby as well?" continues Om Hassan, turning a deaf ear to her daughter's pleas.

"Mother, please . . ." whispers Zanouba again.

"If you won't to talk to him, I will!" Om Hassan finally declares.

"I implore you, mother, leave Abd el Meguid to do as he sees fit."

It is not the first time Om Hassan has prodded Zanouba. Every time she visits she unfolds her list of recriminations. Her complaints have made Zanouba dread seeing her. Why, she wonders, does her mother have to cast this shadow on her happiness? "What difference does it make where I live? I wish she would stop!" her heart cries out. However, in a voice trained to speak with filial respect Zanouba reminds her mother of how convenient it has been living so close to Darb el Magharba. "It will be much harder for you to come as often if I move all the way to Matariyya . . ." she says in her most persuasive tone. Om Hassan will not be moved, however. She purses her lips and grunts with exasperation. Zanouba wonders, "What's all the fuss about, dear God? This must be the work of a neighbor whispering disquieting tidbits in her ear. I can just hear Om

Rida or Om Abd el Hadi telling my mother that she's not treated with the consideration due a mother-in-law!"

Zanouba, who likes living with Fatma, resents her mother's intrusion. Doesn't she notice how warmly her sister-in-law has welcomed her? Fatma is old enough to command respect and also makes Zanouba feel both comfortable and secure. She can obey her as easily she did her own mother. The difference in their ages eliminates the jealousies and conflicts which often arise between sisters-in-law, particularly when living in close quarters. Furthermore, Zanouba has grown very fond of Fatma's niece Zohra, three years her junior. They do their chores together, chatting happily while they work. At night, if Abd el Meguid is not visiting, Zanouba sleeps beside Zohra, as she did with her sisters in Darb el Magharba. It gives her the feeling of being a young girl still, singing and laughing the days away.

Whenever Abd el Meguid is present, Zanouba becomes a wife again. This double life gives the sixteen-year-old bride a certain prestige with her niece. With what admiration she is greeted by Zohra the day after one of Abd el Meguid's visits!

Daily Zanouba's love for her husband increases. Abd el Meguid is careful to nurture his young bride's growing affection; he never visits without a gift or leaves without an endearing glance, tender as a caress. Zanouba always welcomes him with pleasure, admiring his neatly groomed grey beard, his fatherly ways, and the elegance with which he wears his caftans. "How handsome he is!" she whispers to herself over and over again.

Sometimes Abd el Meguid spends the night, leaving at dawn. Other times he stays only a few hours. Zanouba understands; her kind, considerate husband tries to deal equitably with every one of the women in his life. He is particularly cautious not to arouse suspicion in his jealous wife, Mashalla. The secrecy with which he surrounds Zanouba, his furtive visits seem to reinforce, to renew his love for her, rather than weaken it. She is struck by how vibrant he grows in her company. His passion surrounds her. His eyes awaken with feeling as he looks at her. And, when he touches her—always tenderly—she feels herself melt, disappear into him like water on sun-dried soil.

Zanouba will always remember the look in Abd el Meguid's eyes when she announced that she was pregnant. He had instantly taken her into his arms, his eyes wet with tears of joy. How warmly he had embraced her! He could not wait to mark the moment with a gift. Rushing out, he returned an hour later with the biggest and most beautiful diamond he could find. Henceforth, he redoubled his efforts to please her, but also his precautions. Even Om Hassan is warned to make her visits less frequent to keep the gossip mongers from talking. However, Fatma informs Zanouba that Om Mahmood has entrusted Narguiss and Gaulisar with Abd el Meguid's secret. Seeing Zanouba's expression change, she hastens to tell her that she has nothing to fear. Both women are eager to meet her and will help her in any way they can. "They're delighting in the idea that Mashalla might be supplanted," she adds, chuckling.

One night, after her mother leaves, Zanouba carefully combs her long hair and decides to wear a new purple dress as a surprise for her husband. Abd el Meguid is expected for dinner. When he fails to come, she eats alone. The evening trickles away. Zanouba experiences such sadness that no amount of cheering from her companions helps. Neither Fatma's reassurances nor Zohra's tender attention allay her disappointment. Both annoyed and worried, she finally undresses, going to her own bed, still hoping that Abd el Meguid will come. She dozes and wakes, restless. She starts every time a dog barks or a carriage rumbles past the house, imagining footsteps in the garden all night. At dawn she falls asleep, still alone.

The following day, seeing Zanouba's agitation, her sis-

ter-in-law goes to Matariyya to inquire about Abd el
Meguid. When she returns in the afternoon, Zanouba runs
to meet her at the garden gate.

Fatma reassures her. "It's nothing serious, an attack of
rheumatism in his right leg. He has to stay in bed a few
days." "Is he in a lot of pain?" Zanouba asks, her eyes
watering.

"Of course it's painful, but that sort of thing is not unusual for a man his age, my sister. He'll recover, don't
worry, don't worry." After a pause, Fatma smiles. "What's
bothering him more than the rheumatism is not seeing you.
He wanted you to know he hasn't forgotten his young
bride," she says, handing Zanouba a small ring, a token of
Abd el Meguid's affection.

Zanouba is moved to tears again. She asks Fatma to recount her visit in minute detail. What was the room like
where Abd el Meguid was resting? How did he look? Did
he want her to come to Matariyya?

Fatma says that it had been impossible to speak freely,
since Mashalla would not leave Abd el Meguid's side. However, to further reassure her, Fatma repeats that an attack of
rheumatism does not last long. "Abd el Meguid will visit
you as soon as he's able to walk," she concludes, patting
Zanouba on the shoulder.

Days pass and Abd el Meguid is still absent. Fatma,
worried, goes to Matariyya again. Abd el Meguid has scia-
tica, not rheumatism. The doctor recommends bed rest for
several weeks. When she hears the news, Zanouba's tender
heart breaks. In tears, she wonders why she cannot be with
her husband and care for him? "I am his wife, after all!" she
thinks. All at once she understands her mother's relentless
prodding. Now, it is she who pleads with Fatma to take her
to Matariyya. Her sister-in-law promises to speak to Om
Mahmood.

Zanouba does not wait long for an answer. Before the
week is out Om Mahmood sends word that she herself will

come to fetch her daughter-in-law. Zanouba, her heart pounding, packs instantly. Folding some clean clothes into a bundle—a *boga*—she ties the corners of the square with deft fingers and waits.

Early the following day Om Mahmood arrives.

The journey to Matariyya seems endless to Zanouba, impatient with the slow pace of the old mule pulling the carriage. When they arrive, Om Mahmood instructs the driver to take them through the garden, to the courtyard of the *haramlek*. Zanouba, forgetting momentarily about Abd el Meguid, looks around her with admiration. "What a beautiful garden! What a beautiful house!" she exclaims.

Om Mahmood, smiling, points to the *mashrabiyya* windows just above them. "Abd el Meguid is up there, Zanouba. That's the window of Mashalla's harem."

Zanouba looks up with growing excitement and apprehension. She can hardly concentrate on Om Mahmood's instructions, preparing her for the difficult first meeting with Abd el Meguid's other wives.

Once inside the *haramlek,* Zanouba removes her veil. Trembling, she follows her mother-in-law up stairs and down several narrow passages leading to Mashalla's apartment. At last, here is Abd el Meguid! She rushes toward him, past a small woman who appears stunned to see her. Zanouba ignores her. Through her tears she glimpses her husband propped up by pillows. Two women stand at his bedside. Somehow, she instantly recognizes Narguiss and Gaulisar. As if in a dream she kisses Abd el Meguid's hand in respectful greeting. He smiles, saying: "Welcome, my child. The sight of you is enough to heal me."

Before she can respond, a furious voice lashes out: "Hide your face before this man, you shameless girl!"

Zanouba spins around and retorts: "Before this man? Before this man I have every right to show my face." The confidence with which she has spoken surprises her. For a brief moment her indignant response sustains her. Then, all at once she feels as if the ceiling is about to come down about her head. Her forehead is moist with perspiration and her hands turn clammy. She is not sure her legs are going to hold her when Abd el Meguid comes to her rescue. He speaks quietly in his deep voice: "This my wife, Zanouba."

Gaulisar and Narguiss rush toward her, arms extended in a gesture of welcome. Each kisses her repeatedly on the cheeks.

"Welcome, sister, welcome! Ahlan, wa Sahlan!"

Suddenly, behind them, they hear a crash. Mashalla has fainted, knocking over a tray. Zanouba's mouth flies open. Om Mahmood runs to Mashalla. Abd el Meguid tries to get up and cries out in pain.

Narguiss had noticed Mashalla's face flush, then grow deathly pale at the sight of Zanouba. She shrugs her shoulders, calls a servant, points to Mashalla crumpled in a heap on the flagstones and says: "Take this casualty into the bathroom." Within minutes Zanouba hears water running, then a startled cry, then screams. Narguiss returns with an expression of disdain on her face.

Later, Zanouba will discover that, having laid Mashalla on the bathroom floor, Narguiss had stuck pins in her co-wife's hair, to rid her of any ill feelings she harbors toward Abd el Meguid's new bride. She had then forced a piece of charcoal between her teeth, a symbol of the sting of jealousy. Next, she had placed a lump of sugar above Mashalla's heart to sweeten her disposition. Finally, she had doused Mashalla's head with water to bring her to her senses.

"There is nothing like water to get rid of the evil spirits that take hold of a jealous heart, little sister," she later explains to Zanouba. "They're terrified of water!" Mashalla thus chastened had promptly spat out the charcoal (and with it her jealous feelings). She had shaken the pins out of her hair. The sugar had, of course, melted instantly.

Narguiss, returning and seeing Zanouba's consternation, embraces her and says: "Don't worry! You'll see, she'll come out as docile as a lamb!" Gaulisar, standing beside Narguiss, shakes her head in agreement and puts her arm around Zanouba to reassure her. They both congratulate Abd el Meguid on his beautiful young bride.

When Mashalla returns, she does indeed appear transformed. Is it really the effect of the magic or the sobering shower she has received which has caused her to come out smiling? She kisses Zanouba, explaining that she had been taken by surprise, shocked. "Had anyone bothered to tell me who you were, my dear, I would not have spoken to you as if you were a stranger. Now I would like to welcome you properly, like a sister."

Zanouba is taken aback. Can this nice woman be the one she has been warned not to trust? She no longer knows what to think. She looks to Abd el Meguid for guidance, but he only returns her glance tenderly, indicating his delight at seeing her. Om Mahmood and Gaulisar look on, impassive, while Narguiss smiles, full of mischief. Had Zanouba been more vigilant or less innocent, she would never have missed the hardness in Mashalla's eyes which no smile could obliterate.

"Why does life have to be so complicated?" Zanouba wonders with trepidation. Suddenly she wishes she were in the safe haven of Fatma's home, singing, giggling or doing chores with Zohra. Now that she is in Matariyya there is no turning back. Also, she knows in her heart that Abd el Meguid wants her near him.

Om Mahmood, sensing Zanouba's apprehension, takes her aside. "You have nothing to fear, my child. You'll stay with me and sleep in my harem with two of my granddaughters. You'll be safe. What can possibly happen to you?" Om Mahmood's quiet confidence reassures her. She thinks, "What is there to worry about? My Wali, my lord and master is nearby . . ." She smiles at her husband, thinking how noble and strong he is. Abd el Meguid responds by trying move closer to her, but the effort makes him moan. From his bed he gazes so lovingly at her that all of her uncertainty melts away. Abd el Meguid will always protect her.

6 · BREAD

When Zanouba wakes the next morning, she hears familiar sounds: the heavy, rhythmic thud of dough being kneaded and the humming of women's voices rising toward her. Why haven't her mother and sisters called her to help bake? She listens, still drowsy, trying to make out the somewhat masculine voice of Om Badaweyya, the bakerwoman of Darb el Magharba. Gradually, she realizes she is not at home. The voices are not those of Om Badaweyya, her mother or sisters.

She is alone in Om Mahmood's large bedroom. The sun is up. Light is streaming in from the two windows to her right. Filtered through the *mashrabiyya* screens, it dapples the flagstone floor. Her hand wanders over the rug below her mattress. The edges are thick and knobby. Woven of cream colored raw sheep's wool, it gives off a slight odor: Lanolin. It was made especially for Om Mahmood in the village of Matariyya; the wool was collected from several shepherds.

Zanouba props herself up on her elbow to look at a few tiny white clouds moving lightly around the minaret of a neighboring mosque. "I'm in Abd el Meguid's house," she whispers, getting up. Her eyes wander over the room. The ceiling is high, supported by large beams, painted light blue. The walls are bare and have been freshly whitewashed. Against them divans are arranged, interspersed with trunks containing clothes and linens. The divans are covered in flowered chintz with large red roses and blue leaves symmetrically arranged on a gold background. Two large trunks, their shiny brass fittings glinting, belong to Om Mahmood. The smaller ones, standing side by side, are those reserved for children's clothing. The medium-sized trunk beside them, assigned to Zanouba by her mother-in-law, is where the young woman has neatly folded away the few things she brought with her from Abbasiyya.

Between her mattress and Om Mahmood's were two small bedrolls on which Alya and Naima slept. The little girls have already folded them, putting them beside their grandmother's in a special alcove at the far end of the room. How quietly they did all of this, Zanouba thinks. She is amazed at having slept right through. She gets up and rolls her own mattress, stowing it beside the others. Eager to make a good impression on her mother-in-law she shakes and smoothes out the rug. She then dresses and hurries to Om Mahmood's bathroom to wash her face before going downstairs.

Guided by the sound of voices and bustle below, she has no trouble finding her way. Zanouba stands, astonished, in the doorway of the oven room. It is huge, nothing like Darb el Magharba or Abbasiyya. Thirty or forty women, servants, household members, neighbors, bakers are working. Little girls run hither and thither.

More voices emerge from the spacious kitchen adjoining the oven room. As soon as she walks in, however, the laughter and the gossip cease, as do the vigorous hands kneading dough, gloved to the elbows in flour. All eyes turn on her. She blushes and edges toward Om Mahmood and the group of women around her. Gaulisar exclaims, "Welcome sister! Welcome!" Om Mahmood greets her, saying, "May your morning be a sweet as the fragrant rose, daughter. Come join us in making our bread." Narguiss adds, "Welcome, Zanouba, Ahlan wa Sahlan. May your morning be as smooth as cream, my sister. God willing, we'll soon be baking to celebrate the birth of your son."

After this interruption the baking room hums once again. The little girls, delighted with the new arrival, press around Zanouba's skirts, taking her hands tenderly and engaging her in conversation. Meanwhile, the tired kneaders, their blue gowns—*gallabeyyas*—dusted with flour, pause to let another group of women spell them. They offer Zanouba their most radiant smiles. Zanouba, returning their smiles, watches the women who have taken their place. Squatting, strong backs bending, naked arms working the dough, they rhythmically lift and drop it against the glazed, earthenware sides of the knee-high basins. Om Muhammad, a robust Sudanese, senses the young mistress' eyes on her and redoubles her efforts. The dough flies around her, a piece landing on Zanouba's dress. They both laugh at her antics, and Zanouba moves away.

Gaulisar then takes Zanouba by the hand, pulling her toward three other basins where dough is rising. Removing the clean, damp sheeting covering one, she pokes her finger in, tears off a piece, and puts it in her mouth, then gives Narguiss, standing beside her, a taste. Narguiss declares, "It's good. It's ready for the oven," and pops a chunk into Zanouba's mouth. They all laugh. Narguiss calls cheerfully to an old servant squatting in a corner at the far end of the room. "Is the oven warm enough, mother?" The old woman slides open the metal door, testing. "Warm as your heart, my daughter," she answers, breaking into a toothless smile. Then, with a brisk flick of her wrist, she tosses two more dried turds into the lower chamber of the oven. The fire glows.

Later a group of women begin something like a dance around the basins where the dough has risen, dragging them closer to the oven. One removes the sheeting, another covers clean wooden boards with bran to prevent the loaves from sticking. Three women, the sleeves of their dresses rolled up above their elbows, squat between the basins and the boards which are set up on ledges on either side of the oven. Each grabs a chunk of dough, rolls it between the palms of her hands, flattens it into a pita loaf and deftly tosses it on the board. Still later, after the bread has risen a second time, the old woman tending the fire picks up the bread on a square wooden pallet and, with a forward flick of its long handle, tosses each loaf expertly into the oven. They land flat and puff up almost instantly. A few minutes later, another group of women will remove them, spread them out to cool on clean sheeting, and finally store them in large hampers.

Om Mahmood calls to Zanouba: "Come with me, daughter. We need to catch some pigeons for lunch to celebrate your arrival." Zanouba, beaming, follows her out to the pigeon house, trailed by a cluster of little girls. They have just found a new playmate!

At the same time they see Narguiss heading off in another direction, leaving Gaulisar in charge of baking. Each takes a weekly turn supervising the process, counting the loaves and storing them.

The minute Zanouba is out of earshot she becomes the subject of speculation. Some of the servants had seen her the night of her arrival; others are seeing her for the first time. All have noticed that she is pregnant, and Gaulisar confirms it. Everyone agrees that she is pretty and graceful, but what is more important is that she is carrying Abd el Meguid's child. Will it be a boy, the son they have all wished for? Or one more girl?

"God willing, she will give Abd el Meguid a son," one woman declares. "If God so wills it," responds another.

"Who knows if she might not be like Sitt Faika . . ." interjects Khadija, Mashalla's devoted servant. Stunned, everyone stops short. All spin around to stare at her.

"Viper!" cries Om Muhammad, eyes shining with fury in her dark face.

"Is your tongue only good for slander?" echoes Om Hussein, squatting beside her.

"Cursed be your mother, you daughter of a thousand devils!" shouts the toothless Rokeyya from the other side of the room.

"And your children's children," echoes another.

"Is it your mistress who has put you up to this?" asks Khadra, still holding the lump of dough she was shaping between her hands.

"How much did she pay you to throw a curse on this house?" interjects a neighbor.

The robust Om Muhammad suddenly swings away from the basin where she has been kneading, her hands sticky with dough. She grabs Khadija by the hair and spits in her face. The two come to blows. Everyone screams. Although Gaulisar commands them to cease, her voice is lost in the din. She throws up her hands, helpless.

Suddenly, Om Mahmood appears in the doorway. The noise stops. "What is happening here?" she asks sternly.

No one answers. No one wants to bring up the painful subject of Faika. Abd el Meguid divorced her fifteen years ago and she was banished from his house. Since that time he has given strict orders that her name never be mentioned.

"What's wrong?" Om Mahmood asks again. Om Muhammad finally speaks up. "This loathsome bitch said that Sitt Zanouba was no more pregnant than someone whose name I dare not say!"

"That's not true, that's not what I said," Khadija retorts.

"I swear to God, may he strike me dead, that she said it," cries Om Muhammad.

"May God strike her down for this lie!" exclaims Khadija. In chorus, several women confirm: "She did say it!"

All eyes turn on Gaulisar. "She said it," Gaulisar concludes, her voice thick with emotion.

Indignant, Om Mahmood dismisses Khadija on the spot. "Go on, Khadija. We'll make bread without you from now on and you can tell your mistress she'd better find someone else to take your place." The old woman's deeply wrinkled face darkens. Her eyes harden.

As Khadija leaves without a word, she glimpses Zanouba, at the far end of the garden, a bevvy of little girls tugging at her skirts. She thinks of another young woman, her belly rounded like this one's. Faika had given the family so much hope, only to be chased away in disgrace. She too had been young and beautiful. Khadija pauses, remembering. Faika's huge, limpid eyes had seemed to look without seeing. Small and plump, she appeared to be without malice. How had she become embroiled in a scheme which instead of safeguarding her place in Abd el Meguid's home and heart, had crushed it?

Faika had mystified the household. Four years after her marriage to Abd el Meguid, she had announced that she was pregnant. Her housemates rejoiced. They had watched closely as she seemed to grow heavy with child. She had acted the part so convincingly! Visitors who came to see her always found her on a divan, weary, a little distant. Everyone had catered to her needs, particularly Narguiss and Gaulisar. From time to time she would cradle her belly and wince as if in pain. Everyone lived in fear of her losing the baby. They made it a privilege to coddle her.

Who would have thought that Faika could have been so cunning? She was the family's beacon of hope, of course. They had wanted to believe her.

At the beginning of her ninth month, as custom would have it, Faika had gone home to deliver. She would give birth to her first child in her own mother's house.

Word was finally sent to Om Mahmood that her daughter-in-law had gone into labor. She rushed to her side.

Faika's mother lived a good distance away, however, at the far end of Darb el Gamamiz. When Om Mahmood arrived she was greeted with joy cries. Her heart nearly burst with with pride and pleasure. A son at last!

Om Mahmood never could forget the big baby boy the midwife placed in her arms. Also, she would always remember Abd el Meguid's eyes; radiant with joy. In her bed, Faika had smiled. Blood stained towels had been knowingly tossed nearby. Om Youssef, Faika's plump mother, could not stop enumerating the resemblances between father and son. Abd el Meguid nodded, agreed, laughed with genuine pleasure, emptying his purse on the bed. He offered Faika a matching set of gold bracelets and earrings, a piece of heavy blue velvet worked with gold thread for a new dress, promising a thousand other gifts.

Om Mahmood herself had not the slightest doubt that the baby was the spitting image of his father. She was ecstatic. She had insisted on remaining at Faika's side to care for her as she regained her strength. Om Youssef had answered that they wouldn't dream of letting her go to the trouble. But no one could persuade Om Mahmood to go home with Abd el Meguid.

She seemed tireless, unable to take her eyes off the beautiful infant. She had loved him instantly with all her heart and soul.

In time, however, she grew uneasy. She began to notice the women of the household whispering and glancing strangely at one another. She wondered why Faika's bedsheets and clothing were not being changed more frequently and why the baby never stopped crying. Faika put him to the breast, but he came away howling. The baby was hungry, of course!

Om Youssef, with tears in her eyes, had lamented that her daughter did not have enough milk whereupon the midwife had suggested a wet nurse. She informed them that she knew of a clean, healthy peasant woman whose baby had died a few days after birth. She was certain she could hire her. Om Mahmood had insisted they wait, indicating that Faika could still get her milk up and that in the course of three or four days nothing would happen to the baby. The very next morning, however, the wet nurse was on their doorstep and immediately put the baby to her breast. Om Mahmood noted uneasily that the baby nursed a little too avidly for a newborn. On closer observation she noticed an uncanny resemblance between the wet nurse and the child. She did not want to believe her eyes, but could not push aside the doubts which assailed her. That very evening she decided to investigate. Without raising any alarm, she announced that she was going back to Matariyya to prepare for Faika's homecoming. Next, she took aside the peasant woman and questioned her. When she asked her where she was from, the woman faltered, then named the village of Mit el Sireg.

Om Mahmood knew the wife of the mayor of Mit el Sireg who was a cousin of her husband's. She wanted to go directly to her. She resisted. She struggled with her doubts, telling herself one minute that they were outrageous and the next that the evidence was clear as day. Two days went by. On the third she left for Mit el Sireg. What she discovered broke her heart and Abd el Meguid's. Not only was the wet nurse unknown to the village, but no child had been born there in two weeks. Dizzy with anguish, Om Mahmood had stormed back to Om Youssef's house taking the wet nurse aside and threatening her with prison. The woman had wavered. She confessed only when Om Mahmood put fifty gold pieces and the promise of a pardon before her in exchange for the truth.

Faika had never been pregnant. The baby was the wet nurse's son. The midwife had orchestrated everything, including bringing the baby hidden under her veil as Faika pretended to go into labor. The entire situation had been a sham from start to finish!

Om Mahmood would never forget the horrible scene which followed. She had demanded a confession from her daughter-in-law. The midwife had fled, taking with her the wet nurse and her baby, leaving Om Youssef and Faika weeping hysterically.

Om Mahmood and Abd el Meguid were determined to avoid scandal, however. They announced that the baby had died in the night. They simulated a funeral. They buried the imaginary son and with him their hopes and dreams.

Faika, of course, never returned to Matariyya. Two months went by. Om Mahmood and her son grieved. Finally, Abd el Meguid sent Faika her divorce papers. Neither Faika nor any of her relations would ever set foot in Matariyya again nor was anyone in Abd el Meguid's household allowed to mention her name.

Abd el Meguid was deeply affected.

Om Mahmood was never able to forget the beautiful baby she had held in her arms. At the time of Abd el Meguid's marriage to Zanouba he would have just turned fifteen; a young man with broad shoulders and bright eyes, she thinks. He would have led a life of comfort and plenty. As the son of a peasant she knows that he must be harnessed to a menial job, barely making a living.

"What a pity!" she sighs, tears wetting her wrinkled cheeks. "What if I hadn't discovered the truth? Or acted on my doubts? Abd el Meguid would have a son who would be in school now. We would have heard a son's laughter in the *salamlek*. Wouldn't we have loved him as our own?"

Watching Zanouba chasing pigeons, raising one above her head, making the giggling Shafika and Naima reach for it, Om Mahmood reflects: "She's not much older than Narguiss' and Gaulisar's daughters. Look at her, playing with them, not much more than a child herself. Can she be God's gift to us? The one who will bring a son into this house full of girls?"

Om Mahmood brushes away painful thoughts, making

room for hope. The sight of Zanouba frolicking dispels bitter memories of Faika and her fake son. Om Mahmood
smiles when her young daughter-in-law proudly presents
her with the single pigeon she has caught.

"Used up all the grain I gave you and only caught one!"
exclaims Om Mahmood, pretending to be cross. She shouts
to her granddaughters: "Naima, Alya, call auntie Sayyeda
or there won't be pigeon enough for lunch for another
week!" Turning to Zanouba, she explains, "Sayyeda feeds
the pigeons and they flock to her. She'll have a dozen in
hand before you can say 'Allah be Praised'!"

"By the way, where is Narguiss?" she asks.

"She's gone up to her apartment," the little girls answer
in chorus.

Gently, Om Mahmood says to Zanouba, "Look for
Narguiss, my child. She'll give you some sewing or something useful to do keep your hands busy."

"I'm not too bad with a needle, mother. I'd like to do
anything to be of service to you," Zanouba replies, eager to
please.

"You're a good girl," Om Mahmood says, stroking
Zanouba's head. "I've already cut some material for new
dresses for Alya and Naima. Ask Narguiss to give you the
pieces. You could sew in her apartment and she can coach
you on our household routines. You will find Narguiss full
of good advice, Zanouba. She'll take you under her wing."

"You seem to love her very much," Zanouba says.

"That's true. We have lived side by side for a long time.
I have come to love her although she is a slave—a *mahdiyya*—not a wife. It's the same with Gaulisar. They have
been more affectionate to my son than some of his wives.
You see, my child, a wife cannot take credit for being a wife
because marriage is a contract between two families. But a
mahdiyya is chosen for her qualities, her beauty. She can be
proud of what she is."

Om Mahmood notices the little smile forming on Zanouba's lips and says, "I know what you're thinking: Narguiss can hardly be called beautiful now. But once she was beautiful, my child. I can remember the day I purchased her at the slave market, Oukal el Gellaba. She's Ethiopian. It was a long, long time ago, when the Wali Said Pasha died. She was twelve at the time; an adorable little girl. Abd el Meguid was with me and was instantly taken with her. I bought her as a gift for him on his twentieth birthday."

"And Gaulisar?" asks Zanouba.

"What! You haven't heard the story of Gaulisar? I'll tell you. My husband, Abd el Hamid, was playing backgammon with his good friend Murad Pasha one day at his palace. Murad Pasha was losing. He proposed one last game, telling Abd el Hamid that he had received a lovely Circassian slave from Istanbul the night before. He would bet her against what my husband had already won."

"And the Pasha lost?" Zanouba asks, wide eyed.

"And the Pasha lost. The next day Gaulisar arrived at our house. This happened just a short time before my husband died. Abd el Hamid was over seventy years old. He decided, given his age, that it would be better to give Gaulisar to his son. That is how she came to be with us."

"Wasn't Narguiss jealous?" asks Zanouba.

"Well, yes, for a few months. And so was Nafissa who had been Abd el Meguid's wife for three years. Of course, they couldn't help but be jealous. Gaulisar was a splendid girl, with that flawless white skin which is typical of the Circassians. She was tall and just plump enough to be pleasing. Abd el Hamid was giving his son a gift fit for a king. I wanted to make sure there was harmony among us all, so I did my best to console Narguiss. She knew that Gaulisar was considered more beautiful, but Narguiss was brighter," Om Mahmood adds, seeing Zanouba's interest in every detail.

"In any case, Abd el Meguid never openly favored one

above the other. If he spent a night with Gaulisar, he spent the next one with Narguiss. If he offered one a dress or a piece of jewelry, he gave the other a gift of equal value. And, of course, because Gaulisar does not have a grain of malice or meanness in her, she quickly befriended Narguiss and Nafissa and they got along very well."

"Don't you favor Narguiss a little?" asks Zanouba.

"Well, I was the one who bought her and raised her, so naturally she's just like a daughter. She nursed me like a daughter too during the cholera epidemic. It was then that I really appreciated her. She took over the running of the house because half of us were sick, and cared for us without fear for herself. She saved both my life and Gaulisar's. But, sadly, she lost Nafissa and her newborn baby girl, as well as her own daughter, Rokeyya. Through it all she was selfless and devoted, not even taking a single day to mourn. When she buried Rokeyya, she promptly came home to look after the rest of us."

Om Mahmood pauses, then adds quietly, "It's Narguiss I have chosen to perform the last rites for me when I die; to wash and dress me. I have left her and Gaulisar my savings, my jewelry, clothing, all the things I will not need in the other world. You see, Zanouba, the rest of you have families that will take care of you. Mashalla is rich and you will inherit from your parents. Gaulisar and Narguiss have no one other than Abd el Meguid and myself."

Seeing that Zanouba is looking wistful, Om Mahmood hastens to reassure her.

"My child, I hope you're not vexed by what I've told you. My affection for Narguiss doesn't affect my feelings for you. Didn't I pick you for Abd el Meguid? I've placed my greatest hopes in you. It's been painful for all of his wives not to have given him a son. This house has only heard the voices of little girls. God willing, through you a son will be given him."

"From your lips to the gates of heaven, mother. It is my

dearest wish!" Zanouba exclaims, following Om Mahmood upstairs.

She walks up slowly. Her belly is visibly rounded and heavy. The little being growing inside her will determine her destiny. Can it be, she wonders, that I am the chosen one? Can it be that I will succeed where the others have failed? She blushes, stroking her belly tenderly. She feels so young, so small, almost insignificant beside the tall, wizened woman who is her mother-in-law. In fact, she finds her a little daunting. How can it be otherwise? Everything about this harem is still unfamiliar. Although she is proud of the great responsibility she has been given, it is also frightening. This house, despite the cheerful activity buzzing like a hive, lives under a shadow. Is Zanouba destined to remove it? Will she be the one to offer her husband a son, a future master, without whom neither wives who please, nor bread, nor love, nor life itself have any meaning?

7 · JEALOUSY

Mashalla's face is drawn. She has maintained Abd el Meguid's interest in her despite being barren. However, since Zanouba's arrival her recurring nightmare is of being cast adrift, humiliated. She escapes frequently to her room, loathing the company of the other women. Although she is devoured with anxiety, she knows she must be cautious. She feels like howling, crying, biting, yet she has to keep smiling.

Mashalla's predicament is impossible. She cannot trust a single woman with whom she shares her daily life. She certainly cannot pour her heart out to any member of Abd el Meguid's harem, nor even to her own servant. She must silence her heart and her voice. One outburst, one careless word, one impulsive act could lead to divorce. Only at night, with her face buried in her pillows does Mashalla allow her tears to flow. Where can she find strength to continue?

One day, unable to go on, she sends for her aunt Nafissa, the only member of her extended family who understands her, whom Mashalla has not alienated. She desperately needs to be comforted.

When Sitt Nafissa arrives, Mashalla's heart instantly overflows. Weeping bitterly, she exclaims, "Oh, my dear aunt, Abd el Meguid has subjected me to the worst affront! He married a year ago without ever telling me! I suspected nothing. Suddenly, there she was, this Zanouba, this upstart, in my apartment, her face not even covered! I was ready to strangle her! Imagine how I felt when she confronted me, saying 'Before this man I have every right to show my face'!"

Mashalla whispers, but her voice is trembling with rage and her eyes are bloodshot. Her aunt looks at her, distressed. Mashalla's face is swollen from weeping. Aunt Nafissa touches her hand and says, "Go wash your face, my child, and try to be calm. It wouldn't do for the others to see you this way. Your husband has had other wives. How is one more or one less going to make a difference?"

"But he loves her, auntie! It's written all over his face! You should see how he looks at her! When she's there, his eyes, his words are all for her. No one else exists for him but this thing with no chest, her ass as flat as a board and her belly already protruding!"

"She's pregnant?!"

"That's the calamity! What magic spell has this little slut cast on him? What did her parents do to get her pregnant? You should see him, auntie! He's drooling over her! You'd think he'd died and gone to heaven!"

"Calm yourself, Mashalla . . ." her aunt tries to interrupt, but Mashalla will not let her.

"I had persuaded him to accept the will of God," she says. "I thought I could finally live in peace with this old man and here I'm replaced by this big bellied interloper!"

Mashalla's chest heaves and her words are lost in a fit of sobbing.

"Praise be to Allah! Praise be to God the merciful! All is written, my child. Everything is in His hands. Is it for us to question why one woman is given ten children while ten others remain childless? Don't you remember your cousin Zebeyda? How she prayed and prayed for her belly to stay empty just one year!"

"But, auntie . . ." Mashalla protests, regaining some composure.

Aunt Nafissa interrupts her. "If you forget all else, Mashalla, remember what I'm going to tell you and wear it as if it were an earring: A sailor has no say in what wind fills his sails, but a good sailor will master his craft whatever the weather."

"But auntie, if she has a son I'm lost! Do you think I could stand to live here, tossed aside, while she triumphs?" Mashalla sobs. Sitt Nafissa looks at her niece. Her heart fills with pity to see the strong Mashalla reduced to a whimpering heap. Her eyes are wet with sympathy.

Mashalla collapses on the divan, grinding her teeth, trying to stifle her cries of rage with a pillow. "I want to wring her neck, auntie! I want to tear out her eyes and puncture that belly of hers! I can't go on! I can't go on!" She buries her face in her aunt's lap. Stroking Mashalla's head as she used to do when she was a little girl, aunt Nafissa whispers: "You know, my child, some women do have miscarriages . . ."

Mashalla instantly perks up. "Oh, auntie," she says, her eyes glowing with hope, "do you know how we can do it?"

"That's not what I meant, my child. I've only heard that certain herbs by their smell alone . . ."

Mashalla grabs her aunt's hands and exclaims, "Auntie, please, please tell me where I can get some!"

"Since my sister-in-law's unfortunate accident last year, I swore on the tomb of Sayyed el Badawy that I would never get mixed up in such matters again," replies Sitt Nafissa, avoiding Mashalla's eyes.

Mashalla knows better than to insist. She waits. Both women are silent. Mashalla gets up. She splashes her face with cold water. Sitt Nafissa looks at her. Then, almost as an afterthought, she whispers, "My Sudanese maid Behita . . . she knows the merchants . . . the spice market. . . ."

Mashalla jumps at the chance. She exclaims, her voice hoarse, "Please help me, auntie. You know I can't leave the house as long as Abd el Meguid is sick. Would you send Behita to me?"

Her aunt gone, Mashalla feels calmer. She will use her wiles and draw Zanouba into her web.

That afternoon she greets her young rival with a smile, asks after her health, compliments her on her good fortune. She invites Zanouba to her room, displaying her beautiful dresses and jewelry, secretly planning her next move. Zanouba's protruding belly must be eliminated. Mashalla is convinced that her place in Abd el Meguid's heart depends upon it. If Zanouba's child is a son, she will instantly become her husband's favorite. Abd el Meguid's personal belongings would be moved to her harem. She might even be given Mashalla's beautiful apartment! The thought alone of such an indignity causes Mashalla's eyes to glow with fury. She would rather die than be shamed.

"If I fail I will end my life and take them all with me! Zanouba, Abd el Meguid, the whole lot! I'll poison them and then kill myself!" She pictures herself gathering herbs, measuring powders, mixing black potions in glass vials. She sees bodies writhing in pain, faces turning green, eyes protruding. She stands amidst the carnage, downs the last of the poison . . . Her eyes sting with tears of self pity. "Luckily, I don't need to kill anybody, even myself. Just make sure Zanouba loses that baby . . ."

She waits impatiently for the old negress her aunt has promised to send. She is persuaded that Behita is the key to her deliverance. The following day, however, she waivers. "I don't really hate Zanouba. What if she dies?" Suddenly tears come again. Had circumstances been different she and Zanouba might have become friends. She thinks, "It's not Zanouba's fault that Abd el Meguid wanted to marry again. Or that his wives have not given him sons. Another daughter would make no difference. Abd el Meguid has had nothing but daughters until now. It must be God's will. Why would that change?"

Although Abd el Meguid is clearly smitten with his new wife, Mashalla knows that her charms can win him back . . . if Zanouba does not give him a son. If the baby is a boy, all other wives will be eclipsed. Zanouba alone will be the apple of his eye. She alone will enjoy the privileges conferred on the mothers of sons. Mashalla's rage rekindles.

"I must never let this happen!" she exclaims. Suddenly afraid, she peeks out of her room. No one is there. Her head is spinning with thoughts. She sits down to consider her plan.

"Would it be murder? No, an unborn child has no soul. Besides, if all the women who aborted were considered criminals every household would have to have its own prison!"

Mashalla has overlooked the fact that she will be causing another woman to abort against her will.

All at once she panics. "What if Behita were to tell someone . . . What if Abd el Meguid were to suspect something . . . Would he divorce me? Send me to jail? No. Faika was enough . . . He wouldn't want another scandal," she rationalizes, adding to reassure herself, "If one is careful one does not get caught."

At midday Behita finally arrives. Mashalla scrutinizes her visitor. "How ugly she is!" She looks at her greyish black skin, her protruding belly. She imagines sticklike legs and mounds of flesh beneath Behita's black gown. Mashalla is disgusted by the sight of the old woman's long, skinny arms which hang limp at her sides, her pockmarked face, wide, flat nose and fleshy lips which she constantly moistens with her tongue. Mashalla looks at Behita's tongue with morbid fascination. "What a strange pink it is," she thinks, "almost indecently bright!" She notes Behita's strange eyes also, two dark slits, barely visible behind lashless eyelids. Their look is unsettling, even frightening, except when she gazes at her mistress. Only then does Behita's expression soften. Mistress and slave are the same age; Behita is blindly devoted to Nafissa. As a little girl, like Narguiss, she had been bought at the slave market, Oukal el Gellaba. She had been a gift to Nafissa from her father, a playmate for his cherished daughter.

Mashalla struggles to overcome her repugnance. She speaks. Behita listens, her face breaking into a toothless smile. She chuckles when she discovers the extent of Mashalla's fears. "You are neither the first nor the last to be faced with such a dilemma," Behita reassures her. "There's nothing to worry about, my lady; I have the solution to your problem." Untying a corner of her black veil, Behita hands Mashalla seven tiny packages wrapped in pink butcher paper, expertly secured with the thread-thin string used by the spice merchants of the Mousky. Mashalla takes them with a trembling hand and stuffs them into a chest between layers of her clothing. She hands one gold sovereign to Behita who looks at it with disdain. "What's this, my lady? One guinea? I paid four to have this potion prepared and another to have the herbs ground! Three of these herbs come all the way from India and one is from Ethiopia. If you knew what trouble I went to . . ."

Behita crouches down beside the divan, making herself at home. Her voice is high-pitched and carries. Mashalla, afraid of being overheard, tells her to whisper. "May God almighty be my witness, Sitt Mashalla," she begins, "I had to get up at the crack of dawn to run this errand! I posted myself on Hagg Abd el Samad's doorstep even before the breakfast bean sellers had begun their rounds. When he saw me sitting there he exclaimed, 'What brings you here so early, mother? Did you sleep in front of my shop? Or did the devil dancing in your room drive you out at this ungodly hour?' I was the first client in the *souk,* my lady. Instantly, I broke into tears. I had to gain his sympathy, of course, to get what I came for. I said, 'Ah, Sidi, I am the most miserable of women! All my children have died but one girl. There has not been a year that I have not buried the fruit of my womb. My eyes have been disfigured from weeping! I have a child in every cemetery in Cairo and some in Upper Egypt! Allah in all his mercy, finally taking pity on me, left me one daughter. One single daughter is all I have, my good Hagg, and she's now at risk. I am sure to lose her and die of grief if you don't help me, oh Hagg!' And, having said this, I sobbed all the harder. Hagg Abd el Samad then said to me, 'Calm yourself, mother, calm yourself. Your story is sad but how can I help? My business is spices. I neither sell happiness nor do I trade in good luck!' I then replied, 'My daughter's husband has sworn to take another wife, oh, Sidi! She's too thin for his taste.' Hagg Abd el Samad then chuckled and said to me, 'Mother, your son-in-law surely has his eye on a pretty girl he wants to marry and this is just a pretext.' I answered, 'Allah be praised! That's just it, oh Hagg! You can help me and come to her rescue by giving me a potion to put some flesh on the girl's bones. Then if she still doesn't fill her husband's eye we'll know he was lying.' Hagg Abd el Samad stroked his beard and looked at me from under his glasses and replied, 'I might be able to put something together, mother, but you have to swear that you are telling me the truth, that you won't go using this potion to do harm.' I replied, 'Oh, Sidi, may God preserve us from evil!' He then said to me, 'You take the herbs I will prepare for you and mix them with molasses and cook the mixture in sesame oil until you get a paste. First thing in the morning and before going to bed, your daughter must dip her fingers three times into the molasses and lick them clean—she must do this on an empty stomach. At night she must heat up the concoction and inhale it. Make sure there are no pregnant women around, though. The smell is so strong it can induce a miscarriage!' That's what Hagg Abd el Samad said to me." Behita chuckles. "You can imagine that I went to some trouble to reassure him!" Mashalla is silent. Behita looks at her, trying to gauge her reaction. She concludes, "He wanted ten guineas in payment and I bargained him down to four. I had your best interest at heart, my lady!"

Mashalla is convinced that Behita is stealing her blind. She has no choice but to give her what she has asked for. As an afterthought she even adds a tip and says, "I'll let you know when I need your help, Behita. Can you come when I send for you?"

"God willing," Behita replies.

Mashalla feels calmer. Zanouba must be in her seventh month. She can afford to be patient now, preparing to act when the time is right. She will first kiss and coddle her rival. She will feign disinterested affection. She will draw her into her confidence until just before Zanouba returns to her mother's house to deliver, at the start of the ninth month. Then, she will strike.

8 · QUIETUDE

Abd el Meguid has recovered. He has had no pain for several days. He walks around a little, going to the *salamlek* to receive friends. He even spends a night there, gradually returning to the life of a man in good health.

Mashalla will be the first of his wives that he honors with a visit. He plans to have dinner with her and sleep in her harem. He wants to thank her for her devoted ministrations to him during his illness. He offers her a beautiful pair of earrings which she puts on immediately to show her appreciation. His every gesture is intended to let her know that she has not lost her rank in the harem. Abd el Meguid feels like a husband who, having been unfaithful to his wife, redoubles his efforts to please her.

Although Mashalla seems to live in harmony with Zanouba, Abd el Meguid worries, knowing Mashalla's jealous nature. He has been surprised by the friendliness she shows toward his young wife and is even embarrassed to hear her praise Zanouba's beauty and spirited grace. He suspects he is being duped. Having had seven wives, he knows that one wife's praise for another is rarely sincere, particularly when the compliment comes from one as haughty as Mashalla. He remains alert, vigilant.

"Are you planning to send Zanouba to Abbasiyya, Abd el Meguid?" asks Mashalla. "It won't be long now before she goes home to her mother's to give birth. The dear child has confessed to me that she likes being here. Why, Sidi, didn't you bring her to us as soon as you married her? We would have welcomed her like a sister—attended to her needs, instructed her."

Abd el Meguid flushes and says: "You see, Mashalla, there are three of you already, as well as my mother. That makes four women in our household. I didn't want to impose a stranger on you. And then, Zanouba became pregnant so quickly . . . She will have her baby in a couple of months. She will return to her mother's home to give birth, of course, but in the meantime none of you should have to bear the burden . . ."

Mashalla exclaims: "Oh, Sidi! How can you say this! Of course, Zanouba will give birth under her mother's care! But why should she be locked up in that airless house in

Abbasiyya until then? Let her stay here where she can enjoy
the big garden. The fresh air and sunshine will do her good
and her baby will benefit too."

Touched, Abd el Meguid responds, "Mashalla, I'm
happy to see you so interested in Zanouba's well-being . . ."
Mashalla interrupts, exclaiming, "Oh, Sidi! Do you think
I could possibly be jealous of someone who makes you
happy?" She hums, reminding him of a song they had enjoyed in their first year of marriage. The significance of the
words are not lost on Abd el Meguid: "I love all that comes
from my beloved . . ." His expression softens. Mashalla,
smiling coyly, adds, "Have you forgotten, light of my eyes,
that women have only men to fear?" Abd el Meguid smiles.
Softly, Mashalla continues, "I already cherish your son as if
he were my own. I don't know how Narguiss and Gaulisar
might feel, but I would like to offer Zanouba the hospitality
of my harem until she returns to Darb el Magharba for the
happy event." Abd el Meguid, surprised, knits his brows.
Before he can respond, Mashalla says, "Zanouba can have
the room next to mine, Sidi. She can share my meals. I will
hire an extra servant to look after her every need. Is there
more I can offer as a testament of my devotion to you?"

Abd el Meguid, dubious of Mashalla's sincerity, equivo-
cates. "Tomorrow . . . I'll talk to Zanouba . . ."

"Oh, Sidi! Why wait until tomorrow?" Mashalla exclaims and claps her hands, ordering her servant to fetch
Zanouba. An uncomfortable silence settles between husband
and wife. Although he is suspicious of Mashalla's motives,
he also fears judging her too harshly. Mashalla, on the other
hand, is certain she has scored. Her heart beats hard against
her ribs. When Zanouba approaches with a quizzical look
on her face Mashalla puts her instantly at ease. Abd el
Meguid, seeing his two wives side by side, is troubled.
Zanouba is so vulnerable, an easy prey; Mashalla is so de-
vious, formidable. He has a premotion of danger. Instantly
he rejects the thought as preposterous. He says, "Mashalla

proposes you stay with her until your mother comes to take you to Darb el Magharba, my child. How do you feel about this? It's up to you to decide."

Zanouba answers with respect: "It is as you wish, Sidi." Abd el Meguid probes, "But, what do you prefer?" Smiling shyly, she whispers, "I admit that I'm happiest at Matariyya, close to you."

Mashalla's eyes shine as she declares, triumphantly, "Sidi, don't you see how much she wants to stay here!" Turning to Zanouba, she exclaims: "You'll see, darling, how I shall spoil you and watch over you. I'll make sure that you are comfortable, that you come to no harm. And you'll see how much I'll dote on your child since God refuses to give me one of my own! I will love you as my own sister since you, Zanouba, have been chosen to give our dear husband the son he longs for, the son who will carry his coffin at the end of a long life, God willing."

Zanouba answers naively, "Oh, I'll gladly have several children, but I'm afraid. I'm afraid of it hurting, Mashalla. Also last night I had a nightmare. I saw a scorpion coming toward me. I couldn't scream or run away. He stung me and two of my teeth fell out. I don't know what it all means. I can't get it out of my mind."

"God is great! It was nothing but a dream, Zanouba. God forbid that anything bad should happen to you. As to giving birth, its nothing to be afraid of. Look at my cat. She just gave birth to four kittens without so much as a peep. It happens very quickly and the pain is soon forgotten once you have your baby in your arms. We'll feed you a good, rich soup when it's over. Everything will be fine."

Abd el Meguid chimes in, "Nightmares are often the result of indigestion. Go to bed without eating tonight and you will have a peaceful sleep." Mashalla protests, "Oh, Sidi, Zanouba must have dinner with us tonight!"

Abd el Meguid is disturbed at Mashalla's insistence. In her presence he feels self-conscious, neither daring to look at

Zanouba, nor utter a tender word. Furthermore, his young wife's nightmare revives his earlier premonition. His mother had often explained that to dream of losing a tooth means the death of a child while the vision of a scorpion indicates the ill will of a family member. He takes Mashalla aside and, with feigned tenderness, whispers in her ear: "Mashalla, my dear, don't you want to spend this evening together as we are used to doing? We can listen to some songs on the phonograph and you can play your mandolin for me . . . these airs I like so well . . . I would prefer being alone with you. There is no need for this child to be with us."

Mashalla whispers, "We've been married eight years now, Sidi. We don't need to be alone after all this time!" Laughing coyly, she adds, "Or are you afraid my dinner is going to poison our little Zanouba!"

Abd el Meguid has no choice but to give in.

Mashalla's servant lays the low table on which they are accustomed to dining in a small adjoining room. She presents Abd el Meguid's favorite dishes: a large terrine of thick green *mollokhiyya* soup steams in the center of the table, surrounded with little plates of stuffed grape leaves. Tahini, glistening with rich olive oil. A platter of lamb stew. Rice turned out of a mold, forming a perfect dome, slightly crusty on top. Thin, spicy, homemade sausages flavored with coriander. Mounds of fresh bread.

Abd el Meguid, Mashalla, and Zanouba take cushions from the divan and sit on the floor around the table.

Both Abd el Meguid and Zanouba are silent. Mashalla struggles to make conversation.

"I spoke with my mother a few days ago. She told me that the house where I was born, in Bab el Khalig, is being torn down."

"Yes," answers Abd el Meguid, "I understand that they are going to fill in the canal to build a road."

"Our house overlooked the canal, Zanouba. It was a

stately old house, the house of a *bey*. You should have seen it. It had a partly screened balcony jutting out over the water. When the Nile flooded the canal, water almost reached the door. I used to spend hours waiting for a boat to pass. Across the way, on another balcony, another little girl did the same. We slid open a moveable square of screen. We could see each other enough to talk. I wonder what became of her?"

"Wasn't that the house of Mustafa Bey abd el Rehim?" asks Abd el Meguid.

"I wouldn't know," answers Mashalla, "these memories go back more than fifteen years. When we moved from that house I was only just beginning to lose my baby teeth. I can still see us now . . . My sister Aliyya's breasts were just beginning to develop and my brother's beard was just fuzz. Do you know that was the year the British came to Egypt? We were terrified. We fled when we heard that they were approaching Cairo. I was rushed into a carriage with my mother, my sisters, and brothers one night. People went crazy with fear, running every which way in the streets. We were all crying in that carriage, stuffed on top of one another. We took refuge in the house of one of my uncles who lived near the mosque of Sayyedna el Hussein. My mother kept saying there was nothing to fear; no invaders had ever come into this part of the city. As soon as they reached Bab el Futuh, the enemy saw before them the specter of the great-grandson of the Prophet brandishing his sword. Those who did not fall dead in their tracks retreated in terror."

Mashalla stops, telling her servant to fill the glasses with fresh water from the *olla*. She implores Abd el Meguid to take a little more lamb stew and presses more sausages on Zanouba. Abd el Meguid and Zanouba both compliment her on her dinner and she smiles with pleasure. They fall silent again, and Mashalla resumes her tale.

"As long as we remained in Sayyedna el Hussein, we

were forbidden to leave the house. We were told that one never knew with these foreign soldiers . . . My great aunt told tales of the French soldiers who had occupied Cairo long ago. They were very strong and they loved beautiful women. You will laugh when I tell you what mothers who feared for their daughters' safety did!"

Zanouba, fascinated, asks, "What?"

Mashalla says, "They covered the girls' faces and bodies with honey and bits of frayed rag. If they were captured, the soldiers would not touch them, thinking they were sick."

Zanouba bursts out laughing.

Abd el Meguid, amused, asks Mashalla, "Did your mother ever decorate you this way?"

Mashalla answers: "No. We hardly ever saw any soldiers. The Egyptian army maintained law and order and the streets were better lighted and more secure than when the French came. Besides, we were told that the English soldiers did not touch girls from respectable families; they visited prostitutes instead. But the French! They were so gallant and so handsome in their uniforms. They turned the head of many an Egyptian woman. My great-aunt said that harem doors opened to them at night. Some of the girls covered themselves with honey in the morning, then bathed and perfumed themselves for voluptuous nights with the French soldiers." Mashalla falls silent. Both women look dreamy for a moment.

Abd el Meguid takes up the conversation. "At that time," he says, "I had a schoolmate who smoked hashish. He went almost every night to a little coffee house in Gamaliyya to smoke with other *hashasheen*. He told me that just a few puffs on the pipe made him feel weightless. He could go anywhere. No obstacle ever barred his way and walls became transparent. His gaze traversed space, passed through mountains, traveled to countries beyond them where the souls of the dead and even the Prophet Mohammad, prayer and peace be upon him, resided.

"One evening he told me he had seen our hero, Orabi Pasha. The Prophet himself, may peace and prayer be upon him, was offering him a sword to aid his struggle against the British. Another friend smoking with him had even reported seeing Sidi Metwalli handing Orabi Pasha, victorious, the keys to the city and instructing him to take Cairo."

Mashalla says: "Yes, I have heard of such things. But people have extraordinary visions without being under the influence of hashish! A Sheikh praying at the tomb of Sayyedna el Hussein suddenly spotted a dove flying in the direction of Tell el Kebir where Orabi Pasha had set up camp. It had a letter in its beak!"

Zanouba's eyes are wide with wonder. She turns to Abd el Meguid and asks, "Did Orabi Pacha beat the English?"

Abd el Meguid pauses before answering. Finally he says: "He could have beaten them because he was brave and had God on his side. But he was too proud for his own good. He came under the influence of charlatans—magicians, soothsayers, snake charmers, amulet hawkers, dancers, clergymen who spent their time interpreting dreams . . ."

Abd el Meguid's voice trails off, his face pensive.

Mashalla draws him out of his reverie by presenting him with a plate of melon and watermelon cut in half-moon slices.

She says: "Speaking of the English, I am reminded of the story of a British officer who went into a mosque one day. Groups of pupils were sitting around their teachers— ulamas who were reading from the Qur'an. The officer asked his Egyptian interpreter what was being said—he thought the devotees were conspirators. 'Oh, that's the Bokhari,' the interpreter answered, meaning they were reciting verses from a chapter of the Bokhari. The officer, wanting to show off his mastery of the Arabic language, asked 'How fast can it go?' He thought they were referring the the steam engine, the bokhari!"

They all laugh. For a moment they relax and Abd el Meguid says: "One has to laugh over one's misfortunes. Crying is of no use, even in the midst of tragedy. During the cholera epidemic people were dropping like flies. The number of dead was almost greater than the number of living. We lost our share in this house, may God rest their souls. Weepers were never short of work; so many of them paraded in and out of houses that people could hardly cross the street. At that time the first street cars appeared too. When people saw the rails laid and the electric wires installed they thought they were to prevent the epidemic from spreading."

"They did stop it!" exclaims Mashalla.

"Oh, no," answers Abd el Meguid, chuckling. "The doctors did. It was science."

"Science! Science!" exclaims Mashalla, once again. "Do you think doctors are all that strong? The wise people with their magic do just as well, Sidi! Besides, I assure you that the streetcar wires do have magic in them since those who touch them fall dead!"

"I see that you are like my aunt Zeynab, Mashalla. She insists on calling them iron donkeys," Abd el Meguid says, smiling to Zanouba. "She refuses to set foot in a streetcar, claiming to this day that they are the work of the devil, driven by his devotees. She insists that whosoever sets foot aboard one forsakes his soul."

"Well, Satan is not always evil, Sidi! It's said that sages with special powers, 'those who know,' often turn to him for help!" says Mashalla.

They all laugh heartily, their good mood further enhanced by the advent of stewed apricots, raisins and slivered almonds swimming in a fragrant syrup—*mishmishiyya*. The servant presents the crystal bowl to Mashalla who first serves Abd el Meguid and then Zanouba. They relish this special summer dessert in silence followed by steaming mint tea.

They have all eaten abundantly, with the pleasure that comes of sitting leisurely over a meal, relaxing. Zanouba and Abd el Meguid are reclining on the divan, happy, reassured, daring at last to smile at each other.

"You must listen to the most recent song I acquired for my collection," Mashalla says, cranking up her phonograph and placing the hollow, black cylindrical disk—the *kubbayya*—in place.

Zanouba watches her, fascinated.

"What fun Mashalla is," she thinks.

She listens, rapt, to the emphatic rhythm of tambourines accompanying the popular singer, El Koumsariyya. Her voice rises from the primitive machine, light and trembling, filling the room with the lament of unrequited love. Mashalla's eyes glow as she hums along in her seductively hoarse voice, drumming the beat on the edge of the table. She gives herself over completely to the song, "El Helw Mekhasemni," whose words she knows by heart. She sings:

I love him and he doesn't speak to me
Dear God, dear God, have pity on my pain,
   weak woman that I am.
Mother, tell me what to do to win his love.
Tell him that tomorrow,
   from dawn till dusk,
I shall wait for him.
Tell him, mother.
   If he comes to speak to me in the morning,
I shall wear my pink flowered dress and
   dance in the garden among the flowers.
I shall sing and dance for his pleasure,
   so that his eyes may glow with light.
Tell him, mother, that if he comes to speak to me at noon,
   he will find me in my lilac dress
   among the purple blooms.
Tell him that I promise to feed him the flesh
   of a tender gazelle and offer him sweet rose water

to quench his thirst.
Honey will flow from his lips, mother.
If he comes to speak to me at night,
I will be dressed in green,
    my hair bathed in warm perfume,
    spicy 'as the wings of desire.
In his heart, I will plant sweet seeds of love, mother,
    until he is mine once again.

When the song ends, Zanouba is drunk with the music. She begs Mashalla to play another song. The artful Mashalla smiles triumphantly. She takes another *kubayya,* places it carefully on the phonograph, adjusts the needle, and plays a *mawwal* of Abdu el Hamouli, entitled "I Chose to Love Him."

Abd el Meguid, delighted with how the evening has progressed, beats the rhythm on the edge of the table with his fingertips. He is relaxed, his face an image of contentment. His eyes, full of tenderness, gaze on Zanouba's face. The music has given her a special glow.

"She is more beautiful than ever," he thinks.

Mashalla, sitting beside them, innocently speaks. "Now, isn't it delightful to dine like this, just the three of us? Can you still doubt that Zanouba will be happy staying with me?!"

Before her husband has a chance to answer, Mashalla pulls Zanouba toward her, placing the young woman's head on her shoulder in a gesture of supreme affection.

Zanouba, entirely won over, thinks, "Mashalla really grows on you. The others must be wrong. Maybe Gaulisar and Narguiss are only jealous because she's still so young and cheerful! She's so much more delightful to be around than they are! She's just like an older sister and will make life seem even sweeter than before."

On this happy note, Zanouba closes her eyes, trusting, blissfully content.

Abd el Meguid, looking at his two wives, is overcome with tenderness.

"Yes," he thinks, "it will be good to be able to see Zanouba every night, if I wish. We shall be apart soon enough when she goes to her parents' house. I would never have suspected Mashalla of being such a thoughtful wife. I can't believe how I have misjudged her."

When the evening ends, Abd el Meguid accepts Mashalla's hospitality for a delighted Zanouba.

9 · THE NIGHT OF DESPERATION

An evil figure looms. He grins maliciously as he throws a body into a blazing furnace. Hideous red, yellow, and green flames dance and consume white flesh. The victim twists and turns in agony, frantically tossing its head from side to side. A swatch of long hair catches fire. In seconds the entire head is ablaze. The victim's hands flail, in an attempt to stamp out the all-consuming flames. Smoke rises, thick yet strangely transparent. The stench suffocates. The eyes in the burning face are hard, alert, and glow with malevolence. Suddenly, the mouth twists, emitting a stream of continuous laughter from a terrifying depth. The face shrivels into a gargoyle. The mouth . . . Her mouth! Horror stricken, Zanouba recognizes Mashalla!

"Help!" she cries, but no sound comes. Those hard, hard eyes . . . Mashalla's eyes!

"Help! Mashalla's burning! Help! Help!" Zanouba tries to scream, but her throat constricts.

She is glued to the stoop on which she stands, unable to move or make a sound when she sees Satan before her. Yes,

Satan. He sits on his haunches, staring at her. His eyes are vacant, white slits. He wears a strange, red bandana on his head.

Zanouba, panic stricken, tries to flee. "I'm too young to die! Run! Run, while there's still time!

"Help!" she tries to scream again, but remains mute. She can neither look up, nor shout, nor move. All at once the ground moves. She spins and twists, caught in a mad dance with the devil.

What is this? Her head is now where her feet should be. She is hanging upside down like a fly on a cracking ceiling. The smell of burning flesh is making her sick. The air is unbreathable. Satan signals to her. "No, no! Never! I won't go!" Despite her resolve, her feet take on a life of their own, moving slowly as if through a vat of molasses. She lifts one at a time, slowly. She is now face-to-face with the hard eyes, the crazed mouth, cackling in the flames. Her head spins, faster and faster. The flames lap at her feet, lick her legs, sending serpents of smoke coiling around her fragile neck. She brings her hands up to wave them off . . .

Zanouba sits bolt upright in her bed, coughing and retching. Not quite awake, she cries out in a strangled voice, "No! No! I don't want this!" Sweat runs down her back. She touches her face, hot and wet, and whispers, "Where am I?" Her head is spinning, her heart in her mouth. She looks around her—she's in Mashalla's harem.

"How can a nightmare seem so real?" she whispers, falling back on her pillows, her stomach churning.

Satan is gone, yet smoke fills the room. A strange sickening odor wafts her way. "I need help . . ." Weakly, she calls out, "Mashalla . . . Mashalla . . ." then remembers—Mashalla's gone, Behita's here.

Exhausted and still shaken, Zanouba wipes her brow. She is burning with fever. "I must open a window . . ." She calls to Behita who is sleeping on a mat outside her door. No answer. She tries to get up, panting, "I must have some air . . . The window . . . Just a few steps . . ." The room spins. Zanouba collapses, her nightgown drenched, sticking to her body. "I'm going to die!" she thinks. Making one last effort, she yells, "Behita! Help!" Instantly, the old woman appears, holding a candle in her right hand. In the dim light Behita's black face swims before her, eyes alarmingly like white slits, boring into her tender flesh. The room spins again. She is overcome with nausea. Everything is out of focus. "Am I dreaming?" In a daze she watches the flame flicker, hears Behita opening a window, returning to her bedside. "Don't worry, little mistress, it's nothing. Women in your condition can feel this way," Behita whispers.

"But I'm burning up, Behita. My stomach . . ." Behita pulls a basin from under Zanouba's bed. She slips an arm under the young woman's head, saying, "I'll help you get up. Here's a basin. Get it all out. You'll feel better . . ."

"What's this awful smell?" asks Zanouba, trembling, and on the verge of tears.

"What smell, little sister? It's nothing." answers Behita.

"It's making me sick . . ."

"It's probably the wax from this candle."

"No, no . . ."

"There's a little incense in the brazier, left over from last night. In your condition . . ."

"I'm feeling very ill, Behita!" Zanouba cries, pain tearing into her belly.

"Give me your hand, Sitti, give me your hand . . ."

"I'm going to throw up!"

Zanouba is overcome with the nauseating stench. She retches violently, then all goes blank. Behita runs for help.

When Zanouba revives, she has no sense of how much time has elapsed. It is still night. A breeze wafts from the open window. The acrid odor remains. Is it real? Zanouba raises her head but is again overcome with nausea. Her head throbs as if gripped in a vice.

"Oh, dear God! I'm dying!" she cries.

She grabs her stomach and tries to get up. Horrible cramps immobilize her. She feels hollow, her head a poor paper globe, ablaze with fever. Violent spasms make her cry out. She feels her intestines being wrenched out of her belly. Her nightgown, the bedsheets, everything is soaked with blood.

"Behita! Quickly, quickly . . . Behita!" Gaulizar, Narguiss, the household servants all burst into the room. They bombard her with questions. Narguiss orders someone to run for the midwife. She undresses Zanouba. Gaulisar sponges her. A servant takes away the crimson sheets. A fresh bed is made. Zanouba, shivering, still bleeding, is wrapped in towels and blankets. Om Mahmood rushes to Zanouba's bedside.

When the midwife arrives she sniffs the air. She knits her brows, alarmed. A dead silence settles over the room. All eyes are on her as she examines the patient. The damage is serious. She whispers, "Send for Sitt Shafika."

Gaulisar lets out a sob. Narguiss flashes her a significant look. She stops. Om Mahmood hesitates—to call the doctor means all hope is lost. She must consult Abd el Meguid. Where is he? She orders a servant to look for him in the *salamlek*. Narguiss insists on going. "This is no time to falter," she mutters impatiently. Grabbing a veil and *habara,* she rushes out into the night. She runs through the orchard to the barn and shouts to the startled stable boys to saddle their master's horse. Turning to look toward the house, all she sees is a square of dim light wavering in the room where Zanouba is struggling for life. Her body flushes. Under her breath, Narguiss curses the dark day that brought this innocent young woman to live in the cunning Mashalla's harem. She clenches her fists and mutters angrily, "Why wouldn't they listen to me!"

At the *salamlek,* she finds Abd el Meguid in his room. "Quickly, get up! It's Zanouba!"

"Zanouba?" he mumbles. Shocked, he does not immediately grasp the urgency of Narguiss' message.

"Wake up, Sidi! Zanouba's bleeding! You must call the
doctor! Quickly, telephone Sitt Shafika. Tell her to come
right away! There's no time to waste!"

Narguiss helps him with his clothes. Abd el Meguid ex-
asperates her. "This is no time for questions," she cries.
Fully awake, he says, "All right, Narguiss, calm yourself.
I'll go see Zanouba first," but Narguiss cuts him off.

"There's no time for that. You'll see her afterward. Call
the doctor!"

"I'll send one of the servants. I must see her," Abd el
Meguid exclaims.

"They won't listen to a servant, Sidi. This can't wait.
You must go, talk to Sitt Shafika yourself!"

"What shall I tell her?"

"Ask her to bring with her whatever she needs for a
delivery or an operation. Zanouba's life is in danger, Sidi!"

"The child?" whispers Abd el Meguid.

"If you want to save the child you'd better hurry. Your
horse is waiting. Just get to the telephone and call Sitt Shafika in Cairo. Make haste, Abd el Meguid!" Narguiss cries,
aggravated.

Abd el Meguid trusts Narguiss' good judgement. He
races to the village of Matariyya, a half hour away. The
central telephone office is tucked away in a corner of the
small train station.

As the horse gallops, Abd el Meguid's anxiety mounts.
The station is dark and silent. The gates are shut tight. He
bangs insistently on the doors, cursing the night watchman
for taking his sweet time.

"That lazy lout, why doesn't he answer?" Abd el Meguid
mutters.

Finally, the dim light of a lamp appears. A sleepy old
man with a blanket around his shoulders opens the door.

Abd el Meguid tells him to wake up the telephone operator and walks into a little office to the right. The light of the gas lamp flickers. The watchman adjusts the wick so it will stop smoking. Abd el Meguid looks up at the large, round clock on the wall, ticking, ticking away relentlessly. Minute follows minute. Is Zanouba's life ebbing away?

Finally Cairo is on the line. Abd el Meguid grabs the telephone, hears it ring, over and over again until a distant voice answers. It is the doctor herself.

"Hello? Hello!" The line crackles. "Sitt Shafika? It's Abd el Meguid in Matariyya," is all he is able to say.

Sitt Shafika, a woman of experience, understands. She asks Abd el Meguid a few specific questions. She will set out immediately.

"But what a long way off Cairo is! It will take her at least two hours to get to us," thinks Abd el Meguid.

Will Zanouba survive? Can the doctor save her? And the baby? He gallops back in the pitch dark, praying desperately. "Dear God, you whose kindness is boundless, have mercy!" he repeats, to give himself hope.

At the house, looking up apprehensively, he sees the small, wavering square of light.

"Will I find her alive?" he whispers as he runs up the stairs to Mashalla's harem.

1O · ZANOUBA STRUGGLES FOR LIFE

Zanouba is breathing, but her face is colorless. Abd el Meguid remembers how she looked only a few nights

ago, her cheeks flushed, her eyes dancing, listening with innocent pleasure to Mashalla's phonograph.

"How pale she is," he whispers to his mother before
leaving the room. Om Mahmood shakes her head. The
midwife removes the pillows from beneath Zanouba's head
and raises her limp body in an effort to slow down the loss
of blood. "I just hope we can keep her alive until the doctor
arrives," mumbles the old woman.

Everyone is silent until someone begins murmuring a
prayer. The women join in and Abd el Meguid listens, anxiously sitting on a chair in the hallway. The room suddenly
hums like a beehive. Through the door which stands ajar he
stares at the tiny figure of his wife beneath the crimson
comforter on the big brass conjugal bed. How joyous they
had been to have it moved into this room from Abbasiyya!
He remembers Zanouba's delight at being near him and his
own deep sense of contentment.

"She seems no bigger than a doll," he thinks, his eyes
filling. Again he stares at the crimson comforter, the can-
opy, the matching satin curtains, the valence, a lighter shade
of red. His chest tightens. "All this red," he sobs, "it's as if
this bed has drained her of her blood! What can I do, dear
God? What can I do to help her?"

He plunges his right hand into the deep pocket of his
caftan and brings out his prayer beads. The familiar feel of
silky amber slipping through his fingers renews his hope
and calms him. He intones a prayer: "Oh, Merciful God,
Almighty God, you who are the great facilitator, have
mercy on my wife and son, have mercy on your servant
Abd el Meguid . . ."

Zanouba moans then grows quiet. He strains to listen.
Snippets of whispered comments reach his ears.

"I wonder if Sitt Shafika will get here in time . . ."

"She studied medicine in Paris, you know . . ."

"They say that she speaks seven languages . . ."

". . . she wears a white veil . . ."

"Well, of course, she has the right to wear it . . ."
"But she's not a princess . . ."
"Yes, but she's the daughter of a *pasha* . . ."
". . . because of her education. . . ."
". . . I wonder . . ."
"She's a Muslim?"
". . . she's married to Sayyed Metwalli . . ."
". . . children . . ."
"Of course . . ."
"How do you think she'd know what to do . . ."
". . . her education . . ."
"You have to have children to know . . ."
"Maybe she'll say Zanouba has to eat . . ."
"Maybe hard boiled eggs and raw onions . . ."
"Would that stop the bleeding?"
". . . give her strength . . ."

The women's whispers ebb and flow. Abd el Meguid prays, then distracted again stares at the bed as if hypnotized. His eyes travel up and down the curtains. They are sashed, loosely gathered. Each sash is finished off with a heavy gold tassel. One is missing. He is surprised and annoyed to find that this detail irritates him. How can it take on such importance at a time when Zanouba's life trembles on the brink of the great abyss? He remembers her dream—the missing tooth. His heart skips a beat. He shifts in his chair. He tries to return to his prayers but his eye catches sight of the porcelain vase exploding with paper roses and dahlias on the shelf above Zanouba's bed. A portrait of the Khedive Abbas, in uniform, is painted on each side. It was a gift from Zanouba's brother. Ashamed of having been distracted, he accelerates the movement of his fingers on the amber beads.

The midwife takes Zanouba's pulse. Abd el Meguid questions her with his eyes. Narguiss gestures for silence. Everyone listens alertly.

"It's a car," several cry. "God is great!" exclaims Gaulisar, raising her hands to heaven.

Moments later the doctor enters, followed by an atten-
dant carrying a black leather case. "She's not dressed like a
Muslim," one of the servants whispers to another. They
hush, seeing rebuke in Narguiss' eyes.

Indeed, once she has removed her black silk *habara,* the
only part of Sett Shafika's costume which distinguishes her
as a native is the white *yashmak* with its matching, gauzy
veil, worn in the Turkish style of the aristocracy. Otherwise, she is dressed like a European. Her full skirt is cinched
around her slender waist. Her white blouse has long, full
sleeves, a lacy front and collar. When she removes her
gloves and the veil sheltering her fine features, all eyes are
fixed on her.

As she examines Zanouba, the silence in the bedroom
grows tense. Behita's face in particular has turned ashen.
Her teeth are chattering. Gaulisar, that tender heart, suddenly bursts into tears. The doctor, in a firm, clear voice,
orders everyone out. No one dreams of disobeying her.

Some time later she goes out to speak to Abd el Meguid.
"Tell me the truth, Oh, Sitt! Can you save her?"

"I hope so, but I will have to use forceps to deliver the
baby," Sett Shafika responds quietly.

"Can the child be saved?" asks Abd el Meguid.

"I will also try to save the child."

"Do what you must. May God come to your aid," says
Abd el Meguid to her before returning to his chair in the
hallway.

He tries to pray, consumed with anxiety. What will become of his little Zanouba, his cherished little wife, his child
with child on death's door? Will she perish and take with
her his hopes and dreams?

Slumped in his chair, Abd el Meguid is lost in thought,
wondering if God is testing him. The sound of the door

opening startles him. Sitt Shafika comes out, very pale. She sits on the sofa, lights a cigarette from a slender, silver case, and smokes in silence for a few minutes. Abd el Meguid is stunned to see a woman, a Muslim, smoking.

"But, of course, she's a doctor . . . She's different from other women," he rationalizes.

For a long moment, he watches her, mesmerized. She places the gold cigarette holder, decorated with a crown, on the pedestal table between the sofa and the chair. Then, seeing Narguiss and the others returning, Sitt Shafika asks for a cup of coffee. Everyone looks anxiously at the doctor, waiting. Om Mahmood, however, goes directly in to see Zanouba whom she finds fast asleep, chloroformed.

Narguiss speaks first: "Is she all right?"

Sitt Shafika responds, "Thank God, the operation was successful. Zanouba is no longer in danger."

Abd el Meguid looks at her, searchingly. He asks in a trembling voice, "And the boy? Dead?"

He has not asked about a child, but a son. His question is heartrending.

"God willed it so, Abd el Meguid. He works in strange ways, and his wisdom is infinite," answers Sitt Shafika.

In a whisper, she adds, "It was a boy."

Abd el Meguid rises without a word and walks toward the stairs. He hesitates, and as if in a dream, stops by the small window ledge halfway down. He picks up an earthenware water bottle set there to cool and drinks. With heavy footsteps, he walks out carrying his pain.

Sitt Shafika goes back into the room followed by all the women. Gaulisar and Narguiss burst into tears when they see Zanouba, pale, eyelids lowered, her breath barely audible. A little, white bundle lies, inanimate, beside her. Om Mahmood, her eyes filling, looks at her daughter-in-law, taking Zanouba's limp hand in hers.

She wonders, "What could have caused this child to

come now? Zanouba told me she was not due for another two months . . . She was in perfect health . . ."

Sitt Shafika looks compassionately at the women weeping around Zanouba's bed, then asks, "Did she have a fall, by any chance?"

"We would have known about it," answers Narguiss, wiping her eyes.

"Did she take a diuretic or a purgative?"

Om Mahmood says, "I don't know. She's been staying here with Mashalla the last four days."

"Where is Mashalla?" asks Sitt Shafika.

"Yesterday she was called away to see her aunt, who had a fall," answers Om Mahmood.

"Who was staying with Zanouba then?" asks Sitt Shafika.

"I was," answers Behita.

Sitt Shafika turns to her and asks, "What happened last night, Behita? Did she fall? Did she eat or drink anything to upset her?"

"Yesterday Sitt Zanouba was a little tired, but given her condition I didn't think anything of it and told her to rest," replies Behita curtly, tired of having repeated her story half a dozen times.

"Yes, but what happened during the night?" asks Sitt Shafika.

"Late last night she told me she was feeling sick to her stomach, and then threw up. I helped her back to bed, but suddenly she was crying that she had cramps. When I saw that she was bleeding, I called Om Mahmood, who called the midwife. I don't know anything else . . ."

Sitt Shafika does not insist.

As day breaks the doctor gets ready to leave. She instructs Om Mahmood that Zanouba should only be given liquids until the evening when she will return to see her. Narguiss blows out the candles. The cool, thin light of dawn creeps into the room. Suddenly, they hear wailing. Om Hassan, whom someone has fetched, rushes to her daughter's bedside. Narguiss tries to drag her away, worried that she will disturb Zanouba's rest.

"Don't wail like that, sister. She's not dead! Let her rest. Come, come, Om Hassan, drink a glass of tea and calm yourself."

Narguiss' entreaties fall on deaf ears. Om Hassan sinks down on a chair beside her daughter's bed, sobbing loudly.

"Oh, my poor child! My poor child!" she laments, rocking back and forth, tears running down her face.

She wrings her hands and beats her chest in despair.

"Oh, Lord have mercy, Lord have mercy," intone Narguiss and Gaulisar.

"Oh, my poor child! My poor daughter! Why is heaven set against you?! After all the burden of pregnancy, to have it come to this! All of this suffering for nothing? Are you to be forever like the pilgrim who returns without so much as a handful of peanuts to show where he has been?

"Oh, woe is me! Oh, woe is me," cries Om Hassan.

Om Hassan's sobbing puts Om Mahmood under obligation. She must join in the lament or seem uncaring. "Oh, woe is me!" she cries and slaps her old face as her grandmothers did before her—a supreme gesture of despair.

"All my hopes are dashed! No son will ever be born to my son! Not a single male will carry his name, bring him joy!" she wails, besting Om Hassan. "My sister-in-law's house is full of boys, but not a one for my son! What fortune has smiled on her that will not accord me one wish? Oh, woe is me!"

"Oh woe is me," echoes Om Hassan, wailing all the louder.

"Oh Fortune why are you frowning on us?" Om Mahmood begins again. "My son, my son, is the home you have built stone by stone never to be filled with joy? Are these walls never to hear the laughter of the longed-for son?" she questions heaven. The women sob.

Suddenly, in the midst of the chorus of lamentations they hear a man clap three times, seeking entrance to the harem. It is Zanouba's father. The women stop and listen. "Oh, my poor husband," cries Om Hassan, "what will you see when you come into this room?"

Abd el Fattah, waiting for a sign that the way is clear of women, climbs the stairs to Mashalla's harem. He strikes the stone steps repeatedly with his cane and coughs conspicuously to let them know he is on his way. Warned, the women all disappear. Only Om Hassan and Om Mahmood remain beside Zanouba. Om Mahmood deems it sufficient at her age to pull her veil over her head, gripping a corner of it between her teeth in symbolic modesty.

Om Hassan calls out to her husband who walks in with studied dignity. After greeting Om Mahmood, he sinks down on the sofa, his hands crossed on the handle of his cane. He draws his grey-blue caftan about his knees and removes the fez he wears at an angle over his long, grey hair. His thin face is agitated by a nervous tic which distorts his left cheek and the corner of his mouth. He looks over at Zanouba, still asleep. Om Mahmood and Om Hassan have ceased their lamentation and sit, cheeks leaning against their hands, a look of resignation on their faces, still wet from weeping. A heavy silence permeates the room, broken only by Zanouba's shallow breathing. All at once Abd el Fattah hears an animated exchange in the next room. He recognizes Narguiss' voice then Gaulisar's. Other women join in.

"This was not an accident!" says Narguiss.

"She was in perfect health," responds Gaulisar.

Abd el Fattah, listening intently, wonders: "Could it be that what they are saying is meant for my ears?"

"Your husband won't let this matter go until he's found out the truth," insists Narguiss, "He's too intelligent to be fooled, my sister. He knows this evil is someone's doing!"

Gaulisar responds: "I've heard that Abd el Fattah is endowed with a sixth sense . . ." "And besides, he's educated" adds Narguiss.

"Yes, he speaks French," adds Gaulisar.

Raising her voice, Narguiss says, "He knows the language of the Europeans, and every year he's invited by the French community to a big reception for notables at the Ezbekeyya gardens!"

"That's not all. He even invites them back for a lavish reception!" exclaims Gaulisar.

"I heard that ambassadors and consuls visit him at home . . ."

"And you should see the feasts he gives," says Gaulisar.

"He has twenty hens slaughtered for each couscous that is cooked in his kitchens . . ." adds a servant.

"His neighbors respect and fear him," says Gaulisar.

"They know that when he takes someone to court he doesn't have to use the ones in Gamaliyya like other Egyptians," explains Narguiss.

"Yes, Om Hassan told me that he has the right to go to the tribunals in Ezbekeyya where the rich and powerful go," says Gaulisar.

"He never has to go to Gamaliyya?" asks a voice.

"Never. And he has never lost a case," says Narguiss.

After a brief silence, someone says, "He has the protection of the French . . ."

"He won't let this matter rest," answers Narguiss, confidently.

"Someone is going to regret this," concludes Gaulisar.

A door slamming silences the speakers.

Abd el Fattah has taken leave of Om Hassan and Om Mahmood. They look at each other. They too have overheard, but no one dares say a word.

Once Abd el Fattah is out of the harem, Om Mahmood alerts the other women who return. Again, the midwife takes Zanouba's pulse. Zanouba opens her eyes and whispers, groggy, "The baby?"

"May you live long, my child," Om Mahmood responds, tears trickling down her wrinkled face.

Zanouba, disbelieving her ears repeats, "The baby . . ."

The midwife echoes the traditional response which indicates that someone has died: "May you live long, sister."

"Dead?" questions Zanouba, her eyes filling.

"I rubbed him with alcohol, I passed a raw onion under his nose. Sitt Shafika was here. She signed the death certificate," whispers the midwife.

Om Hassan begins to sob loudly again.

Om Mahmood signals her with her eyes, leans toward her and whispers, "Think of your daughter, Om Hassan."

"Lord have mercy!" exclaims Gaulisar.

"Lord have mercy!" all the women respond.

"God is great and infinite in his wisdom," says Narguiss.

Om Hassan, daubing her eyes, exclaims, "If Zanouba doesn't step over the body seven times, she'll stay barren seven years!"

"Zanouba is too weak to get up, Om Hassan," replies Narguiss, looking at the midwife for reinforcement. "The doctor said to keep her quiet. If she moves she'll start bleeding again."

"We can't bury the baby without Zanouba doing this," persists Om Hassan.

"Do you want to kill her?" asks Narguiss, indignant.

Om Mahmood suggests instead that they pass the dead child seven times across Zanouba's bed.

"What about the water left over from washing the body?" asks a servant.

"Sprinkle it on the floor of the room," instructs Om Hassan. "It's the only way to chase out evil spirits."

When Abd el Meguid returns, everyone falls silent. Where has he been? Hearts brimming with sympathy, their eyes question this big, kindly man. Did he walk on the narrow path along the canal? Did he lie down in his fields wishing to die? Did he pray in some dark corner of the mosque? No one knows. He has brought with him his most precious caftan, the white silk one he wears on ceremonial occasions. Walking two steps behind him is the man who will wash the little body in preparation for burial. Abd el Meguid whispers some words into his son's ear, words that will help him get into heaven. Then, unravelling his turban, he wraps it around the little head before covering the body with his caftan as a shroud. Zanouba looks on, dazed, tears running down her cheeks. Abd el Meguid touches her forehead gently with his lips. He then tells Om Mahmood that there is to be no wailing or lamenting after he leaves. "It might be fatal to Zanouba," he whispers.

Without another word, Abd el Meguid takes his son in his arms and leaves. In the courtyard, the men of the neighborhood have assembled to walk with him to the cemetery. After the funerary procession, Abd el Meguid delivers his son to the earth that has welcomed his ancestors. Placing the tiny body beside his own father's, he says: "Oh, father, here is your grandson who was not meant to stay on in the world of the living. Here is the son I waited half a lifetime to welcome. Welcome him, father, your grandson who refused to enter the land of the living. Welcome him, father, to the world of the dead and make a place beside you for me. There is nothing left for me but to take my place between my father and my son. I am but a passing shadow, father, a man cursed by God, condemned to leave no trace of himself in the world."

Although Abd el Meguid's eyes remain dry, his face has aged ten years. His voice is the voice of a parent shattered by the immensity of his suffering.

Part Three ▪ *Justice in the Harem*

11 · ACCUSATION

At her parents' house Zanouba rests on a divan, lost in thought. Her youngest sister, Aziza, nestled on the wide ledge of a window beside her, pulls her out of her reverie.

"Look! Look at what's coming!"

Zanouba props herself up on her elbow and looks out of the window. Her eyes brighten when she sees Mohammad, the doorman, and Ramadan, the gardener from Matariyya, crossing the courtyard. They leave two huge hampers by the kitchen door.

"Oh!" exclaims Faika, another sister, "what's in those baskets?"

"They're mangoes," replies Zanouba.

"I'm so excited, I've never eaten them!" both sisters say in chorus.

The men return each carrying large earthenware pots.

"That's probably butter or honey!" exclaims Zanouba.

Seeing the gifts from Matariyya, her heart races. She knows that Abd el Meguid is expected tonight and that these are gifts heralding his arrival. She lies back down, smiling. This visit will be her husband's first since she came home after the horrible accident, a week ago. She sees Abd el Meguid in her mind's eye as she last saw him. As she was leaving Matariyya, he had looked intently at her with his big, tired eyes. His face had been drawn with fatigue and his

95

beard, usually so carefully trimmed, had been neglected. She had been struck then by how deeply the baby's death has affected him.

Om Mahmood has told her that since her departure Abd el Meguid, inconsolable, has not set foot in the *haramlek*. He has withdrawn to the *salamlek*. A *fiky* has come to read the Qur'an to him daily. His meals, his clean clothing, his linens, everything were brought to him there. He has received visitors offering their condolences with an absent look. He even smokes his water pipe without pleasure. He has become indifferent to everything.

"Well, perhaps not everything," thinks Zanouba, "after all, when I was still in Mashalla's harem, burning with fever, he came to see me every morning after the doctor left."

She remembers how attentive and tender he was toward her as she struggled against death. When she emerged from that period of darkness, as she called it, how gently he took her hand in his, kissing it, his eyes full of love.

Does she love him? Her eyes fill with tears and she feels a pinching sensation in her chest. She knows how sorely she misses him. How eagerly, that first week in her father's house, she had looked forward to Om Mahmood's talk about Abd el Meguid!

"Perhaps this is love," thinks Zanouba. "Dear God, why did my mother make me come home?"

Om Hassan would not listen to Zanouba when she pleaded to be left in Matariyya. Her mother's face had assumed the set look it had on her bad days. Zanouba was powerless against her.

"What was she afraid of?" she wonders.

Zanouba is surprised to find herself annoyed at being back in the old house in Darb el Magharba, although she had cried when first leaving it, thinking she would never be happy anywhere else. She now finds her old rooms cramped, and she is constantly running into Faika's mattress, or Aziza's chest.

"Maybe this is because I don't belong here anymore," she reflects.

Even the corner of the sleeping porch where she loved to spread her mattress on summer nights is now occupied by Faika. She remembers lying under the windows to catch the evening breezes, and the hole she made in one of the *mashrabiyya* screens so that she could look up at the stars. She doesn't have the strength to carve a place for herself. And her sisters' giggling and their silly games annoy. When they refuse to stop, she feels like beating them, breaking into tears of frustration instead. The little girls do not understand.

In addition she has to put up with her mother's moods. Om Hassan has become so impatient, so secretive, that it mystifies her. "What's the meaning of all those questions she asks me?" wonders Zanouba. Om Hassan interrogates her all day long, wanting her to recount the details of that fateful night!

Zanouba churns the events over and over again:

"Is it my fault that I can't remember everything? Just because I said something about a bad smell, now I'm supposed to remember just what it was! Maybe it was a dream. Behita said what I smelled was the remains of some stale incense. Why doubt her? Why does my mother question everything that Behita did that night? She keeps asking whether she was alone in the room with me, and whether the window was closed or open when I woke up. This is the fourth time I've had to tell about that awful nightmare! Doesn't she realize this is torture for me? Why doesn't she stop? I'm not the first woman to lose a child! Of course, it's a misfortune. Still, I'm young and I can have as many children as Abd el Meguid wishes.

"What about Mashalla? Why does she hate her so? Mashalla let me have the best room in her harem. What did my mother mean mumbling and gesturing at her when her back was turned? She clenched her fists and extended her index finger and her little finger like two little horns, to chase away the evil eye. What could have possessed her? What could this all have to do with Mashalla, who treated me like a sister?"

Zanouba is shocked by her mother's attitude every time the subject of Mashalla is brought up.

"Don't mention this woman's name in my presence! She's evil and she wants to hurt you," she snaps.

Zanouba feels confused and guilty. "Why am I such a coward? Instead of coming to her defense, I break into tears. What do they all have against poor Mashalla?

"Could they all be jealous because she's rich and proud? But why would Om Mahmood be jealous? If Mashalla had been with me nothing of all this would have happened. She told me so herself. How she berated Behita for not looking after me! I practically had to stop her from beating the old woman! And how she wept at the loss of the baby! One would have thought she had lost her own son. She would have gladly given her life to save him, she told me. Even Abd el Meguid was touched. She's still dressed in black, wears no makeup, hasn't put a touch of *kohl* in her eyes, or henna on her hands. She's constantly sobbing with her headscarf mournfully pulled down over her forehead. She's deprived herself of everything she likes. Even the men in the *salamlek* say they can hear her wailing. What does everyone have against this woman?"

Despite her trusting nature and her innocence, even Zanouba is puzzled that Mashalla's expressions of grief are greater than her own, her tears more copious even than Om Hassan's and Om Mahmood's. She thinks, "She never even saw the baby. Why does she speak of loving him?"

And Zanouba, although saddened by the loss, particularly at coming home empty-handed, tells herself that her task now is to get well again. She is determined not to spend the rest of her days mourning.

"I almost died," Zanouba muses. As her strength returns, she is almost elated. "I never knew how good the blood running through my veins could feel! As soon as I'm recovered, I'll have another baby," she concludes.

Her heart sinks, however, when she remembers Abd el Meguid's grief. She would like to be near him, to console him. She is certain that he needs her. "I'm strong enough to return to Matariyya now," she whispers, deciding to ask her husband to take her home when he comes to visit her in the evening. Never mind if her mother is not pleased. A woman's place is in her husband's home. She will know how to choose her words so that her request cannot be refused.

When Abd el Meguid arrives, Zanouba hoists herself up on her elbow, peering intently through the *mashrabiyya* screen, hoping for a glimpse of him. She knows he is in the *salamlek* with her father. Her brother, Ibrahim, has told her that her husband is coming to see her. She is burning with impatience.

Finally, Abd el Meguid emerges. She watches him raise his eyes to the windows of the *haramlek*. "He's searching for me," she thinks, her heart pounding.

Their eyes meet, yet only she knows it. "He doesn't see me, but he knows I'm up here. Oh, Sidi, why are you taking so long . . ." whispers Zanouba. She resists the urge to shout out his name when her mother appears at the door with Om Mahmood. Playing the role of the dutiful daughter, she feigns interest in their conversation, but she can only think of her beloved Abd el Meguid. What is he doing? Will he come up before or after dinner? "Mother, I'm getting very tired of lying down. Could you put some pillows under my shoulders?" asks Zanouba. In this position she can watch the two men chatting in the *mandara,* across the way. Her eyes are level with two large openings in the *mashrabiyya* screen beside the bed, although the carved rosette in the screen only permits a glimpse of the precise spot where the men are seated.

Om Mahmood and Om Hassan are engrossed in talk about a cousin they have in common. Zanouba can look to her heart's content at her father and Abd el Meguid. Seeing four men joining them she exclaims under her breath, "Oh, what a nuisance! Did those sheikhs from our mosque have to come now?"

As long as there are visitors, her father cannot invite Abd el Meguid to come up and see her. And, Abd el Meguid would never ask to see his wife in her father's home without being invited.

"Oh, I hope they won't stay long," sighs Zanouba.

When she notices that they begin to smoke a *narguila,* she whispers to herself, "They'll probably be here all evening."

Zanouba watches them sipping coffee, as the *narguila* makes the rounds. Each guest brings his lips to the amber mouthpiece, making the water bubble in the thick glass body of the pipe. She watches as the fragrant rose petals swirl with every puff taken. Her frustration mounts.

"What do they care that Abd el Meguid and I are waiting!" For them time does not exist. They can sit for hours, placidly smoking and sipping.

Zanouba takes some consolation in the fact that her brother is among the guests and has promised to report to her on what was being said. Every now and then he looks up at the *mashrabiyya* window and winks at her as if to say, "I'll let you know everything that is being said, don't worry." In exchange for his spying she has promised him a new suit, a green silk shirt, a bow tie, and a fine red fez, a real *tarboush.*

In the company of her mother, mother-in-law, and sisters, Zanouba pretends to show an interest in the gossip about her cousin Amina and her children. Zanouba asks about their ages saying just enough to keep her mother distracted. She then retreats into her own thoughts.

Downstairs on the *mandara* a servant removes the

narguila and coffee cups, setting a low table down in front of the men. Abd el Fattah has no doubt invited them to stay for dinner. Zanouba realizes that her mother has known this all along and that is the reason for such elaborate preparations.

"Abd el Meguid is really stuck now; he won't be up to see me before dinner."

Om Hassan had in fact given her daughter a description of the meal but had not told her that there might be guests other than Abd el Meguid. Zanouba regrets not having helped to prepare this meal for her husband particularly as Om Hassan has gone to great lengths to impress him. The roast duckling on a bed of raviolis filled with a mixture of meat and pistachios are a favorite of Abd el Meguid's.

Om Hassan and Om Mahmood leave for the kitchen in order to supervise the serving of the meal and Zanouba relaxes. She and her sisters now watch every move of the company below, pressing their noses against the *mashrabiyya*. Ibrahim glances up at the window and mimics everyone's appreciation of the meal. This pantomime suddenly irritates Zanouba. In a fit of temper, she chases her astonished sisters out of the room.

The hours seem endless to Zanouba. She has pushed aside the dinner tray that was sent up to her. But the men continue to linger over tea. When Om Hassan returns Zanouba cries, "What are they waiting for?"

"Patience is the key to deliverance, my child," answers Om Hassan, but both she and Om Mahmood have also begun to wonder why Abd el Fattah has not invited Abd el Meguid upstairs.

"Something is not right," thinks Zanouba. Noticing that Abd el Meguid is making a move to leave, she says, "See how considerate he is, mother? He's reminding my father that he wants to see me . . ."

To Zanouba's consternation, however, her father does not invite his son-in-law to go up. Abd el Fattah insists that

Abd el Meguid and Om Mahmood spend the night in Darb el Magharba. "You can stay with me in the *salamlek,* Abd el Meguid, and Om Mahmood can spend the night with Om Hasssan and the girls."

Zanouba senses that something is not as it should be. She broods. "Why is my father keeping Abd el Meguid from me?"

She blames the ill-timed visitors for having deprived her of the pleasure of seeing her husband, although she cannot help resenting her father's insensitivity too.

"Even if the hour is late, why couldn't he let Abd el Meguid stop in for a few minutes? Or is it Abd el Meguid who doesn't want to see me?" wonders Zanouba, fretting.

But would he have come all the way to Darb el Magharba if he hadn't wanted to see her? Zanouba feels sure that he does not hold her responsible for the loss of the child. It was an accident. In fact she is certain he loves her as much now as when they were first married.

"I'll see him tomorrow . . . But will I be able to sleep? How long the night will seem!" she sighs.

Before she knows it, however, she opens her eyes to the cool light of dawn playing on the stone floor. Her sisters are still fast asleep.

Her first thoughts are of Abd el Meguid.

"I hope he hasn't left. Oh, that's really silly. It's still early," she thinks, watching the sun just clearing the top of the courtyard wall, casting horizontal shadows on the glass of the windcatcher above her head.

Zanouba hears movement downstairs and rushes to the window. "Dear God, he's up!"

Her father and her husband, two men of the same age, are kneeling, their foreheads on their prayer rugs. When they lift their faces to the sky, Zanouba's eyes meet Abd el Meguid's. She is shocked, but quickly realizes that he cannot see her. She almost cries out, however, when she notices how tragic Abd el Meguid's face looks.

"What could have happened? Why can't I rush down to console him? He's my husband! I will not let him go home without me. I will say to him, 'Take me with you, Sidi, my master! A woman's place is in her husband's home, not her father's. I'm your slave! Take me with you!' That's what I'll say. If only he would come upstairs!"

But, what is happening? Om Mahmood comes in with Om Hassan. Her mother-in-law has put on her *habara* to leave.

Zanouba turns imploring eyes on them. "What is the meaning of this? Abd el Meguid is not coming to see me?" she cries.

"Your father has not invited him to come up," answers Om Mahmood.

"But I want to see him! I want to go home to Matariyya with my husband!"

Om Mahmood's eyes are hard as pebbles and her mouth is pinched. "Peace be upon you, daughter," is all she says.

Walking stick in hand, Abd el Meguid stands silently in the courtyard, his shawl under his arm. He is erect and dignified. Neither he nor Abd el Fattah utter a word.

"What's happened! What's the matter!" she wails. Om Mahmood has joined Abd el Meguid. Zanouba bursts into tears.

"Am I going to let him go without a word? Am I such a coward that I cannot run away from this house which is no longer my home? You should be ashamed of yourself, Zanouba!" She collapses on the divan, weeping. The hurt little girl has emerged.

Looking up at Om Hassan she sobs, "What have you done, mother?"

"My little girl," Om Hassan responds, "it is important for you to know now that your father and I are convinced that your miscarriage was not an accident. Someone induced it . . ."

Zanouba tries to object. Om Hassan stops her.

"Don't protest," she says, "we are not the only ones who believe this. Even your husband speaks of it openly now. Both the doctor and the midwife agree."

"Who could have done such a horrible thing?" Zanouba sobs.

"I cannot accuse anyone just yet. Your father wants you to stay with us until the matter is cleared up. That's why he didn't send your husband to you last night. He wanted Abd el Meguid to understand that he could not turn a blind eye. We won't stand for it!" says Om Hassan, emphatically.

"But what if he never comes back?" Zanouba sniffles.

"He will, my child," comforts Om Hassan.

"But he's so proud, mother!"

"He's a just man. Your father didn't want to embarrass Abd el Meguid yesterday; he told him that you were still too weak to leave. But Om Mahmood and I spoke. We understand each other. I knew that she had her own doubts, but, of course, she doesn't want a scandal. I spoke to her about your father's connections with the French consul and the judges who preside over the mixed tribunals."

"Oh, mother!" cries Zanouba.

"I did this only to let her know that we were in earnest, my child," says Om Hassan. Then, taking pity on her daughter, she adds, "We cannot send you back to Matariyya where that viper lies in wait for you, my child!"

Zanouba is stunned. "You can't mean Mashalla, mother! She's my friend!"

"We'll see, my child," answers Om Hassan, getting up.

Zanouba persists. "I'm not afraid and I want to go back to Abd el Meguid. I want to go now!"

"Your father has made it a point of honor to seek justice," answers Om Hassan.

"But what if Abd el Meguid gets angry and divorces me?" cries Zanouba.

"These things are in the hands of God, my child," replies Om Hassan, "But I think that Abd el Meguid loves you

too much to do that. What we are asking him to do should
not make him angry. He has been hurt too."

"But I don't want to lose him. I love him and I know he
loves me, mother, because he gives me gifts all the time,"
persists Zanouba.

"Listen. I've asked Om Mahmood to gather all the
women of the household, both wives and servants, and to
have them solemnly swear by all that is holy, that they had
no hand in your misfortune," says Om Hassan.

"And if they all do that?" asks Zanouba.

"If they all do that and none is struck down by God,
then you can go back to your husband, Zanouba," says Om
Hassan.

"And what if Abd el Meguid refuses to let his wives
submit to this test?" asks Zanouba.

"Om Mahmood has promised to persuade him to let
them take the oath," answers Om Hassan.

"Oh, mother! I'm so afraid I'll not see him again!" cries
Zanouba.

"Silly girl! Haven't you noticed that he cherishes you
more than his eyes?" replies Om Hassan, smiling.

Zanouba, reassured, whispers a prayer, asking God to
give her patience.

12 · THE OATH

The following morning, Mashalla is in an agony of in-
decision. "Should I leave?" she whispers to herself,
"when they're all at the mosque it would be easy. I could
return to my parents' house, or go to one of my aunts. I
have money and jewelry. But leaving would make me look
guilty. I would lose Abd el Meguid for sure. And if I'm
gone Behita might talk. Abd el Fattah would send the au-

thorities after me. I would be publicly shamed . . . No, no, I have to stay calm and deny everything. After all, no one can prove anything . . ."

Mashallah smiles, thinking of the gloomy faces of the other women as they had gathered to leave for the mosque at daybreak. "They deserve what they got," she chuckles.

The night before, she had agreed to go with them to pray before taking the oath. She had seen them from her window, gathered in the courtyard in the cold grey light of dawn, hugging their black silk *habaras*. Narguiss, Gaulisar, Om Mahmood, and all the servants, in their cotton *milayas*, standing around uncomfortably. And there she was, hidden behind her *mashrabiyya*. How she had relished making them wait! She had watched them glance up at her balcony every few minutes, until Narguiss, taking charge, had sped up to hurry her along. Mashalla had gleefully sent Behita to head her off at the top of the stairs to say that she had her period. In this impure state how could she have gone to the mosque?

"That will serve them right!" Mashalla had whispered to Behita and watched as eleven pairs of furious eyes looked up at her window. She knew they didn't believe her, but amazingly enough this time she was telling the truth.

"What a stroke of luck," she thought.

Through the *mashrabiyya* of her bedroom Mashalla had seen Narguiss arguing with Om Mahmood. Her mother-in-law put a hand on Narguiss' arm to hold her back. Narguiss finally threw her arms up in defeat. Shortly after, the troop, like a dark centipede, left without her. Om Mahmood had insisted that Behita go with them, however. Mashalla could not raise any objection without seeming culpable.

That morning all the women had washed themselves carefully, purifying their bodies before going to the mosque to purify their souls. They had gleefully anticipated seeing Mashalla take the oath. But Mashalla had eluded them since her condition precluded her touching the Qur'an.

"Behita will have to swear on the Qur'an . . . I wish I

could have sent her back to my aunt's house, but then I would be suspect; they would think I had something to hide . . ." thinks Mashalla. She knows she should not let the old woman out of her sight. Behita might be indiscreet.

"Had I known that Behita might have to take the oath I might have taken a chance myself, but now it's too late. Well, I hope I've persuaded the old witch not to betray me," thinks Mashalla.

Behita had come running to Mashalla when Om Mahmood had insisted she go with the group to the mosque. She was terrified at the thought of swearing on the Qur'an. Mashalla wished then that she had decided to go along to give Behita moral support. But it was too late.

"She's sick with fear. She's sure that she will be struck dumb, or go blind, or be instantly paralyzed if she gives false testimony. I'm glad I told her that if she is saying something but thinking something else, no harm will come to her."

Mashalla had made Behita repeat, "I swear that I am innocent, that I had no hand in the death of the child," while thinking, "I swear that I am innocent, that I had no hand in the death of the lamb." She is sure this ploy will keep Behita from faltering. Mashalla had also given her fifty gold coins and promised to send her back to her mistress in Cairo the very next day if she did as she was told.

"She'll take the oath. She won't die of it, not with all that Behita has on her conscience! What a lot of mumbo-jumbo! If I'd decided to take that silly oath, I certainly would have, but I'm glad I got out of it. Besides, they can't prove anything; I wasn't even there the night of the accident. This gaggle of geese thought they had me cornered? Well, they don't know Mashalla!"

It had been humiliating enough to be questioned by Om Mahmood the day before. Her mother-in-law had looked at her suspiciously when she had told her she would rather be divorced than take the oath. Om Mahmood had responded

"Don't you know what people will conclude?" Mashalla had wanted to strangle her on the spot. Om Mahmood had even gone so far as to say that she would take the oath first to show that there was no shame in proclaiming one's innocence. Mashalla had then decided it was in her interest not to resist. But the next morning, she was ecstatic to discover that her period had come, preventing her from going to the mosque. Mashalla, remembering the women waiting for her, chuckles.

"They probably think I'll be trembling like a leaf. I'll show them! I'll attend their little ceremony when they return from the mosque. In any case it's a good idea to be there to keep Behita in check. They think they've set such a clever trap, but I'll show them what Mashalla is made of! So they hate me? Well, I'll send the same right back at them! I am a little sorry for Zanouba. She's so trusting. For a while I was really afraid she would die on me! It's all this old goat's fault! Why did Abd el Meguid have to marry a sixteen-year-old? Did he really think I would let her take my place without a struggle?"

In the midst of this internal monologue Mashalla hears the old hinges of the massive courtyard door squeaking. Running to the window, she observes the troop accompanied by Om Hassan and followed by a blind cleric with a cane—the *fiki*.

"That busybody certainly got up early enough to start trouble brewing! This hocus-pocus must be her idea," thinks Mashalla, cursing Om Hassan under her breath. "I wish I could see Behita's face. She's so bundled up, she looks as if she's been swallowed up by her *melayya*. I hope she didn't lose her head!"

Just as she decides to go down to meet the other women, Mashalla hears their footsteps on the stairs. She whispers, "Oh, no! They're coming to my rooms! That's really too much! Nothing I can do now but pretend to welcome them."

"Welcome, welcome," says Mashalla, smiling as the women remove their *habaras* and *melayas*.

"How are you, my child?" asks Om Mahmood. "We decided to have the ceremony in the room where Zanouba slept; I hope we are not intruding."

"Not at all, not at all," says Mashalla, determined to put her best foot forward.

"I see no reason not to meet here and I only regret that I cannot take the oath along with you," she adds quickly.

"We're sorry too, daughter," says Om Mahmood, "but I'm sure you will take the oath as soon as you are able."

"God willing," replies Mashalla.

The blind *fiki* stands by the door, his vacant eyes raised toward heaven, his yellowish-white beard trembling as his lips mumble a prayer. Someone has to take him by the hand and lead him to where Zanouba had lost her baby. He puts a hand on the bed, as the women all line up against the wall. Mashalla stands a little apart, scrutinizing Behita who seems distracted, her eyes darting wildly back and forth.

Om Mahmood takes the oath first. Holding the Qur'an in one hand, resting the other on a loaf of bread, she repeats after the *fiki,* "In the name of God the Merciful, the Great, and in the name of his prophet, Muhammad, and all his saintly followers, I swear that I had no hand in Zanouba's miscarriage."

Om Mahmood passes the Qur'an back and forth three times in front of her eyes then, breaking the bread, she does the same with it. All eyes are intently fixed on her every gesture. Gaulisar, Narguiss, and four household servants follow her lead.

When Behita's turn comes, she takes the book and the bread with trembling hands and faces the Fiki. Her back is turned to the other servants, but Om Mahmood, Mashalla, Gaulisar, and Narguiss can see her from where they stand, to the left of the *fiki.* They watch her intently. Her eyes look huge. Her lips quiver. She licks them nervously.

Mashalla stares at Behita, trying to get her attention, but the old woman stares straight ahead, repeating after the *fiki:*

"In the name of God the Merciful, the Great . . ."

"In the name of God the Merciful, the Great,"

"And in the name of his prophet . . ."

"And in the name of his prophet,"

"I swear that I had nothing to do with Zanouba's miscarriage . . ."

"I swear that I had nothing to do with Zanouba's miscarriage."

A dead silence falls over the group, all staring at Behita. She suddenly gasps for breath and crashes to the ground. The old woman's eyes stare pathetically, her tongue swells inside her mouth. She tries to cry out, but cannot make a sound. The women scream and scatter. Only Mashalla, Narguiss, and Om Mahmood remain self-possessed. They bend over the writhing mass of flesh and bones on the floor, trying to revive the miserable Behita. Her mouth is screwed up in a horrible grimace. Her right eye, half closed, glazed over, looks dead. In her left eye they see terror. She flails her right arm as if waving some horrible apparition away and her left leg beats the ground. Suddenly she grows rigid, the right side of her body paralyzed. They pinch her and prick her with a hairpin, but she seems to feel nothing. Narguiss calls to a servant to bring a loofa; they rub her leg with it, but to no avail.

"We have to call a doctor," says Mashalla, her voice so uncharacteristically high-pitched that it startles her. She suddenly feels as if she were standing outside of her own body, watching a drama in which she is a player. Her head spins, but all at once a strange calm settles over her.

Inside her a little voice whispers, "It's over."

The blind *fiki,* bewildered by the flutter of activity he cannot see, asks what is happening. Once again it is Mashalla who speaks, "It's nothing. Behita has always been subject to these attacks."

Om Mahmood puts her hand on the Fiki's elbow and leads him out of the room. "We will send for you another day," she says quietly, directing a servant to see him down the stairs.

The women reluctantly move Behita onto a mattress which someone has unrolled on the floor. They speak in whispers. Everyone avoids Mashalla, who looks at them with cold indifference, her head held high. When she calls one of her servants, the girl grabs a veil and runs as if for her life. Mashalla, who normally would have heaped insults upon her at such behavior, shrugs her shoulders.

In the courtyard the women hear the clapping of hands to warn them that the doctor is on his way up. Everyone withdraws except Mashalla and Om Mahmood who take up their veils. After he examines Behita, he says: "Her right side is paralyzed. There is nothing that I can do about that, but her life is not in danger." Once the doctor leaves, the women gather up their *habaras* and *melayyas* and turn their backs on Mashalla. Heels ring on the stone steps as the women go down.

Narguiss, the last to leave, exclaims loudly enough to be heard, "Can anyone have any doubt now about who is guilty?" "God is great," says Gaulisar. "God's wisdom is infinite," respond the other women.

"Behita has been silenced forever for lying with her hand on the Qur'an and the blessed bread," comments one of the old servants.

"Did you see the terror in her eyes?" asks Gaulisar. "She should have been struck dead not dumb!" responds Narguiss.

"I couldn't stand to look at her," says one of the women. "Did you see how the whites of her eyes rolled up into their sockets?" "I couldn't stand to look at her either," says another.

"And that mouth, and that hand reaching, I couldn't help feeling pity for the old woman, hideous as she may be," one of the women says. "Did you see how she was imploring to be rescued?"

"I don't know what I would have done had it been me," says another. "How awful to be paralyzed, struck dumb, not even able to ask to be finished off!"

Mashalla hears the voices trail away. She is alone, abandoned. Falling on the divan, she weeps in desperation, suddenly overcome with weakness.

At noon a little girl of seven or eight brings her lunch. Mashalla understands that not a single one of the servants wants to get near her.

"Is there no one else at home?" asks Mashalla, sternly. "Where is Khadiga? Where is Safeyya?" The little girl puts down the tray, a look of pure terror in her eyes. Without a word, she bolts out of the room.

Mashalla rushes to the top of the stairs cursing her and shouts, "Tell Om Mahmood that I want to see her!"

Facing the hostility of the entire harem, Mashalla has to think, to calculate. Behita will never be able to confess. And, although the women perceive her to be guilty, she is sure they cannot prove anything.

"Of what use is their certitude in a court of law? They'll never get me to reveal the truth," thinks Mashalla.

As she ponders, Mashalla hears footsteps in the hallway. "You asked for me, Mashalla," says Om Mahmood, coldly.

"Where are my servants?" Mashalla asks.

"They said they no longer wanted to serve you, Mashalla. They went home to their families," answers Om Mahmood.

"And you let them go? Leaving me to take care of Behita without help?" snaps Mashalla.

"All the other servants refuse to come up to your rooms, but I will try to hire someone to help you, maybe by tonight," answers Om Mahmood.

"Another servant? Everyone will turn her against me before she sets foot in my harem!" retorts Mashalla.

"Calm yourself, Mashalla . . ." says Om Mahmood. Mashalla interrupts her.

"You're telling me to calm down, Om Mahmood? I know what you think of me! Isn't Narguiss your mouth-piece? She let me know what all of you thought! Can you deny this?" exclaims Mashalla.

"Well, you have a way of proving your innocence, Ma-shalla," Om Mahmood answers quietly.

"Me? Beg? Why bother when you think I'm guilty?! Don't think for a minute that I'm afraid. What happened to Behita has nothing to do with divine justice. All I want now is to see Abd el Meguid. Ask him to come see me and I'll not trouble you further," says Mashalla, regaining her self-confidence.

"You will not have to wait," answers Om Mahmood, turning to go.

As soon as Om Mahmood leaves, Mashalla opens one of her coffers and pulls out a dress of blue silk. She refreshes her face and adds *kohl* to her eyes.

"I will soon know if Abd el Meguid is for or against me," whispers Mashalla.

Looking at herself in the mirror she begins to say, "You'll fight to the bitter end, my girl, and stay proud to the end."

Mashalla waits expectantly. A little later she hears foot-steps on the stairs. But they are not Abd el Meguid's.

"Her again!" mumbles Mashalla, with indignation.

Standing in the doorway just long enough to convey her message, Om Mahmood says, "Abd el Meguid is waiting for you in the *mandara*."

"Well, that leaves little hope," thinks Mashalla.

In the privacy of her harem she had felt confident in winning him over, but in the *mandara* . . . Her husband's icy expression confirms her fears.

"He too thinks I'm guilty," she concludes. She knows

that no smiles, nor protestations of love that she has prepared will have any effect.

To save face, she takes the first step. Her head held high she says, "Sidi, I have come to ask your permission to spend a little time with my family."

"I see no harm in that," answers Abd el Meguid, courteously.

"I would like to leave tonight."

"I'll send for your carriage as soon as you want it."

"In an hour."

"It will be ready."

"May God shed his peace upon you, Sidi," Mashalla concludes proudly as she turns to go.

Abd el Meguid has not asked her why she was leaving, or for how long. She is stung, but returns to her rooms to pack without volunteering any explanation. No servant is there to give her a hand. What should she take? What should she leave? She knows that her departure is final and packs accordingly, starting with her jewelry, clothing, and personal effects. The heaviest of her chests is in the room where Behita has been moved. Mashalla pulls it out into the hall with great difficulty as she cannot stand to see the old woman's grimacing mouth or her upturned eyes. The left one seems to follow her every move. Exasperated, she silently curses her.

Om Mahmood enters Mashalla's rooms a half hour later and sees chests open and empty. Mashalla's *bogas* are unfolded, the cloth squares carefully laid out on the divans, ready to be filled before their four corners are gathered together. Om Mahmood contemplates this spectacle in silence. In the white, silk ones, intricately embroidered with silver thread, Mashalla's most beautiful dresses will be packed. Beside them are the lace-bordered linen ones for lingerie. On the floor are patchwork *bogas* for shoes and slippers. Mashalla's silverware is tied in *bogas* of sturdy cotton and canvas. On a large tray, an array of smaller velvet ones, embroidered with gold thread, contain her jewelry.

Mashalla herself comes and goes from one room to another, looking to make sure she has left nothing behind. She ignores her mother-in-law.

"So you are leaving, Mashalla?" asks Om Mahmood.

The young woman shrugs her shoulders.

"Mashalla, I'm speaking to you," says Om Mahmood.

"Stop pretending, Om Mahmood, you know I'm leaving and never coming back. You all hate me and I don't care. But now you have managed to turn Abd el Meguid against me. There is no reason for me to stay in this house. I'm leaving and it is my intention to ask for a divorce!"

"And what chance do you think you would have of getting it?" asks Om Mahmood, her wrinkled face flushing.

"I know what I have to do," Mashalla answers.

"Well, my girl, Abd el Meguid will be doing the divorcing!" exclaims Om Mahmood, indignantly.

"We shall see! I will miss neither you, nor Narguiss, nor Gaulisar, nor your old man of a son! I hope Zanouba will put you all in your place and that the day will come when you will regret losing Mashalla!"

"And Behita," says Om Mahmood, ignoring Mashalla's tirade, "What are you going to do with her?"

"You will do with her as you please," answers Mashalla, with a bitter smile. "I'm giving her to you. It was you who caused her to be in the state she is in! You take care of her!" Om Mahmood turns abruptly and leaves the room.

Mashalla, ready within the hour, looks around the harem where she spent so many years and where she has experienced happiness. Her throat contracts and she suppresses a tear. And, although she is relieved to be leaving with her pride intact, she knows that the fate of a woman who goes back to her father's house is not enviable. Mashalla sighs. There is no other choice.

"How will I be received? How will I explain my return?" she wonders. She is grateful that her mother has left
her enough money to be independent.

"I don't have to ask anyone for anything!" she says, but
then she wonders what good independence will do her.
"Can I eat it? Drink it? A woman alone is always looked
upon with pity or disdain . . ."

Mashalla thinks of her aunt Nafissa, who never married,
and shudders. "A woman's place is in her husband's
harem," she thinks. But there is no turning back now. She
stares at Behita, desperately imploring her with her good
eye, grunting in a terrible effort to speak.

"She must realize I'm leaving without her," Mashalla
thinks, then reconsiders, "It might be safer to take her
along. What if she should regain her speech? My aunt won't
take her back after this incident. What am I going to do
with her?" She leans over and whispers into Behita's ear,
"I'll send for you soon."

She hears a carriage pulling up below. Mashalla puts on
her veil and *habara* and walks slowly downstairs, trying to
hide her agitation. As she climbs into the coupe, the old
driver goes up to collect her things. No one is there to see
her off. Abd el Meguid is conspicuously absent and Om
Mahmood is nowhere to be seen. Mashalla feels their eyes
upon her and hears voices behind the *mashrabiyya* of Gaulisar's apartment.

"Does she think she will be safer in Cairo?"

"Well, her father's rich enough to protect her."

"She's got influential relatives."

"So does Zanouba."

"Don't you know Abd el Fattah is protected by the
French consul himself!"

"She can boast all she wants about her wealth, and her
father's friends, and her mother's eunuchs, she'll get what
she deserves all the same!"

"She'll end up in prison like the common criminal that she is!"

13 · THE DIVORCE

Shortly after Mashalla's departure, Abd el Meguid receives the visit of the governor of Cairo, who folds his legs beneath him on a divan with ease. The two friends gaze at the little pond in the garden. It is a beautiful November day. The water ripples gently, dappled with light. Yellowing leaves float down, miniscule boats grazing the surface. Dragonflies dart among the trees; bees hum in the orchard. A fresh breeze carries the perfume of orange blossoms.

Abd el Meguid knows that the governor has come for a reason. He wonders what it could be but, courteous as always, he betrays nothing of his curiosity. He heartily welcomes his friend and the two of them exchange compliments. They will get to the point of the visit after circling around it.

"You know, Abd el Meguid, I would come to see you more often if you lived closer to town," begins the governor.

Abd el Meguid answers, "Your visit, Excellence, is a great honor. I hope you will frequently grace our home despite the distance. As you know I am quite attached to this old house which I built myself which is near my final resting place beside my father and grandfather. I particularly cherish this garden. I cannot think of living elsewhere."

"It is understandable that you should wish to remain here, my friend. Yet, business calls you so frequently to Cairo that you should consider having a second home there," says the governor.

"I have thought about it," answers Abd el Meguid.

"Did you know that the old gardens of Ibrahim Pasha, near Abdin palace, are being subdivided?" asks the governor.

"I had heard something to that effect," answers Abd el Meguid.

"The streets have been laid out and some of the best families are buying land and beginning to build houses there. You could do the same," says the governor.

"When I have to be in Cairo for a week, it would certainly be more convenient than staying in a hotel," says Abd el Meguid.

The two men discuss prices and the future of such a new neighborhood. As they sip coffee and enjoy a pipe together, Abd el Meguid wonders if the governor has come only to persuade him to buy land. His mind wanders. He watches the reddening coals upon which a perfumed tobacco is burning and listens to the water gurgle in the glass body of the pipe. His visitor's voice pulls him out of his reverie. The governor asks him casually if he knows his old friends Ibrahim el Aal and his brother Mahmood. Abd el Meguid senses a significant story coming, something that relates to him in some way.

"I think I met them last year," he answers.

The governor says, "As you must know then, these two brothers have lived together since their father's death. They own a house, a factory, and land in common. The eldest has two sons and the younger has two daughters. It was always understood that the boys would marry their cousins. Everyone had agreed on this plan, but, when the time came to sign the marriage contracts, the sisters-in-law quarreled. This put the brothers in conflict and the weddings were cancelled. The young people were eager to get married and asked me if I would intercede on their behalf. I promised them to try to guide the waters back into their proper channels, as we say. The next day I sent word to the families that I was coming to their house that very night with the *maazoon* to marry the young people. The conflict between the sisters-in-law had been over dowries and wedding gifts, you see. So, I also chose the gifts myself and had them delivered to the families. At last everyone got what they really wanted: marriage between the cousins."

"How kind you are, Excellence! You never fail to use your lofty position to do good and to prevent discord. He who reunites two souls is assured a place in heaven!" exclaims Abd el Meguid warmly.

"Yes, my friend, it is always my dearest wish to reunite those who are in conflict. Today, however, I am charged with doing just the opposite. I have come to ask you to release a member of your household, however painful that may be. As a friend, I plead with you to act on this matter now," says the governor, finally coming to the point.

Mashalla had written to Abd el Meguid shortly after her departure informing him that she would never return to Matariyya. She also reproached him for his suspicions and indifference toward her and asked him to initiate the divorce proceedings, threatening to go to court herself. Abd el Meguid had refused, although not out of any desire to have Mashalla return, but out of pride. Divorce, particularly when the woman is from a good family, disgraces the husband as much as the wife. He was also stung by the fact that Mashalla had left Matariyya of her own accord and wondered how this might reflect on his manhood. He feared that people would think that she really had another man.

Mashalla's father came to see him and Abd el Meguid had had no choice but to say that he was considering her request. He was quite certain that Mashalla would not go to court, for fear of precipitating an investigation as to why she had left her husband's harem. Yet, he knew Mashalla would not hesitate to act out of pride. He made sure to act so that no one could fault him with neglect of his duties. Monthly, without fail, he sent the ten gold pounds that were her allowance. Religiously, without delay, she returned them. She was intent on letting him know she was above needing his support. Now she had sent the governor to plead her case. Abd el Meguid knew he could not further delay his decision.

Passing the pipe to his visitor, he watches a bee circling above the pond. How can he deny the request of such an important person? And, complying allows him to divorce Mashalla without losing face.

After smoking for a few minutes in silence the governor says, "Islam renders divorce as easy for us as marriage, Abd el Meguid. We are allowed to have four wives as long as we are loyal to them and treat them equitably. But, if through no fault of your own, one of your wives is unhappy and no longer wishes to live under your roof, my friend, or say for some reason can no longer live under your roof, what can you do? You are duty bound to grant her her freedom, Abd el Meguid. Islam teaches us that by pronouncing one word a man and a woman are united. In the same way a word can terminate an unhappy union. Marriage is joyful, Abd el Meguid, but divorce must be granted without rancor when necessary. I am sure you do not disagree. You know which of your wives I am referring to . . ."

Abd el Meguid shakes his head in assent, "I know you mean well in interceding on behalf of the daughter of El Mallaoon, Excellence."

"I am a friend of her father's as well as your loyal friend, Abd el Meguid. I wish to see a resolution for the sake of both families."

"I thank you, Excellence, for your generous intentions," responds Abd el Meguid, not conceding too easily, "but I'm certain you would be the first to say that I do not deserve the indignity of such a divorce. I have lived many years with Mashalla and my heart is heavy at the thought of never seeing her again."

"My friend," responds the governor "I know that she

has lost her place in your heart, although I won't ask you to explain the reasons why. Under the circumstances, it is in both of your best interests not to prolong this matter, Abd el Meguid. No one will think the worse of you. Mashalla has assured me that she does not wish either the return of her dowry or the three months of alimony which is her right."

Abd el Meguid exclaims, "Do you think, Excellence, that I would hesitate over a matter of money? My honor is at stake . . ."

"Your honor is not in question, Abd el Meguid. Everyone has the greatest respect for you. You should also know that Mashalla says that she has no intention of marrying again."

After a moment, Abd el Meguid says gravely, "Excellence, you know that I would give my eyes for you, so how can I refuse? If you will kindly remain a little longer, I will fetch a witness and what you asked for shall be done."

When Abd el Meguid returns, he is accompanied by a neighbor who will serve as the required second witness. Thrice, in a quiet voice, he pronounces the formula for divorce before the two witnesses: "I declare that I divorce Mashalla, that she is no longer my wife and that, henceforth, she is as a sister or a daughter to me."

At once the divorce is in effect. Abd el Meguid takes the prayer beads from his pocket and quietly fingers the amber, gazing at the rows of trees in the orchard, his lips moving silently. The witnesses, sitting down, leave him to his thoughts. Abd el Meguid remembers a dream. He had been looking at a woman leaning over a young sapling, pulling it up by the roots.

The meaning of that dream is clear. He will never forgive Mashalla. Divorcing her had been necessary.

When the prayer is over, Abd el Meguid's visitors make a move to go. Always the courteous host, he tries to detain them, but the governor insists he must leave. Abd el

Meguid hands him a pouch containing eighty gold pounds and asks him to kindly give it to Mashalla. It is her dowry plus alimony for three months. As he bids farewell to the governor at the garden gate, Abd el Meguid's thoughts are not of Mashalla, but of his young wife. He can hardly wait to see her.

Om Hassan has taken Zanouba to a cousin's house in Helwan. She had persuaded Abd el Fattah to let her move Zanouba to this small town where the dry climate would speed her recovery. Abd el Meguid thinks that his news will do more to help her than the best of climates. "If I get on the five o'clock express to Cairo, I can catch the connecting train to Helwan and be with her tonight."

In his mind's eye he imagines the carefully laid out streets of Helwan, the green gate leading to the quiet garden and the trim white house. He sees himself opening the garden gate, the door, and finally entering the bedroom. Zanouba's adoring eyes look up at him. He imagines himself pressing her childlike head to his breast. His heart fills with tenderness and the smile he had lost returns. His cherished Zanouba, recovering under her mother's doting care, smiles back, her face flushing with pleasure as he tells her he has come to take her home.

14 · ZANOUBA VISITS DARB EL MAGHARBA

Zanouba's clothes are folded in their *bogas*. The few belongings she and Om Hassan have brought with them are packed. Om Hassan exclaims, "Oh, my Zanouba, you will return to your husband's house in triumph, mistress of Matariyya!"

Before going on to Matariyya, however, Zanouba spends a little time in her father's home in Darb el Magharba. Neighbors stop to say *Hamdullah alal Salaama*—Thank God for your recovery—and, of course, to gossip. Om Hassan, her spirits soaring, announces her daughter's happy news to every visitor.

A servant lights a fire in the *mangal*. Squatting before it, she makes one pot of coffee after another. "Zanouba is returning to Matariyya?" asks a neighbor, "May Allah be praised!"

"I understand that her husband has been asking after her and is coming to fetch her tomorrow," says a visitor. "We wanted to keep her here a month, but Abd el Meguid will not hear of it," replies Om Hassan proudly.

A woman interjects: "But why doesn't he live in Cairo?" Her neighbor exclaims, "Why would a rich man want to live in this crowded city and be squeezed into cramped quarters like the rest of us?! Look at my courtyard, and even Om Hassan's. They're not much bigger than a pocket handkerchief!"

Om Hassan, taking the cue, boasts, "Imagine that in Matariyya the garden alone is more than ten acres!"

"Ten acres? Why that's more space than three Cairo neighborhoods put together!" exclaims one woman.

"Three? More like four!" answers another.

Om Hassan informs her visitors that the women of Abd el Meguid's harem go out for donkey rides in that garden and that Om Mahmood even has her own mule. "When you see her, a servant holding the bridle and another with his hand on the animal's neck, you'd think she was the governor's wife," she says.

"Your son-in-law is that rich?" exclaims one woman, further prompting Om Hassan.

"Rich? He owns seven houses in the countryside, and half of the shops in the quarter of Gamaliyya!" exclaims Om Hassan.

"I've heard it said that if he touches sand, it turns to gold," says one of the visitors, flattering Om Hassan.

"It's quite true," she responds.

"He must have such beautiful things!" exclaims one of the visitors.

"You cannot even imagine how much he has!" exclaims Om Hassan.

"Tell us, Om Hassan," says a visitor.

Om Hassan does not wait to be asked twice. She begins: "In some rooms he has three or four rugs, and what rugs! Some are worth more than a hundred guineas!"

Seeing her impact, she continues.

"There is a special room for meals with furniture made in Europe. He has a huge table for writing which he calls an office, surrounded with cupboards full of books. He even has a book about Noah! And that's only the tip of the iceberg."

"What about the kitchen?" asks a visitor.

"I can't begin to describe all the store rooms! They show a man's true worth. There are stacks of drums full of hundreds of pounds of oil, and at least fifty giant earthenware tubs of clarified butter. There must be enough soap drying on the shelves to last twenty years. Jams and preserves of every sort: rose petal, date, fig, bitter orange, condiments from Syria, Turkey, India . . . Abd el Meguid buys everything in bulk: hard candies, Turkish delight, nuts, everything."

"Allah be praised!" repeat several women at once. Om Hassan exclaims, "And I haven't come to the fruit stores filled with harvest from his gardens!"

"I've never seen an orchard," interjects a neighbor. "I thought only the Khedive and his family and the *pashas* were allowed to have them!"

"Well, Abd el Meguid's gardens are a match for any *pasha*'s. You can visit them when Zanouba goes back to Matariyya."

"You know," says one of the neighbors, "my cousin's son-in-law is an engineer with the irrigation department. He tells me that there are fruits in the Khedive's orchards that have never before been seen in Egypt. There is a green fruit as big as a fist, round and full of cream-covered black seeds . . ." Her neighbor interrupts, "It's called *ishta*—cream. They say it smells like perfume and you eat it by sucking the creamy flesh off the seeds."

"Abd el Meguid also has new fruit in his orchard," brags Om Hassan.

"I've heard of one like a big, green egg with orange flesh and a huge seed inside," comments a neighbor.

"Also I've heard about a tiny, red fruit, which is very fragrant and has a little green collar around the stem . . ." adds one of the women. "It grows close to the ground."

"Abd el Meguid's garden is like paradise on earth," says Om Hassan. "If you could see the oranges! They're as big as pomegranates. And the pomegranates are as big as watermelons. Trellises shade the garden paths in summer and they're loaded with green, black, and red grapes!"

"God is great! Allah be praised!" exclaim the visitors.

An old neighbor has listened to Om Hassan without comment. She thinks, "That foolish woman is going to attract the evil eye on her family with all of this boasting." Finally she says, "How everything changes, my sister. In my day who would have dared think of such strange fruit, or oranges bigger than God intended them to be. Does man's arrogance have no limit? Since those streetcars have invaded us, religion has gone by the wayside and the devil's work knows no bounds."

"God is Great, grandmother," laughs a young visitor. "Why aren't these fruits also his creation?"

Om Hassan, absorbed in her narrative, charges on. "I still haven't told you anything about the vegetable garden . . ." she begins again. An exasperated neighbor interrupts her. "Aren't all vegetables the same, sister?" she questions.

"There are some that neither you nor I would know how to cook nor even eat, sister," responds Om Hassan.

A neighbor, sensing ruffled feathers, tries to smooth them out. She turns to Om Hassan and places a hand on her shoulder. "I've heard about these wonders, sister—one such vegetable grows on a long stem and looks like a flower," she says. "That's the one I'm talking about," answers Om Hassan, pleased. "It looks like a globe with a lot of hard, green leaves packed very tightly together. It's called *kharshoof*—artichoke!"

"I've heard it's very bitter," says one woman.

Om Hassan responds, "I've never tasted it, but I'm told you only eat the heart. I've tried *arnabeet,* though."

"What's *arnabeet?*" asks a young woman. Om Hassan happily explains. "Imagine a plump head of cabbage and in the middle of it a white ball, like a big flower, made of little branches. You pull the branches apart, dip them in batter and cook them in hot oil. It's as delicious as fried brains!"

"Praise be to Allah!" proclaim the women in chorus.

Om Hassan grows incautious. She neglects to guard against the evil eye of the envious. "She should say at least one negative thing about Abd el Meguid," thinks her wise old neighbor. Om Hassan adds, impetuously, that fresh milk and thick cream are brought to the door of each of Abd el Meguid's wives for breakfast.

Exclaiming on Zanouba's good fortune the neighbors finally take their leave despite Om Hassan's polite insistence that they stay a little longer, have another cup of coffee . . . They kiss Zanouba, wish her well and promise to visit.

15 · ZANOUBA'S RETURN TO MATARIYYA

The next day, Om Hassan helps her daughter get ready for her triumphant return to Matariyya. They fold Zanouba's clothes lovingly into the many *bogas* that have been sewn as part of her trousseau. Om Hassan also creates a tiny charm to insure her daughter's continued good fortune and happiness. A number of ingredients are placed in a small pouch which she ties securely: seven hairs taken from a black dog, seven hairs from a cat, a feather plucked from a crow's wing and one from the head of an egret, and a dead man's tooth. She instructs Zanouba to hide the charm beneath her husband's pillow, warning her to guard against anyone else knowing about it.

When Om Mahmood arrives in Darb el Magharba to fetch her daughter-in-law she finds Zanouba eager to accompany her. Om Hassan is invited too. She brings with her a huge hamper of homemade cakes, cookies, and sweets to share with the women of Abd el Meguid's household.

When the party reaches the village of Matariyya, their carriage is delayed. A huge tent has been erected before a house, and spills over onto the road. Their passage is blocked by a celebrating crowd. Women's joy cries are interspersed with melodious recitations of the Qur'an.

"What is happening here?" asks Om Hassan, turning to Om Mahmood.

"The oldest son of the household is a student at the Al Azhar University. He just received his three loaves of bread," she answers.

"What does that mean?" asks Zanouba.

"When a student successfully completes his first examinations, the university awards him a daily stipend consisting of three loaves of bread, which recognizes him as a novice member of the clerical community. The success of an Azharite gives honor to his parents and his whole village. It also marks his passage into a different kind of life. Since he has gained stature and respect, he has to act accordingly."

"What does he have to do?" asks Zanouba, intrigued.

"Well, it's what he has to stop doing, for one thing," responds Om Mahmood.

"What does he have to stop doing?" asks Zanouba.

"He can no longer go to coffee houses, or look at belly

dancers, for example. Three loaves that he gets are blessed and anyone in need of help can ask for a piece. The sick can come to him, girls who want a good husband, people who are signing contracts, that sort of thing . . ."

Om Hassan, hearing Om Mahmood's explanation, pleads with her to ask the coachman to fetch a piece for Zanouba. He brings back only a tiny morsel since the takers are numerous. She and Abd el Meguid will share it to insure a fruitful union and keep them out of harm's way.

Finally, making a passage through the crowd, the carriage continues. At home Zanouba finds Narguiss and Gaulisar eagerly awaiting her. They have had a calf slaughtered in her honor. The animal's blood is still bright red on the threshold over which she must step. Om Mahmood explains that this makes sure her foot is firmly planted in the household. Om Hassan recognizes the significance of this ritual which declares the importance of Zanouba's presence in her husband's harem. She expresses her appreciation by letting out a volley of joy cries, which are immediately echoed by the other women.

Having been carefully instructed by Om Hassan to step on Narguiss and Gaulisar's feet as she greets them, Zanouba pretends to stumble as she rushes to kiss one and then the other. Her mother had carefully explained that she must do this to stamp out any possible jealousy.

Meanwhile, Om Hassan's eyes take in every detail of the homecoming preparations. She flushes with pride when she sees in the kitchen the figure of a portly cook hired for the occasion. The quantity and quality of the food offered in Zanouba's honor indicates how much Om Mahmood values her new daughter-in-law. Om Hassan knows that Abd el Meguid's feelings toward Zanouba are ultimately determined by his mother's acceptance of his wife.

Gaulisar and Narguiss both exude mystery and anticipation. The one restrains a little smile, the other's eyes wrinkle playfully. Om Hassan guesses that they have a surprise for Zanouba.

All three women are so eager to see the effects of their pains on their young companion that they rush her upstairs to Mashalla's old apartment. Om Hassan climbs the old stone stairs panting behind them. Zanouba opens the door and gasps. What miracle has taken place here? Is this really the same harem which witnessed her trusting happiness and her accident? Will it become hers now? Cautiously, she steps in.

The great hall has become a room from an enchanted fairy tale. Om Mahmood, Narguiss, and Gaulisar thrill at the wonder on Zanouba's face and smile at her mother's exclamations. Om Hassan invokes God, his prophet, and all the saints as her witnesses. She declares Abd el Meguid the best and most generous of husbands, repeating that there are not two like him in the world.

Zanouba is mesmerized. A strange light, as if emanating from a magician's lantern, dapples the room with red, blue, and lilac. Looking for the source, she discovers new stained glass windows above the *mashrabiyya* screens, similar to those she has seen in sanctuaries she has visited with her mother. The small pieces of colored glass are set in thick, brilliantly painted white plaster. The sight fills her with a sense of reverence.

Looking up at the high, beamed ceiling, she sees a new chandelier, like a graceful crown. Suspended by chains, its three concentric circles of carved brass are studded with twenty lighted pink candles. Their glimmering gives the room an air of tender warmth. The walls have been freshly decorated. Stunning panels—light blue, edged in red, highlighted with a thread of gold—form rich rectangles all around the room. The ceiling is now a night sky, crisscrossed with fine gold lines outlining lozenges. The white stars catch the light deflected through the stained glass windows and even seem to twinkle, caressed by the candlelight.

On the stone floor, a giant Persian carpet has been spread. The deep earth colors, the rich reds and blues interspersed with lighter tones, enchant Zanouba. Her eyes grow wide with delight when she discovers the intricate patterns of flora and fauna woven into the thick pile.

Mashalla's old harem has also been refurnished from top to bottom. On the right and left of the room, along the walls, are long, deep divans adorned with fine Bokharas. The wine-colored wools used to weave the geometric designs of these exquisite rugs are offset by a profusion of pale silk cushions. These invite one to recline and savor life. On either side of the room, facing each other, are two massive dressers, inlaid with ivory and mother of pearl. Crowning these are deep niches with shelves, closed off with little doors fitted with carved silver hinges. Above them are large mirrors with frames intricately inlaid and shaped to simulate the doors of a mosque.

Scattered throughout the room are *sandaliyyas*—twelve-legged tray tables supporting large, circular silver trays. The table legs are inlaid with mother of pearl, matching the dressers. Around each tray table Zanouba sees adorable little square settees, upholstered in crimson velvet. Between their pale, stubby legs are lacelike panels of a darker wood exquisitely carved with motifs resembling those in the large Persian carpet.

Zanouba flutters from one end of the room to the other, emitting little cries of excitement and surprise. She reaches up to touch an ivory ostrich egg, hanging from the center of the chandelier by a string of multicolored beads. She opens the doors of the niches and exclaims at the little lead statues snuggled there. She fingers the knickknacks and, like the child she is, tries to decide which is her favorite. One of the figurines is a Qur'anic reader, squatting, looking up, his mouth open. Another is a placid waterpipe smoker. A third represents a bedouin with a shotgun under his arm. A couple is enjoying a game of backgammon, sitting cross-legged on a rug. Chess players are sitting on a bench with an onlooker standing behind them. Zanouba exclaims at the tiny chess pieces, perfect replicas of king, queen, vizir, judge, lions, soldiers . . . Unable to contain her delight, she claps her hands, feeling happier than she has ever been.

In the bedroom where Zanouba has left her veil and *habara,* she sees her own furniture, moved from Abasiyya. She does not linger there, but rushes back to the living room.

For a fleeting moment she remembers Mashalla, sitting before the *masharabiyya* window where she liked to spend lazy hours in repose. Zanouba thinks of her vanquished rival. The Mashalla she sees in her mind's eye is not the criminal who caused the death of her unborn child, but the older sister who told her stories, initiated her to the mysteries of the harem. But these thoughts are fleeting. All traces of Mashalla have been removed. This room is no longer the sinister site of Zanouba's nightmare, but a giant jewel box, richly upholstered, silky and luxuriant, prepared with love by Abd el Meguid for his cherished little wife.

Hafiza, a young girl with round, red cheeks and blue eyes appears at the door with a tray of refreshments. Zanouba is pulled back to the present. Hafiza is the cook's oldest daughter. Om Mahmood has assigned her to be her daughter-in-law's personal servant. Zanouba kisses the pretty little girl affectionately, thinking with pleasure that she will become a friend and confidante. The child seems delighted to be assigned to such a young mistress and relieved of tedious kitchen duties. Zanouba imagines the bonds of affection that will grow between them, and her simple heart soars.

Toward the end of the evening, when Zanouba notices that her mother does not intend to leave, she grows apprehensive. She wants to be able to see Abd el Meguid tonight. If Om Hassan stays over, she will sleep in her daughter's harem, and her husband's visit will have to be delayed. Om Hassan, in deep conversation with Narguiss and Gaulisar, seems oblivious of Zanouba's distress. Her mother-in-law, however, senses her impatience. As if reading Zanouba's mind, Om Mahmood says, "Don't worry, my gazelle, Om Hassan will spend the night in my harem . . ."

Gaulisar and Narguiss, overhearing, smile. Zanouba blushes. Embarrassed to have been so transparent, she looks for a pretext to run out of the room, but Narguiss calls her back.

Om Mahmood takes Zanouba's hand and pulls her down beside her on the divan. "Don't run away, child, we were just going to discuss how to divide our household responsibilities." "Anything you say, mother," answers Zanouba, averting her gaze.

Om Mahmood gets right down to business. She suggests that Narguiss and Gaulisar continue supervising the cleanliness and upkeep of the house, meal preparation, and baking. Zanouba, like Mashalla before her, could be responsible for Abd el Meguid's wardrobe which would be kept in her harem. This vote of confidence touches Zanouba's heart because it establishes her as the head wife. Innocently, she agrees.

Alert, Om Hassan instantly raises objections. "This is too much of an honor for my daughter right now. It might create discord between the wives," she says, explaining that every time Abd el Meguid took a bath Zanouba would have to provide him with fresh clothes. That would be embarrassing after he had spent the night with one of his other wives.

"It's best for each wife to have some of her husband's clothing in her apartment and have its upkeep be her responsibility," says Om Hassan.

"Well, perhaps," answers Om Mahmood, accommodating.

Om Hassan, who is superstitious, also believes that having full responsibility for Abd el Meguid's wardrobe would put Zanouba at risk. She is convinced that all it would take to turn her husband against Zanouba would be for one of her potential rivals to put a spell on his clothing, particularly a piece which touches his skin. Also everything which absorbs his perspiration must be carefully protected. Under no circumstances should any undergarment, hankerchief, or nightcap ever be sent out to be washed, not even given to a household servant.

Om Hassan suggests that Zanouba, who is clever with numbers, be given responsibility for the safe. "She could distribute allowances, pay the servants and tradesmen, and keep accounts," says Om Hassan. "She's very clever!"

Om Mahmood's face flushes with indignation. She says, "Have you ever heard of a mother-in-law receiving her allowance from her son's wife, Om Hassan!"

"I didn't mean it that way," responds Om Hassan, knowing better than to insist.

"It's just that Zanouba, who is still so young, would be ashamed not to do more to help out," she explains.

Om Mahmood curtly informs Om Hassan that she has performed this task for over twenty years without anyone ever daring to suggest that it be done otherwise, not even Mashalla.

"As to the keys which open the safe, my son holds them, as is his right as master," says Om Mahmood, emphatically.

Zanouba, mortified by her mother's brazen suggestion, shrinks back into the cushions of the divan, wishing she could disappear.

Om Hassan, realizing she has blundered, tries to smooth out the awkward situation. She turns to Om Mahmood and, in a conciliatory tone, says, "Zanouba must make herself useful, sister. What would you think about her helping Narguiss one week and Gaulisar the next?" Her suggestion is accepted without argument but she secretly hopes that one day, when Zanouba has familiarized herself with the workings of the household, she will indeed step into Om Mahmood's slippers.

Part Four ▪ *The Musharrara:*
Witchcraft Which Renders
Its Victims Sterile

16 · STERILE WOMEN

Several months have elapsed since Zanouba's joyous return to Matariyya.

"Zanouba, my daughter, your husband is not such an old man that he cannot have children," says Om Mahmood one day.

"Sitt Shafika, the doctor, has assured me that your miscarriage has not left any scars, my child, and yet you are still not pregnant. Abd el Meguid is consumed with grief. He is losing his taste for life and can think of nothing but his desire for a son. He is neglecting his business and even his friends," says Om Mahmood, looking dejected. Narguiss adds, "You know that neither Gaulisar nor I can have children now, Zanouba, and Abd el Meguid won't hear of taking another wife. What can we do, my sister?"

Om Hassan, who is visiting, pipes up, "I've said over and over again, Om Mahmood, that this is the result of a curse. I know a Sudanese Codia, and I've suggested more than once that we hold a *zar* . . ."

"Don't even mention the word, Om Hassan," says Om Mahmood, "You know how Abd el Meguid feels about magic. He is a pious Muslim and a sheikh, don't forget it!"

Om Hassan's face flushes. She protests: "How can you call getting rid of evil spirits magic, Om Mahmood? Is there anyone who would dare deny that they exist? How can anyone be against a ritual which is designed to rid us of the harm they do?"

"Be that as it may, Om Hassan! No *zar* will be held in this house, not even in secret!" answers Om Mahmood, curtly.

"Well, have it your way, Om Mahmood. But I won't hide my feelings from you, my sister. My heart aches to see my daughter in this predicament and this house without a son. But, since you refuse my advice, you cannot fault my Zanouba," replies Om Hassan.

Narguiss intervenes to smooth things over. She says, "Well, of course everyone knows there are ways to counteract the *musharrara,* Om Hassan. You are quite right. In fact, I was a victim of the *musharrara* myself. I remained four years without children. One day, on the advice of our old Aisha—you knew her, Om Hassan, she died last year, God rest her soul, I took my courage in my hands and went to the far end of the village where the trains pass, and I did as I was told. I lay down between the railroad tracks. I think you can imagine my terror . . . I made myself lie perfectly still until the locomotive and all the cars had passed over me. Then, I went home. It was winter and I remember trembling. I don't know if it was cold or fear. Anyway, by Sham el Nessim, that next spring, I was pregnant with Shafika."

"Well, now you see!" says Om Hassan, triumphantly, "It takes an extraordinary act to overcome sterility. It's the only way to dispel the effects of the *musharrara!*"

"Narguiss, my sister, you are braver than I could ever be. I would have certainly died of terror!" cries Zanouba, shivering suddenly.

"I heard of a woman who became pregnant after passing seven times beneath the belly of a *gamoosa,* a female water buffalo," contributes Gaulisar.

"Everyone knows that the number seven is magic," answers Om Hassan.

Gaulisar adds "Of course this was a *gamoosa* belonging to the Khedive. It was in his gardens, in Shubra."

"There is a wonderful *hamman* in those gardens. The waters of that bath heal and also work against the *musharrara*. A number of women have been cured of sterility there. No other baths are like it!" says Fatma, a visiting relative of Om Mahmood's.

"Why go so far? What about the sacred tree of Matariyya, where the holy mother Mary rested on her flight into Egypt?" questions Om Mahmood.

"I've been there, and I wasn't alone, mother," says Zanouba, looking at Om Mahmood.

"Yes, I went with you, child, and I told you not to breathe a word to Abd el Meguid, that's true," confesses Om Mahmood.

"But, of course, it's all superstition, and you can see that it didn't do any good," she concludes.

"My success is proof of what Om Hassan said about an extraordinary act," Narguiss insists.

"There are easier ways of doing these things, though," comments the visitor.

"Like what?" asks Om Hassan.

"Like going into a pyramid, for example," the visitor replies.

"I've heard of women who go to the museum in Bulac to circle the mummies of the ancient Egyptians. It seems they have power over the *musharrara*," says Gaulisar.

"Yes, you go around them seven times," says Narguiss.

"My cousin, Zaynab, is very pious and never visits pagan sites, or does anything else against the teachings of Islam. Yet, she has a child almost every year," comments Fatma.

"Well then, what does she do?" asks Om Hassan.

"When I asked her for her secret, she told me that she prays at the tombs of saints buried in certain sanctuaries."

Om Hassan, her eyes lighting up, exclaims, "There is

none better than El Maghrawi! How could we have forgotten him? Abd el Meguid could not possibly object to Zanouba going to pray there, could he, Om Mahmood?" asks Om Hassan.

"Abd el Meguid doesn't like the sheiks at the mosque of El Maghrawi. And I've heard that visitors do more than pray there," answers Om Mahmood.

"Well, then, how about the sheikhs of the Bekhtashi order? They are pious men who follow the teachings of Islam to the letter, Om Mahmood. They would never have you do anything sinful," says Om Hassan.

"Well, perhaps," answers Om Mahmood reluctantly.

Om Hassan says, "The trouble with living so far from Cairo is that expeditions to these holy tombs are difficult. How would it be if Zanouba returned to Darb el Magharba with me for a few days?" And, turning to Zanouba, she adds, "Also, you haven't seen your father and brother for a while, my daughter."

Zanouba is tempted, but is reluctant to show her enthusiasm for fear of displeasing her mother-in-law. She looks to her for a sign. Om Mahmood simply shrugs her shoulders. Seeing Zanouba getting a little teary-eyed, she says, "It's for Abd el Meguid to say, my child." Turning to Om Hassan, she warns, "Don't even think of having a *zar*!"

"A *zar*?" answers Om Hassan, "Who would pay for it? Abd el Meguid won't hear of it and my husband complains that I'll be the ruin of him if I ask for twenty piasters to buy a new veil. Zanouba, tell your mother-in-law! If I even mention money, he raises his hands to heaven and curses me, my mother and my mother's mother! No, no, Om Mahmood, a *zar* is expensive! But visiting sanctuaries is free, except for the little gifts to the sheikhs when we ask them for a special prayer." Om Hassan cannot resist adding, her voice trailing off, "But a beautiful *zar* would be so much better . . ."

17 · EL MAGHRAWI

At Darb el Magharba, Om Hassan says to her daughter, "I was surprised your husband let you go so easily, my child."

"He knew this trip would please me and said I could stay a week. He's really very good to me. This morning, just as I was leaving, he gave me five guineas to pay for transportation and buy gifts for the sheiks. He even told me he would pray along with me to ask God to grant us a son," responds Zanouba.

"God willing, you will have one, and maybe many," chimes in Sitt Habiba, Zanouba's grandmother, who has come to join her daughter and granddaughter. "I have great confidence in the powers of El Maghrawi. Did you know that I once took your aunt Galila there? She had been childless for three years and now she has seven children, God give her health and long life," adds Sitt Habiba, referring to her eldest daughter, with whom she lives.

Om Hassan says, "I must confess that I've never been there, mother. Of course, I had Zanouba within a year of my marriage, then her brother, Hassan, God rest his soul, then Ibrahim."

"May God give them health and long life and reward them with many children," says Sitt Habiba.

Zanouba is anxious about the visit to the Maghrawi mosque and, asks her grandmother what she will have to do once they get there.

"You'll have to climb a lot of stairs, my child, and then you'll do what the *fiki* tells you," answers Sitt Habiba.

Zanouba has heard about this extraordinary mosque, a deep cavern carved out of the Mokattam hills. Sitt Habiba gradually remembers what Galila had to do there years ago. She tries to explain to her granddaughter, but Om Hassan constantly interrupts. Zanouba is confused. She thinks, "I'll find out soon enough."

Sitting with her cheek cradled in her right hand, her mind wanders. "I'll never really be considered a woman until I've had a son. Gaulisar and Narguiss have daughters and they're never called mother of Fatma, or mother of Zakiyya. They're just called Gaulisar and Narguiss. My mother and my mother-in-law are never called by their names. They are Mother of Hassan and Mother of Mahmood. That's how I want it. And it would make Abd el Meguid so happy . . ."

On the chosen day the sun shines brightly. It is not as hot as is usual this season. The March winds, the *khamseen,* just beginning their hot and dusty fifty day reign, have given them a reprieve.

"What a pleasure to be let out of the harem," thinks Zanouba.

On the way, peeking out from the curtains of the carriage, Zanouba relishes the sight of the copper craftsmen along El-Nahaaseen Street. She listens with delight to the cries of the fruit and vegetable sellers, the strident voices of the donkey boys, the clanging of the cymbals used by lemonade vendors to attract business. "I wish I could get out and walk," she thinks, imagining herself window shopping, her face well hidden behind her heavy black *boro.*

They pass the gold street, the *sagha.* She wishes she could look at the rich display of jewelry in every store front and then in the Khan el Khalili. She has heard one finds there the most beautiful silks for dresses. The perfume merchants will put a drop of dizzying amber or jasmin oil on the back of your hand. None of these places are far from Darb el Magharba. She thinks, "Maybe I can persuade my mother to take me there on foot some day."

Finally, the Mokattam hills come into view. The carriage climbs a steep road to the Citadel. As it travels along the massive sand-colored walls of the fortress, the driver points out the place where a Mameluk Bey on horseback took a flying leap, trying escape being murdered. He shouts in order to be heard. "His companions were all killed by the soldiers of the great pasha Muhammad Ali."

"How could he have survived?" asks Zanouba. "He was caught in midair by an angel," interjects Sitt Habiba. "Then what happened to him?" asks Zanouba. "Well, it seems Muhammad Ali Pasha accorded him a pardon," declares the driver.

"That's because he saw that he was saved by God's angels," repeats Sitt Habiba.

Zanouba looks and listens. How fantastic this all is! She imagines the horse, falling, the horseman standing erect in the stirrups, his great coat flying behind him. An angel holds him gently by the shoulders, slowing his descent to the firm ground.

Suddenly the carriage turns into a sordid little alley, under the dirty walls of the prison of Manchiyya.

"How sinister!" Zanouba thinks and shivers.

She almost expects to see hairy hands, frantically grasping the bars on the tiny windows, or the menacing face of a bandit coming over the wall.

The alley twists and turns. Garbage is everywhere. The driver pulls on the reins and the horse picks its way carefully amidst the debris.

"Look!" says Zanouba, her voice full of emotion.

Simultaneously, three pairs of eyes turn above their black face veils. Each cylindrical gold *asaba* holding the cloth in place between forehead and nose glints in the sun.

The ruins of a once superb complex of buildings loom to the right. The remaining walls, crenelated into giant clover leaves, are silhouetted against the sky. A square tower rises alone, surrounded by thickly fluted domes and slender minarets. What is left of the fine, lacelike stonework attests to long gone grandeur. These tombs, the pride of the Mameluk Beys who built them, mark their final resting place.

The three women, lost in thought, ride in silence until the driver's voice startles them, announcing, "El Maghrawi!"

With his whip, he points to an opening in the golden cliffs ahead. A small, green oasis with a few scattered eucalyptus trees is visible.

Zanouba is disappointed. She had expected to see domes covered in gold, minarets rising to meet the sky, and a magnificent mosque. Instead, she sees buildings with plasterwork so dilapidated that they practically blend into the desert tan of the mountainside. A few barely surviving trees dot the rocky landscape. Scraggly climbers cling to bits of wall. A scattering of red leaves reminds Zanouba of the *Bent el Onsol*—pointsettias—which bloom in winter in the garden of Matariyya.

The carriage stops next to a ledge which leads to steep stone stairs, bleached by the sun. The three women look up and see a small opening at the top. They begin to climb.

Step by step they go up, curiosity motivating their ascent. Sitt Habiba, with her arthritic knees, moans every inch of the way. Zanouba and Om Hassan stop and wait for her, looking at the carriage far below. "How high it is! It's dizzying!" exclaims Zanouba. They look at the driver watering his animal in a sliver of shade. "He doesn't look much bigger than a doll," says Om Hassan.

Near the top, they come to an overhang, a sort of porch and a flagstone walk leading to an opening in the mountain. It looks like nothing more than a black hole with a small wooden fence across it. Sitt Habiba informs them that this is the sanctuary. They must remove their shoes before entering. On a worn grass mat are six pairs of shoes, and two pairs of slippers, side by side. They add their own.

"This must be the mosque," thinks Zanouba.

"Allah be praised!" exclaims Om Hassan, out of breath, "I'll never set foot in there! This looks like a doorway to hell!"

Zanouba touches her mother's arm, motioning with her head to a courtyard, just beyond the entrance. It looks cool. She hears the gentle gurgling of water and sees a small marble fountain surrounded by wooden benches. Two bearded men sitting there are members of the order. Their flowing robes are cinched at the waist with cummerbunds. Zanouba is astonished at the large earrings they wear. Their strange turbans are like tall, fluted cylinders, brilliantly white.

"They don't look like any sheikh I've ever seen," she whispers to her mother.

Before Om Hassan has a chance to respond they witness an amazing scene. A woman is on the other side of the little gate. A sheikh recites verses from the Qur'an, places the holy book on her head, and strikes her on the shoulder with a stick. As if she were a puppet on a string the woman kicks the air both to the right and left. The *fiki* then hands her a glass of water which she drinks. She leaves without looking at anyone or saying a word. Sitt Habiba, leaning toward her daughter and granddaughter, whispers knowingly, "That was to get rid of aches and pains."

Om Hassan and Sitt Habiba take Zanouba by the hand and lead her into the cave. She has been instructed to drop a silver twenty piastre piece, a *talari,* in the offering box on her way in. Once she is inside and her eyes are accustomed to the dark, Zanouba makes out a *fiki* coming toward them. He strikes a match, lights a candle, and leads them down a long corridor. This passage at first is fairly wide but narrows as they go deeper into the flank of the mountain, finally reaching the chamber where the saint is buried.

The tomb is surrounded by a small fence. The dark shapes of women are circling around it. More tombs on raised platforms are on either side. The *fiki* explains that monks are buried beneath them. The headstones are columns topped with curious, fluted turbans not unlike the ones worns by the bearded men at the fountain. These, however, are more pointed at the top.

Turning to her grandmother, Zanouba whispers, "They're just like the domes of the *mameluk* tombs we saw on the way here, Sitti."

Sitt Habiba explains that they represent the headdresses worn by monks in days gone by.

The *fiki* motions to a tomb in the deepest recesses of the chamber. The headstone is composed of four turbans rubbed smooth and yellowed by the hands of visitors seeking blessings. Sitt Habiba goes forward, touches each one and then her own head, shoulders, and knees. She invokes the saints to preserve her from the infirmities of old age.

Zanouba touches each turban then touching her belly, she murmurs: "May a child traverse my body as I traverse this passageway."

Suddenly, the dark form of a woman hurtles toward the open door of the mosque, twirling, spinning around and around on her way out. The visitors press against the balustrade surrounding the tomb, trying to avoid her.

"Do I have to do this in order to have a child?" Zanouba asks, apprehensive. The monk responds, "You must do this whether you are here to ask for a cure or a bridegroom, to get rid of a rival or appease a husband's anger, or to dispel a curse. The only way to have your prayers answered is to leave the mosque this way. It's the same if you're asking God to protect you from the ill will of your husband's sisters or to put you in your mother-in-law's good graces. You cannot just walk out."

Zanouba looks questioningly at her mother and wonders, "Can I really do this?"

"Courage, daughter!" Om Hassan responds.

Sitt Habiba adds, "It will be easier than you think, child."

"Oh holy man," exclaims Sitt Habiba, turning to the monk, "If my little Zanouba has a boy, I will sacrifice two calves on this spot and you shall have their meat!"

"No blood can be let in this holy place, mother. But if

your wish is granted, on the tenth day of the month of Mo-
harram, you can bring us two full *zembils* of rice for the
feast of Ashoora," says the monk.

As Zanouba's eyes become accustomed to the dim light
in the cave, she notices women rolling around on the
ground, others circling the tomb. A few kneel in prayer before the *kebla,* their faces turned toward Mecca. The three
sheikhs in attendance place the holy Qur'an on the women's
heads and instruct them to touch certain amulets attached to
their cummerbunds. They follow them as they roll down a
dark tunnel and out of the mosque.

"I'm not sure I can do it, mother!" cries Zanouba.

"My daughter, we have not come all this way for nothing! You have a head and you have eyes. Just look at what
the others are doing and imitate them."

Zanouba resigned, circles the holy tombs. Seven times,
she goes around them, rubbing her belly against each headstone. She repeats, "All powerful Allah, grant me a boy. All
powerful Allah, grant me a boy . . ." Then she goes to the
fiki who places the Holy Qur'an on her head and recites
some appropriate verses. He tells her to touch an amulet,
a glass ball on his belt. Finally, she lies face down on
the ground and prepares to roll out of the sanctuary like a
barrel. She is followed by the *fiki,* Om Hassan and Sitt
Habiba.

Once they reach the open door, Om Hassan helps her
daughter up and brushes the dust from her dress. "You did
very well, my daughter. Allah willing, your wish will be
granted."

Zanouba is trembling and can only stare ahead. At the
open door of the mosque, high up one side of the Mokattam hills, the three women pause, catching their breath.
Looming before them are the slender minarets and imposing
domes of Cairo, the City Victorious. Beyond is the Nile,
shimmering. The distant pyramids are enveloped in sunset's
golden haze.

18 · THE HAMMAM OF MUHAMMAD ALI

In a hired carriage, Zanouba and several members of her family are going to visit Muhammad Ali's palace in Shubra, one of Cairo's most prestigious districts. Ibrahim, riding beside the coachman, calls out greetings to every English soldier they pass. His mother, exasperated, reprimands him. "If you keep on yelling at every English soldier, you'll have to get out!"

"He's pretending to know English!" razzes Zanouba.

"I do know English! And French too! Just watch me read the signs on the European storefronts!" exclaims Ibrahim, vexed.

"Set straight your *tarboosh* and quit your tomfoolery or I won't let you come to the palace with us!" chides Om Hassan.

"So what! I'll go to Gezira!" answers Ibrahim, insolently.

Zanouba, using the sassy tone reserved for her younger brother, retorts, "I bet you'd rather be off to the races anyway!"

Ibrahim looks furiously at his sister. Earlier that week, he had extracted a *talari* from her to bet on some horses. Since then, she has hounded him and accused him of putting on airs. When he became a student at the exclusive Khede-wiyya Secondary School, he began to wear western clothes, bet on horses, and play the role of the thoroughly modern young man. Zanouba let him know she thought he looked ridiculous. When she teases him in the carriage he gives her a significant look meaning, "How dare you talk about horses in front of mother!"

Om Hassan has pricked up her ears. She demands: "What races? Is that another one of those newfangled British pastimes? Is that what you do in Gezira? I must let Abd el Fattah know about this!"

"No, no, mother, I go there to watch football and tennis," replies Ibrahim quickly.

"Football and tennis, indeed," Zanouba mocks, "It's the bare ankles of the 'misses' you go there to watch!"

"Ankles? Legs?" cries Sitt Habiba. "Aren't their bare faces enough of an affront? God spare us such blasphemy!"

Ibrahim blushes. He is annoyed at his sister for having gotten him into trouble. However much he relishes peeking at the unveiled face and ankles of a European, he would never marry such an immodest girl. Still, he is mortified to have his secret exposed before his mother and grandmother.

The carriage quickly passes the train station of Bab el Hadid, and crosses the tracks. Rumbling along at a good clip, they reach Shari' Shubra, once a royal road, linking Muhammad Ali's palace to the pond in the Azbakiyya gardens—the Birket el Azbakiyya. Zanouba and her family enter the tree-lined avenue, now a fashionable promenade. Few people are out because of the noonday heat. Shari' Shubra, straight as an arrow, is shaded by luxuriant branches of ancient sycamores. From one end of the avenue to the other, they form a cool, green tunnel. The horse slows down and Om Hassan sighs with relief.

Ibrahim assumes the role of guide. As they pass, he calls out the names of princes and notables whose villas are encircled by lush gardens and flowering hedges. The profuse bougainvilleas catch Zanouba's eye, their papery pink and peach blooms offset by their dark green foliage and the mottled bark of the sycamores.

An hour later, they reach the gates of the palace grounds. Om Hassan presents her permit to enter the gardens, procured by her husband, Abd el Fattah, probably in exchange for a favor. The porter ushers in the carriage.

"Allah be praised! This must be paradise!" exclaims Sitt Habiba as she is helped out of the carriage by a watchman.

He escorts them down the wide, tree-lined alley leading away from the palace and toward the baths—the *hammam*. Zanouba's eyes widen before the manicured lawns, magnificent flower beds, and bushes.

Zanouba and Ibrahim, still childlike, run ahead. They find the baths deserted. They climb up the first few steps and stop, struck with wonder. The water in the great marble pool glistens reflecting the delicate columns of the deep-set galleries surrounding it. A marble fountain at the center is decorated with lions slumbering in the great calm of this wonderland. On all four sides, stone crocodiles spout jets of water.

When Om Hassan and Sitt Habiba catch up with the young people, Om Hassan says, "Daughter, let's not forget why we've come here . . ." Her voice rings in the still afternoon.

Ibrahim and the watchman, taking the hint, leave.

"I don't know if Abd el Meguid would approve of this expedition," says Zanouba, suddenly guilty. Om Hassan, raising an eyebrow, smiles at her daughter and asks, "How long have you been married now, Zanouba?"

"Five years, mother," answers Zanouba.

Om Hassan says, "After all this time, you're still telling your husband everything? You're not doing anything wrong . . ."

"But he only gave me permission to visit the mosques and tombs of saints, mother . . ." interjects Zanouba.

"My child, Abd el Meguid doesn't want to know that you've been to visit the mummies at the museum in Bulac, or that you've been inside a pyramid. Or for that matter, to know the details of what you did in the mosque of the Bekhtashi sheikhs. Zanouba, an honest woman must still decide what to tell and not to tell her husband. You know I wouldn't mislead you, my heart!"

Sitt Habiba discovers a little staircase going into the pool. She calls to her granddaughter: "Take off your shoes, my child, go up and down these stairs seven times washing your face and feet, then go around the pool seven times."

Zanouba obeys.

As she circles she notices decorative fish on the sides of the pool. Since the number seven brings good fortune, she touches seven of them for good luck. Then she rests on one of the deep ledges in the shady recesses of a gallery. Ibrahim finds her there an hour later. Above their heads is a sculpted medallion of Ibrahim Pasha, surrounded with coats of arms and weapons. Her brother recounts the general's exploits as they explore the other galleries. They stare in awe at the ceilings with the murals of landscapes and seascapes. Ibrahim particularly admires a nude woman rising out of a seashell. The watchman opens the doors to apartments surrounding the pool, hoping for a good tip. They peek in at Ibrahim Pasha's vast, opulent salon with its massive mirrors, gilt ceiling, imposing chandeliers and candelabras, and call to Om Hassan and Sitt Habiba.

"There must not be two more beautiful rooms in the entire world," says Sitt Habiba, tipping the guard to let Zanouba go inside.

"Walk around the rooms seven times, my child," she instructs.

Having done all they can around the pool, Om Hassan tells Ibrahim to wait for them at the gate. The three women explore more of the gardens, searching for locations which can further enhance Zanouba's fortune.

Seeing a tree with huge, exotic looking fruit, Sitt Habiba exclaims, "This must be a mango tree, look at the size of that fruit!"

Om Hassan says, "It's just like the one in Abd el Meguid's garden, mother."

"There are mangoes and there are mangoes," answers Sitt Habiba, telling Zanouba to go around the tree seven times, anyway, just for good measure. "This is, after all, in the Khedive's garden," she explains.

When she hears the squealing of a *sakia*—a water wheel—coming from a distant orchard, Zanouba reminds her mother and grandmother of the story of the woman who went under the belly of a pregnant *gamoosa*—water buffalo—belonging to the Khedive and the following year had a child. They walk toward the sound, hoping that the *gamoosa* attached to this *sakia* will be a pregnant female.

They enter an orange orchard and see the animal, its eyes covered to keep it from becoming dizzy as it goes around and around. A boy of ten on her back keeps her moving with a switch. Sitt Habiba gives him a few coins. He stops the animal and leaves. The *gamoosa* is visibly pregnant.

Zanouba, after making sure the coast is clear, crawls under the animal's belly and goes back and forth seven times. The water buffalo, relieved to rest, does not budge. Sitt Habiba tells Zanouba to sit on the bar attaching the animal to the wheel and to ride around seven times. She tips the little conductor, who has returned, to prod the buffalo along her plodding rounds. The *sakia* sings and squeals. The red clay pots attached to the vertical wheel lift water from the canal and rhythmically pour it into narrow ditches leading to the thirsty fields. Zanouba rides around and around, her face radiant with childlike happiness.

Om Hassan suggests that it is time to leave if they wish to be home before nightfall. Shari' Shubra is now bustling with activity. Men on horseback, open carriages full of young men reclining on cushions, covered *landaus* with curtained windows perhaps shielding women—all follow one another on either side of the avenue. The coachmen's cries are strident as they urge the horses with their whips and caution pedestrians. Suddenly, a cluster of officers on horseback races down the avenue, yelling commands to clear the way. All carriages halt in a golden haze of dust rising slowly like incense.

Ibrahim shouts, "It's the Khedive!"

He quickly clambers down to the street, joining others

eager to see the sovereign. His grandmother, mother, and sister are left to see what they can through their veils.

"What a good omen this is, my child," murmurs Om Hassan.

Sitt Habiba adds, "God willing, your wish for a son will be granted. Do you know, Zanouba, every time I have prayed for something and seen the sovereign, my prayers have been answered. I've had the good fortune of seeing him five times. Do you remember your uncle Hassan? When he was on mission in the Sudan, I hadn't heard from him in five months. I was frantic with worry. On the very day that I saw the Khedive, Hassan came home. That was years ago . . ."

"You seem very fond of the Khedive, grandmother," Zanouba remarks.

Sitt Habiba responds: "Doesn't everyone love his sovereign, my child? God has chosen him above other mortals as the one to look after his flock and to make sure we are well governed. May God preserve him as he preserves our land and the blessed waters of the Nile."

A hush settles over the great avenue. Only the thumping of horses' hooves can be heard—the palace guard in procession, mounted on white stallions. Ahead of the royal carriage a pair of *sais,* in gold embroidered costumes, runs barefoot waving long sticks and shouting to clear the way. The women inside their carriages and the men standing on the street bow in deep reverence. Nonetheless, no one fails to peek at the sovereign as he is conveyed to the palace. He rides by alone in his open carriage, his bearded face sadly staring straight ahead.

After he has gone Sitt Habiba continues, "After God, it is the Khedive whom the whole world venerates. Did you notice the silence when he passed? If you had dropped a pin, you would have heard it ring!"

"Look, grandmother, the European women did not cover their faces," cries Zanouba suddenly.

"Did you wish for a boy?" asks Om Hassan, dismissing her daughter's comment. Zanouba has been far too caught up in the spectacle to even think of a wish.

19 · AT THE PYRAMIDS

Zanouba is awakened at dawn by Sitt Habiba after having spent the night at her grandmother's house. Om Hassan and Ibrahim are up and dressed. The only sound they hear at this early hour is the patter of tiny hooves and the cry of a goatherd, hawking his fresh milk: "Laban, laban, laban."

Zanouba says, "I hope I won't have to roll on the ground inside the pyramid too, Sitti."

Sitt Habiba laughs. "Allah be praised, child! You're barely more than a girl. I'm the one who should be worried! I've worn out one whole pair of shoes following you from one end of Cairo to the other. In all the years that I was married, I only wore out two! If you don't have a son after all that, Zanouba, then you're surely under a terrible spell!"

Zanouba yawns. She and her grandmother help themselves to hot buttered rolls and tea brought in by Om Hassan. Ibrahim is waiting outside to hail a carriage. Zanouba has just enough time to splash her face and put on her veil. The happy sound of brass charms clinking like bells on a horse's bridle tells her it is time to go.

"What a beautiful morning!" she sings out, her veil fluttering in the cool breeze.

The streets are still deserted. As the family approaches the Kasr el Nil bridge the sun has just cleared the top of the Mokattam hills. On the opposite shore of the Nile, flowers are in bloom. Camels are being herded to slaughter. The flatbeds of donkey carts are creaking with the weight of squatting women as they head for market.

Soon they inhale the heady perfume of the grey green laurel hedges, dripping with pink blossom, surrounding the Khedivial palace in Giza. Just beyond is the countryside. Farmers are already working, their animals tethered on the edge of the emerald green fields of alfalfa.

Ibrahim feels self-important as the man of the family and points out sights along the way. He explains that the road was built in 1869 by the Khedive Ismail so that Empress Eugenie of France could visit the pyramids, when she attended the opening of the Suez canal.

Zanouba breathes deeply. The air is so light and fresh, the sky so blue that she is glad to be alive. The great pyramids of Giza, which she has often seen from Cairo rooftops, come into view, framed by the ancient sycamores lining the roadway.

"How small the third pyramid looks up close," she thinks, as the carriage comes to a halt.

Instantly, a group of bedouin in flowing white robes appears offering to guide them.

"We don't need anyone," says Sitt Habiba.

"But we are the *ghafeers*—watchmen," says one of them.

"Then tell us where the door to the pyramid is," she demands.

"Up there," answers the oldest one pointing to a tiny opening among the stones, a quarter of the way up one of the pyramids.

"I don't see anything. Why didn't they put the door at the bottom? We'll never be able to climb up there!" exclaims Sitt Habiba.

"With all due respect to you venerable mother, maybe you can't, but it's really not that far up."

"Will my granddaughter be able to get up there?" Sitt Habiba inquires.

"Women usually don't like to do that," says one of the *ghafeers*.

"She has to go in! That's why we're here!" declares Om Hassan.

"Why is that, mother?" asks one of the men.

"So she can have a son," replies Om Hassan.

"She really must see the Pharoah's tomb!" insists Sitt Habiba.

"With God's help, we'll get her up there," the *ghafeers* say reassuringly.

Ibrahim has already climbed the first stone block. He extends a hand to his sister. Zanouba gathers up her cumbersome *habara* and follows him.

"Be careful," shouts Sitt Habiba.

"Ibrahim, watch out for your sister," adds Om Hassan, who has decided it is sufficient to say a prayer. She watches anxiously as Zanouba goes up, hindered by her long dress. Encouraged and helped by the *ghafeer* and Ibrahim, she finally reaches the platform in front of the opening to the tomb. Looking down, she notices how small her mother and grandmother seem waving to her down below. She waves back. Despite her fear, she is very pleased with herself for having climbed all this way.

She thinks, "It won't be long now, just a few spins around the tomb and this ordeal will be over."

Looking with dread at the forbidding opening through which she must pass, she turns to seek comfort in her brother. Ibrahim is playing the fearless one, joking with the men. The *ghafeers* light candles and they begin their descent into the black hole. One of the bedouin behind Zanouba encourages her. She declares, "There is no God but Allah," stoops and follows the others. Darkness engulfs her. She hesitates, then focuses on the dancing light flickering ahead in the *ghafeer*'s hand. Her throat tightens with fear. She is thinking that it is getting hard to breathe in this stuffy passage when the men ahead of her stop.

"Praise be to Allah," she whispers, thinking they have reached their destination. But this is not so. Now they must climb up. One of the guides uncoils a rope and attaches the end around Zanouba's waist. Ibrahim brags that he needs no help.

Zanouba's legs begin to tremble. Ibrahim takes her hand to steady her as they inch their way up the low, narrow passage. The flickering light of the candle and her brother's chattering give her heart, however. The bedouin reassures her that she has nothing to fear with the rope around her. But how long and tiring this expedition is! The ground is uneven. Holes are just barely visible by the candle light. Zanouba is terrified of falling or cracking her head on the low ceilings. Stooped, she has walked what seems like a long time. All at once, judging by the echoing of Ibrahim's voice, she senses a vast space around them and imagines bats and vampires. She fears stepping on a snake and cries out when she feels a warm breath on her cheek.

When will this end? Zanouba can no longer tell if she is more tired or more afraid. Why didn't anyone tell her she had to walk endlessly in dark and sinister passages? Why did she let herself be persuaded to enter this cavernous world of the dead? What would Abd el Meguid think if he were to see her now? Would he be angry or sympathetic? Would he acknowledge that she was enduring this ordeal to give him a son?

"Courage," she whispers to herself, "this can't be worse than Narguiss lying between the train tracks!"

At last, they can stand up straight. The guide announces: "The Pharoah's chamber!" Ibrahim yells to see if his voice will echo.

It is impossible to make out the details of the chamber, although it seems big to Zanouba. "Maybe I can rest here a while," she thinks. Sitting down, she peers into the darkness and sees what she thinks is a bathtub. "*Hammam!*" she exclaims. Ibrahim is indignant. "How could you mistake the Pharoah's resting place for a bathtub!" he chides her. She inches over to the massive granite sarcophagus, afraid to look in. "Is the pharoah's body there?" she wonders. But the tomb is empty. Finally, mustering courage she circles it seven times, quickening her pace on the seventh round, eager to get out.

The descent from the tomb is even more difficult than the ascent. Zanouba trembles with fear. She trips. Ibrahim catches her and the *ghafeer* assures her that they are nearly to the opening.

"I can't wait to see the daylight. What if I had fallen in one of those caverns?" she worries. She is tired and thirsty. A rising odor nauseates her. She feels as if she has been walking for hours. The passageway they have taken seems unfamiliar. She is suddenly panic-stricken. Where are they taking her? She yells: "I don't want to go any further! I want to get out of here now!"

The *ghafeer* says, "Don't you want to see the tomb of the queen, my lady?"

"I want to get out!" Zanouba insists.

"We're almost there," he tries to encourage.

"I have to get out or I'll drop dead!" cries Zanouba.

They turn back, inching along the cramped passageway once more, stooping, knees bent, walking backward. Zanouba nearly faints. Standing behind her, one of the *ghafeers* bolsters her. Another holds onto the rope. Ibrahim, raising a candle above their heads, is silent. They go down, turn, and lo and behold, the daylight!

Zanouba is helped to the doorway. She drops down on the stones, unable to go further. Her head is heavy and her face is drenched in sweat. Her eyes glaze over and she barely understands what her brother is saying to her. His voice seems muffled and distant. At least she can breathe. She sighs with relief and stands. She gazes far below and sees fields of ripe, golden wheat, and brilliant alfalfa rippling in the breeze. Orchards are beyond and further still, Cairo. With a cry of delight, Zanouba points to the Mokattam hills and the Citadel.

Ibrahim shouts to the women below. Om Hassan and Sitt Habiba, anxiously awaiting them, wave. Zanouba's head is still heavy and her throat dry. All she wants is to feel her feet on firm soil. Finally she is steady enough to climb down. Helped by two of the guides, she reaches the bottom and collapses at her mother's feet, crying, "Water, mother, water! Dear God, I've had such a fright!"

Om Hassan is alarmed and remorseful. Ibrahim reassures her. Sitt Habiba, however, is resolute: "Don't drink now child! Hold onto your thirst and your fright as long as you can! God willing, you will have a boy!"

"Oh! That's too much!" explodes Zanouba, nearly in tears. "How will being driven mad with fear, having my feet worn out and my body wrecked from rolling and stooping get me a boy? Thank God this nightmare is over! Tomorrow I'm going back to Matariyya!"

"Be patient, my girl," says her grandmother, stroking her head. "Since we are here, let's not overlook going around the pyramid and the sphinx."

"Let me rest a little and for pity's sake give me something to drink. I feel sick. If only I could have a cup of coffee!" cries Zanouba.

The sun is directly overhead and there is no shade anywhere. A faint humming rises toward them, the call to prayer. An old man, Sheikh el Batran, overhears Zanouba's plea and says, "Allah be praised! You must come to my home for coffee!" Gratefully, the family follows him to a group of tattered tents pitched behind the great pyramid. Sheikh el Batran ushers them into the biggest, cleanest one. His women welcome them warmly and invite them to sit on a rug spread on the sandy ground. The visitors seem as much at ease sitting cross-legged there as they are on the silk covered divans of their harems. Ibrahim follows his host into another tent where several men are gathered.

As Zanouba recovers, Sheikh el Batran's wife prepares coffee and asks why they have come to the pyramids, whereupon Sitt Habiba eagerly recounts their tale of woe. "Our family's troubles are so great they cannot be described, mother!" she cries.

The bedouin grandmother presses her. "In the name of the Prophet and of his grandson who reigns in the hearts of men and sheds his light upon them, protecting them with his sword, what is wrong? Speak, I beseech you. It will relieve your anguish. Don't you know the saying 'If it were not for my neighbor's ear, my heart would burst,' sister? Tell me what ails you."

"Our misfortune is great, mother," says Sitt Habiba. And, sighing, she explains, "Here is my grandaughter, in the flower of her youth and beauty. She is married to a rich man, a kind man. She has everything but what counts most, children."

"And does her husband have any children, sister?" asks the woman with genuine concern.

"He does, but all girls. He longs to have a son. Do you think that our visit today will do any good?" asks Sitt Habiba.

"If God wills it," replies the old woman. She motions to a younger member of her family who gets up to offer them corn bread and goat's cheese. She presses them to eat.

All three thank her and, as custom dictates, politely refuse, saying that they have eaten. But the bedouin presses them twice more. Finally, they accept, relishing the fare and even more the coffee.

When they get up, their hostess says, "Come back to see me before you leave, I'll have something for you."

"What could she possibly have for us?" asks Om Hassan, looking at her mother.

Zanouba wonders too.

Their host returns to fetch them, bringing Ibrahim with him. They mount little donkeys, saddled and ready to take them around the pyramids and the sphinx. By the time they reach the great head sticking out of the buff colored sand, the sun is beginning to set.

"Here is Abul Hole!" exclaims Om Hassan who instantly recognizes the giant statue, although she has never seen it before. Zanouba remarks that she understands now when people say that something is as big as Abul Hole. Sitt Habiba asks Ibrahim if he knows the story of the sphinx. Not giving him time to respond, she tells it:

"Once upon a time there was a queen in Cairo. She was in love with a handsome officer. But he didn't love her. One day, tired of her persistence, the young man ran away. She followed him in hot pursuit, together with her army. But he succeeded in crossing the Nile into the desert. Realizing she had lost him, she cursed him and turned him to stone for all eternity."

"How did she have the power to do that, Sitti?" asks Zanouba.

"Well, this queen had been nursed by a Djinn and had her protection, so her wish was instantly granted by her spirit mother."

"If you dug in the sand, I'm sure you'd find his body!" concludes Sitt Habiba with a flourish.

"Abul Hole's not handsome now, with that broken nose . . ." observes Zanouba, laughing.

Ibrahim replies, "Bonaparte broke it with his cannons. The story Sitti just told is just a tale. The sphinx was built by the ancient Egyptians, just like the pyramids. It's true he has an animal body. I read it in a book."

Sitt Habiba, pursing her lips, says, "What do you mean, the pyramids were built by the ancient Egyptians! They're much older than mankind, my boy, and were put here by spirits who lived on earth even before God created Adam and Eve! You shouldn't believe so much of what you read in books, Ibrahim. Scholars today think that everything can be explained by science. They're nothing but jackasses, my son; true knowledge resides in God alone."

Glancing over at her granddaughter, Sitt Habiba frowns. Zanouba, listens, sleepy-eyed, sitting on her donkey.

"Don't just sit there yawning!" her grandmother scolds. "Go around Abul Hole seven times so that no one can accuse us of not having tried everything to combat your *musharrara*!"

Zanouba obeys. When she is done, they return to the foot of the great pyramid and the tent village. The bedouin grandmother motions them in and offers them more coffee which they finally accept.

Closing her eyes for a moment, Sheikh el Batran's wife says: "I have thought about your problem and I beseech you, in the name of God the Merciful, and in the name of his Prophet, Muhammad, to heed my advice."

She hands them a few beads, a scarab, and a piece of blackened linen. "This scrap of linen is from a bandage which was wrapped around a mummy. The scarab and the three blue beads are older than the Prophet himself, may prayer and peace be upon Him. They were found in the tomb of an Egyptian queen," she explains.

"Thank you, mother, these are precious talismans, but what is my daughter to do with them?" asks Om Hassan, perplexed.

Addressing Zanouba, the old woman begins: "First, my daughter, soak the scarab in water, and sprinkle this water on the four corners of your bedroom—don't forget your bed and your husband's bed. Use what remains to wash yourself just before the second prayer on Friday. When you get down on your knees have these objects beside you. When you have kneeled three times and risen, cross over them seven times."

The old woman pauses, pressing more coffee on her guests, then continues: "When you are done, hang the beads and tie the linen to one of your necklaces and never take them off until you know you are pregnant. May these talismans soon make you the mother of a son, my child," says the wise woman.

"If this comes to pass, auntie, I will be in your debt.

You can ask for anything and you will have it," says Zanouba, trying to slip a few silver coins into her hand. The
old woman pushes them away. Gently, she says, "If you
wish to make an offering, you can make it to my husband."

"And who is your husband?" asks Om Hassan.

"Sheikh el Batran, keeper of the pyramids, the one who
brought you here," she answers.

Sheikh el Batran waits outside the tent to escort them to
their carriage. Zanouba is impressed with his noble demeanor. He stands tall and dignified in his flowing white
robes, his face weathered beneath a full grey beard. The
sheikh's headdress is also brilliantly white, secured low over
his forehead with a thick twist of gold thread, the traditional
okal. Zanouba discreetly offers him her gift, asking for his
blessing.

"May Allah lavish his blessings upon you, my child.
May He in all His benevolence bestow peace and good
health upon you and yours," he murmurs, raising his hands
to heaven.

"If I am blessed, uncle, I promise you a camel and my
son shall be your disciple."

"Our destiny is in the hands of God, my daughter, and
His wisdom is impenetrable," replies the old man.

This phrase echoes in Zanouba's mind as she climbs into
the carriage. She gazes thoughtfully at the blackened scrap
of linen, the tiny glazed scarab, and the blue beads which
were once a queen's. She is not sure she believes in the
power of charms but . . . Tomorrow is Friday, she will pray
and do as she has been told. One never knows . . .

Zanouba can hardly wait to be back in her own harem
in Matariyya. The thought of seeing Abd el Meguid on her
first night home fills her with happiness. Her six days away
have seemed like an eternity.

Part Five ▪ ***The Child***

20 · ZANOUBA IS PREGNANT

O m Mahmood's voice is triumphant as she throws open the shutters of the *mashrabiyya* windows. She calls to Narguiss, "Zanouba's pregnant!"

In a few minutes the entire household knows.

"Thanks be to God—*Il Hamdulilah!*" everyone exclaims. Zanouba's apartment fills with well wishers. Her eyes twinkle with happy tears. She smiles at her visitors, confirming the good news.

"Thank God, thank God!" shouts Om Mahmood and everyone echoes her.

"Oh, dear heart, Abd el Meguid will be so happy!" exclaims Narguiss, hugging Zanouba.

"He'll stop at nothing to please you now, my sister! You can ask him for anything!" adds Gaulisar.

"He'll travel to the ends of the earth to bring back the sweets you long for!" says someone.

"If you must have oranges out of season, and they are no bigger than olives, he'll plead with the sun to smile down on his orchards!" adds yet another.

"If it's the milk of a bird you want, dear soul, he'll pray for a miracle!" continues one of the servants.

"That's true," confirms Om Mahmood. "Abd el Meguid will stop at nothing to please you, my daughter," she beams.

Zanouba's face is radiant.

"Be sure to ask your husband for the impossible, my

child," continues Om Mahmood. "Make believe you're suddenly overcome with crazy longings. That's how you'll let him know. Ask for something that cannot be found or bought at any price."

"Ask him for a baby donkey!"

"A blue one!"

"Ask him for a green lamb!"

"Ask him for a camel no bigger than a cat!"

"Ask him for a deer with six legs!"

"Tell him that you want every animal born in his stables during the months of your pregnancy . . ."

"None of the female babies, though, they'll bring you bad luck!"

"Only the little males."

Zanouba laughs at the banter, her heart brimming with happiness. For several days now, she has felt a great hope growing within her. Fearing disappointment, she had not breathed a word to anyone. This morning, certain that she is pregnant, she divulges the news to Om Mahmood. She will at last be able to call herself a woman, she thinks. And this time she is determined to take every precaution to prevent another accident.

She thinks of Abd el Meguid's reaction. Tears of joy run down her cheeks. Can the child she is carrying this time be another son? "God willing," whispers Zanouba.

Earlier that morning, knowing Abd el Meguid was away three days visiting one of his farms, she thought, "If only he could be the first to know!" Her eyes filled with tears. Om Mahmood had found her weeping. At once she was alarmed until Zanouba confessed she was pregnant and was crying because her husband would not be the first to hear the good news. Instantly, Om Mahmood let out a strident joy cry and shouted to Narguiss and Gaulisar. She also informed Zanouba that Abd el Meguid was expected before nightfall.

"Now, now, my daughter, wipe your face and dry your

eyes. You don't want your husband to come home and find you crying, do you?" Om Mahmood said, handing her a perfume soaked handkerchief.

Zanouba immediately knew that she was being tested. It was said that pregnant women lose their sense of smell. There was no way she could not smell that perfume, it was so strong! However, she knew better than to admit it! She was learning! Having dabbed her nose delicately and wiped her eyes, she returned the handkerchief to her mother-in-law without a word. She found it hard to suppress her laughter.

Om Mahmood knit her brows and stared at Zanouba. "Don't you smell anything, my child?"

"I smell nothing at all, mother," Zanouba said.

"The perfume on my hanky, child," Om Mahmood insisted, "didn't you smell it?"

"What perfume, mother?" Zanouba replied, feigning surprise.

Om Mahmood promptly left the room. She went to Gaulisar and Narguiss with the hankerchief. "Smell this. I just gave it to Zanouba and she doesn't smell anything!" she exclaimed.

"Allah be praised!" repeated Narguiss and Gaulisar, rushing to tell everyone.

The good news has put the entire harem in a state of joyous upheaval. Will Abd el Meguid's house finally be graced with a son? A son!

Zanouba, pregnant, suddenly gains extraordinary importance. She is no longer just a woman, but a living sanctuary. Everyone in the household, wives, servants, relatives, feels that they have a stake in the little being growing inside Zanouba's body. They all believe they have some responsibility for the unborn guest. Each watches vigilantly over the mother-to-be, vowing to make sure that, this time, Zanouba's child will see the light of day.

Everyone offers help and advice:

"Don't go into the kitchen from now on . . ."

"We won't let you lift a finger to do anything . . ."

"Don't ever walk down any stairs by yourself!"

"Yes, anything could happen, it's too dangerous!"

"Take someone with you to walk in the gardens."

"But don't walk too much and tire yourself . . ."

"I will sleep in your harem from now on, so that you'll never be alone," announces Om Mahmood.

"I'll prepare your food with my own hands. Just let me know in the morning what you'd like to eat every day," says Narguiss.

"Would you like me to make honey pastries for you today?" asks Gaulisar, "I know you're fond of them."

"How about pigeons stuffed with rice for lunch?" asks Narguiss.

The milk maid chimes in, "I'll put aside the yellow cow's milk. It's pure cream!"

"Don't forget to perform your prayers five times a day so that God will bless you and the child you're carrying. I'll come pray with you," says Om Mahmood.

Pausing for a moment, she adds, "But be careful when you kneel. A careless movement can cause an accident, my child . . ."

Zanouba takes naturally to all of this attention, delighted to find herself the cherished queen of the harem. She savors the admiration of her fellows, particularly the glowing eyes of the little girls squatting at her feet.

In the afternoon, Om Hassan arrives. Tears of joy run down her face as she kisses her daughter.

"Didn't I tell you that it was the *musharrara,* and that we could stop it!" exclaims Om Hassan.

"I will promptly make an offering to the Bekhtashis, and to the Sheikh of the Pyramids!" she adds enthusiastically.

"What Behktashis? What Sheikh of the Pyramids?" asks Om Mahmood suspiciously.

"Oh, just some holy men who have prayed for Zanouba," Om Hassan replies, catching herself.

Zanouba says nothing, too happy to want to remember her terror in the bowels of the great pyramid. She caresses the blue beads attached to her necklace, resolving to keep them there even after her child is born.

Om Hassan has brought with her a healer from Darb el Gamameez, a wizened old woman by the name of Sheikha Souida. She unties a scarf knotted at the corners, pulls out a small copy of the Holy Qur'an, a jar of bees' honey, a skein of silk thread, and a little gold lock. Everyone watches curiously.

"With your permission, Om Mahmood," begins Om Hassan, "Sheikha Souida will pray over Zanouba to prevent another miscarriage."

Om Mahmood knits her brows. What is all this claptrap? There has to be more to this than simple prayer. Finally, she agrees, saying to herself, "There can't be any harm to this. She can't possibly do anything that would really go against the teachings of Islam in my presence . . ."

At once Sheikha Souida measures Zanouba's height and waist with the skein of silk. She cuts the thread to size, dips it in the honey, and instructs her to swallow it.

Zanouba hesitates, stupefied.

"Swallow it, my child," encourages Om Hassan, "the honey comes from a young hive and the thread will hold the baby in place. Swallow, my child, swallow!"

Zanouba obeys. "After all," she thinks, "the honey is sweet and fragrant, and the thread will go down easily." She takes several more spoons of honey, licking her lips, and then stretches out on the divan, face down. Sheikha Souida asks one of the little girls present to help her, handing her the little gold lock. "Hold it open and put it on her back, then snap it shut, my child," she instructs. She explains that this procedure will insure that the child can remain in its mother's belly the full nine months. The little girl, wide-eyed, obeys.

Finally, Sheikha Souida tells Zanouba to turn over on her back. She places an open Qur'an on the young woman's belly, and repeats the *Surat Youssif* four times. They hope that this evocation of Joseph, the son born to an aging Jacob, will induce Zanouba to have a baby boy.

The reading from the Holy Qur'an reassures Om Mahmood. Seeing her mother-in-law's face relax, Zanouba smiles.

"There's really nothing wrong with any of these rituals," thinks Zanouba. "After all, doesn't the proverb say 'Precaution is a sacred duty'?"

When coffee is served, Sheikha Souida reads the dregs in Zanouba's cup. Do the grounds convey whether the baby is a boy or a girl? After the dregs have dried, the sheikha lifts the cup gingerly. Holding it between her thumb, index, and middle fingers of her right hand, she turns it slowly, mysteriously peering inside. Finally, she whispers, "I see a form . . . a baby . . ." She confesses, however, that she cannot quite make out a boy or girl.

Noticing the apprehension on the faces of the women, she hesitates, then finally says,

"It might be a boy . . . Yes, it's probably a boy."

"God be praised! *Il Hamdulilah*! A boy at last!" everyone choruses.

Although everyone is relieved, none of the women would dream of accepting Sheikha Souida's prediction as gospel. Each one has a special sheikh, or sheikha, an astrologer, a numerologist, a reader of cards or of seashells, a soothsayer, whom they promise to themselves to consult immediately. Every one of them will also boast that she knew the gender of the baby all along.

"What name will you give your son, Zanouba?" asks a visitor.

Zanouba is caught off guard and blurts out the first name which comes to her mind: Abd el Meguid.

Everyone laughs with good humor.

"Look at this woman! She's putty in her husband's hand! Look at what love does! She can't think of a single man's name that is not his!"

"Come on, Zanouba, try again," teases one of the visitors.

"Why not call him Muhammad? Is there a more beautiful name than that of the Prophet?" suggests Om Mahmood.

"That definitely would be the best name to give a first-born son," confirms Narguiss.

"You're right, my sister, yet half the men in the world are called Muhammad," says Gaulisar.

"Why not call him Sayyed—'Lord,' a name that would insure his place in the world and his happiness?"

"Why not Saleh—'Virtuous'?"

"How about Karim—'Generous'?"

"Wouldn't it be wise to find a name which would insure him divine protection by declaring him the servant or slave of God?"

"In that case, how about Abd el Latif or Abd el Hamid?"

"I would pick Abd el Wahid, myself—'Servant of the Unique.' That's my favorite of the ninty-nine names of God!" exclaims one of Om Mahmood's cousins.

"My choice would be Abd el Rehim—'Slave of the Merciful,' says another visitor."

"Let's wait and let Abd el Meguid decide. Don't you think he'd like to choose his own son's name?" Zanouba says, laughing.

"Whichever way you look at it, there's plenty of time," says Om Mahmood, philosophically.

"I have a feeling that you will find the wait longer than you expect, my child," she adds, stroking Zanouba's head.

Night falls. Several women light candles. Narguiss whispers something into her daughter's ear. The word makes the rounds. Suddenly, with an air of mystery, all the girls leave the room. A few minutes later, the pitter-patter of their slippers is heard on the stairs as they rush back. They jostle one another and descend upon Zanouba, giggling. Several tug at her dress, others pull her up by the hands. They have all stuffed their dresses with rags and pillows, pretending to be pregnant. Each has tied a bright shawl around her hips and begins to dance and gyrate. Laughing, with Zanouba in their midst, they finally sit in a circle—some fifteen girls, daughters of servants and mistresses alike, big, small, fair, dark. Zanouba joins them as they gaily sing the song of the nine months, clapping their hands.

> Baby, my baby, how happy I am
> You're here, you're present.
> Baby, my baby, my own little child
> today marks your first month of life.
> Baby, baby, cherished one,
> Take care not to hurt the one carrying you.

Cheered, the women join in, clapping to mark time. Zanouba raises her arms as if dancing. She snaps her fingers, moves her body rhythmically, first right, then left. Joy cries mark the end of the first verse. Then the youngest girls join in, mimicking the older ones, learning the words of the song.

> Baby, my baby, in your second month of life
> I feel weary and wan.
> I'm too sleepy and weak to serve my dear
> master. What will he think?
> I live and breathe only for you now.
> In your third month of life
> you've become so demanding.
> You cause me longings
> I cannot satisfy,
> a taste for strange fruit,
> nowhere to be found.
> In your fourth month of life
> my belly is swelling.

I feel cherished, I'm
showered with gifts.
These gifts are for you.
I'm happy but heavy, my darling, my own.
Baby, my baby, in your fifth month of life
I am stronger.
I feel life stirring, your little
heart beating.
Baby, my baby here comes the sixth month.
Your movements grow brisk and proud.
Beware not to hurt me my own little one,
or I'll have to punish you.
In your seventh month of life
you grow restless, thumping and squirming.
Are you a gazelle or a fierce lion roaring?
Who are you, baby, my baby, my own?
Day and night you knock at the walls
of my heart . . .
You must be a lion!
In your eighth month of life
you move restlessly right and left.
Oh! naughty, naughty baby!
Will you not let me rest?
Mysterious baby, my darling, my own,
my heart races with anticipation.
A boy or a girl?
Will your birth bring tears of joy or tears
of sorrow?
Will I laugh when I see you?
Or will I cry bitter tears?
Oh, baby, my baby, make my wish come true!
Gladden the heart of the one carrying you.

During the last stanza the singing voices become graver.
Faces grow serious. Finally, Gaulisar belts out a long joy
cry, then a hush settles. Mothers think of their children,
those who are with them and those already gone. Little girls

dream of that mysterious state called motherhood evoked in their song. One day, they too will be mothers.

Zanouba is pensive. She sits in the circle of flickering lights, feeling life within her stirring. It is a miracle. The eternal cycle has vividly taken shape in her mind. She imagines her child, nursing at her breast, a boy, of course. She conjures up a radiantly happy Abd el Meguid, contemplating his son and his son's mother with infinite tenderness.

21 · PREPARATIONS

One morning, Om Hassan says while helping her husband on with his caftan and adjusting his cummerbund: "Have you given any thought to the preparations for the last month of Zanouba's pregnancy?"

Abd el Fattah frowns, knowing that he is about to spend money.

"Are you planning to make all the arrangements, Abd el Fattah?" she continues, "Will you get all the things we need for before the child's birth and for when Zanouba delivers?"

Abd el Fattah does not answer. The prospect of all the expenses puts him in a bad mood.

"Abd el Fattah?" insists Om Hassan.

Her husband finally grumbles, "All we need! All we need! What do I know about all we need!"

"Don't you remember what you bought when I had our children?" persists Om Hassan.

"It's been fifteen years! Do you think that my head keeps records? Why don't you go buy what's needed!"

"All right, I'll do it. Give me fifty guineas, then," replies Om Hassan.

"Only fifty guineas! Where do you think I'm going to get fifty guineas?"

"Abd el Fattah . . ." begins Om Hassan.

"Oh, Abd el Fattah, Abd el Fattah! Since you insist, Om Hassan, I'll do the shopping myself. At least I know the merchants and can get a better price. But, really, is all this necessary? After all, it's only for a girl's first lying-in that her mother is responsible! Why can't we call this her second?"

Throwing her hands up, Om Hassan cries, "Merciful God, preserve us! Lord have mercy on us! Do you want to dishonor your family with your avarice? Man! Did that tragic miscarriage cost you a penny? What a calamity to be the wife of such a miser!"

Abd el Fattah, realizing he is about to have a mutiny on his hands, finally exclaims, "Don't be upset, my heart! I'll do as you say!" He pauses and adds, "But what's the hurry, woman? What if Zanouba were to have another miscarriage? The money would be down the drain . . ."

Om Hassan's face flushes with indignation. He catches himself. "All right, all right, don't get angry! I'm saying this both in your interest and that of the children. How would you manage, Om Hassan, if I ran out of money?"

Seeing his wife's expression of outrage, however, he concedes. "Well, make me a list. But, try to be reasonable, woman! Abd el Meguid is richer than we are and we can't impress his family with our extravagant purchases," he says.

"It will take her at least one day to figure out what she wants, one day of respite for me," thinks Abd el Fattah and heaves a sigh of relief as he leaves the house.

Little does he know! He barely has time to open his shop when Ibrahim comes down the street, bringing the list which his mother has dictated to him. Abd el Fattah, busy with his clients, stuffs it in his pocket to look at while having lunch, after his noontime prayers. When the busboy from the neighboring restaurant brings him his meal, he sits down with the list. He reads and rereads it, shrugging his shoulders and knitting his brows. He is so absorbed in his calculations that he does not notice Youssef el Metwalli, his neighbor, come in. Youssef stands looking at him, smiling. Finally he says, "What can possibly be on that piece of paper, Abd el Fattah? You're talking to yourself, shaking your head and rolling your eyes. You have the look of a man who has just lost a court case!"

"Tell me if you don't think women are mad!" demands Abd el Fattah.

Youssef el Metwalli chuckles.

Abd el Fattah continues, "Here's what my wife is asking me to buy for my daughter's lying-in: one calf, three goats, two billy goats, a barrel of honey, two barrels of butter, ten *okka*s of *boughasha* paste to offer to the guests who come to visit after she has given birth, five *okka*s of Caraway seed to make teas. Also, for my daughter, three bolts of sheeting, two pieces of white calico, twenty cushions, four dresses, two veils and six head scarves. And, a large mortar and pestle. I'm going to pulverize Om Hassan's head in that mortar!"

"You're quite right, Abd el Fattah. Your wife's not thinking straight! She's forgotten to include almonds, hazelnuts, candles for the seventh day celebrations . . . There's no mention on that list of the ingredients to make spicy jam for the new mother, to bring on her milk . . . Nor do I see gifts for the midwife . . . And where's the baby's layette? That deserves a list to itself!"

Abd el Fattah ponders, stroking his beard. Youssef el Metwalli puts a hand on his neighbor's shoulder and says: "My friend, don't look so distressed. What has to be done on such occasions has to be done. A father must not mind the money he spends on his daughter at a time like this. I went through it myself only last year as you may remember. I'll tell you what to do."

"What?" asks Abd el Fattah.

"For starters, keep everything that you buy here in your shop until your daughter's time draws near. When the girl's mother-in-law comes to stay with you, load your purchases on two or three carts, and send them home. Make sure that the horses have showy bridles with lots of bells, and that the drivers shout your praises all along the way. When they have delivered everything in full sight of your mother-in-law, believe me, Abd el Fattah, you'll not regret the expense. The family will hold you in greater esteem. But if all of this is done quietly, then it would hardly be worth your trouble!"

While Abd el Fattah juggles his calculations, Om Hassan and her mother prepare Zanouba's room. Sitt Habiba comments that using this room is auspicious since all of the men of the family were born in it.

"Yes," adds Om Hassan, "and none died except of natural causes."

The room is now being used for storage—the family's seasonal clothing, clean rags, worn bedsheets, bolts of new cloth, odds and ends, and a sewing machine. Standing in the doorway, Om Hassan and Sitt Habiba agree that the room must be furnished with great care. She tells her daughter that a great-uncle, Sheikh Soliman, venerated by the entire family as a saint, left his furniture and belongings to a granddaughter.

"We must try to borrow them!" exclaims Om Hassan.

"They would be a blessing and protection for your daughter," agrees Sitt Habiba, turning to see Zanouba coming up behind her.

"What would be a blessing, Sitti?" she asks.

Sitt Habiba explains about Sheikh Soliman. "He was so pious, my child, that he guided his own coffin to the cemetery after his death. The men who carried the coffin said that it moved by itself. In fact, it's said to have paused before the doors of seven mosques along the way and avoided passing before any houses inhabited by sinners and nonbelievers!"

When approached, Sheikh Soliman's granddaughter agrees to lend the family the saintly man's furniture and personal effects. His bed, a table, four chairs, and a rug are loaded on a cart and delivered to Abd el Fattah's house. Sitt Habiba even manages to secure the dead man's turban which she displays conspicuously on a small shelf facing Zanouba's bed. She hopes it will help her granddaughter safely deliver a baby boy.

Having made a pilgrimage to the sainted shrines of El Rifai and Saidna el Hussein, Om Hassan acquires two velvet panels said to have covered the saints' tombs. Both embroidered with verses from the Holy Qur'an, one with gold thread and the other with silver, they were in the possession of a local cleric.

"The sheikh was not eager to part with them, mother," she says.

"Surely he wouldn't have taken them off the tombs and given them to you!" exclaims Sitt Habiba in dismay.

"No, no, new ones had been offered to the shrine and these old ones were just tossed in a cupboard," replies Om Hassan.

"How did you persuade him to part with them, my daughter?"

Om Hassan boasts that her clever negotiations as well as a reward finally persuaded the sheikh. She calls for help to hang the panels on either side of the only window in the room, like drapes. On the opposite wall, for luck, she places a color print of the Khedive's son, the little Prince Abd el Moneim, who came after a long wait, following the birth of three daughters. She adds a portrait of Sultan Abd el Hamid, a view of the Holy seat in Mecca—the Ka'ba—and some appropriate verses from the Qur'an, penned by a skilled calligrapher and framed.

When it comes to discussing the baby's layette, however, Sitt Habiba advises her to hold off.

"It's best to wait, my daughter. For his protection, he should first be swaddled in old clothing, something worn by someone virtuous so that he too will be virtuous."

"I've heard people speak of a certain Sheikh el Fellaheen as a virtuous man, mother," says Om Hassan.

"Yes, daughter. He's a very old man, no one knows how old, but they say that his teeth are green with age. His real name is Sheikh el Dardiri and he lives near Al Azhar. People have said that he stayed twelve months in his mother's belly, just like Sayyed Badawy of Tanta," answers Sitt Habiba.

"He performs miracles! Even the notables of the city send for him," says Om Hassan.

"When he walks beneath people's palm trees, their date crop is certain to be abundant," answers Sitt Habiba.

"I've heard the same said of wheat crops," adds Om Hassan.

"I've been told that women who only touch the hem of his caftan give birth to boys," whispers Sitt Habiba, conspiratorially.

This revelation impresses Om Hassan who hastens to arrange a visit to the saintly man. They find him living in poverty at the end of an alley near Bab el Ghurayyeb. He is old and blind, jealously guarded by family members as if he were their personal treasure.

Om Hassan, Sitt Habiba, and Zanouba greet the sheikh and his entourage. Om Hassan sings his praises saying that his ability to perform miracles is well known throughout the Muslim world. A chorus of voices affirms her compliments. However, an old woman, heavyset, blind in one eye, scrutinizes her. Firmly she says: "The sheikh despite his piousness and many virtues is poor and has a large family to support. He does not perform his miracles free."

Om Hassan has brought only a small gift of money, but as soon as she reveals that Zanouba is the wife of Abd el Meguid of Matariyya, the woman's tone changes. They are treated with deference and offered gifts: a shawl and prayer beads belonging to the holy man. He instructs them to place the beads around Zanouba's neck when she goes into labor and to wrap the newborn baby in the shawl so that they may enjoy divine protection through the sheikh's intercession.

Om Mahmood watches vigilantly over her daughter-in-law in the final weeks of her pregnancy. One day, declaring that Zanouba's time is near, they travel to Darb el Magharba. After they arrive, Zanouba climbs the stairs of the old house two at a time. Om Mahmood shouts, "Don't run like that, you foolhardy girl!"

Zanouba, reaching the top, laughs and bursts into the room where her grandmother and mother are seated. She kisses them, crying, "If only you knew what I just saw!" She tosses aside her veil and *habara*. Her face glows and her eyes sparkle.

"How plump and white and fresh you look! The Lord be praised!" exclaims Sitt Habiba.

Om Hassan's hands fly up to her cheeks in a gesture of alarm. What could her mother be thinking? Has she forgotten the evil eye? She has put Zanouba in jeopardy with her impetuous compliment which cannot fail to attract the wrath of the envious!

Quickly Om Hassan counters, hoping to prevent a calamity. Even before greeting Om Mahmood she cries, "Oh, my child, my heart, how sallow you look! How weak, how ugly you've grown! God preserve you!"

"Mother," cries Zanouba, paying her mother and grandmother no mind, "I went past Bab el Hadid and guess what I saw?"

"What did you see, my dove?" asks Sitt Habiba, smiling tenderly.

"I saw a cart without a horse running all by itself!"

"It's just the streetcar, Zanouba! You know that! It's been running up and down Mohammad Ali street for years now!" answers Om Hassan.

"No, no, it's not the streetcar, mother! I know what the streetcar looks like. This has no rails under the wheels and it has a roof and doors and it's no bigger than a carriage!"

"Was anyone in it, child?" asks Sitt Habiba, skeptical.

"Oh, yes! And he was holding a wheel between his hands, Sitti! You should have seen him!"

Seeing Om Hassan and Sitt Habiba glancing at one another with doubt written in their eyes, Om Mahmood confirms Zanouba's story.

"What a noise it made, my sisters!" she says, emphatically, further validating her daughter-in-law's report.

"It was noisier than a train!" exclaims Zanouba.

"Well, my child," says Sitt Habiba, "You've just seen something new. That's a good omen. There's no doubt now that you're going to have a boy!"

No sooner has Sitt Habiba drawn her hopeful conclusion than their conversation is interrupted by a great clamor below. They rush to the *mashrabiyya* windows.

In the courtyard, Abd el Fattah is issuing orders to six men. Two of the men are pulling goats, another a calf, a fourth is struggling with a pile of cushions, a fifth unloads bolts of cloth, carrying several at a time over one shoulder. The last man is stacking barrels, crocks, and huge tins against a wall, near the stairs. Their loud voices and the ruckus they are creating, while full of good cheer, would lead one to think there were a hundred of them, not six.

Zanouba, seeing this spectacle, claps her hands and laughs happily. Om Hassan puffs up with satisfied pride. Covertly looking for Om Mahmood's reaction to her husband's display of generosity, she orders two servant girls to run down and help.

Om Mahmood instantly understands the significance of the scene. As becomes a rich woman, she admires the gifts without being too effusive. When the provisions are brought in, she fingers the cloth, tastes the honey and the butter, and appreciates their quality. However, as she wants to get home before dark, she prepares to depart despite Om Hassan's insistence that she stay. She kisses her daughter-in-law more warmly than before, reminding her to be careful. Zanouba presses her not to go and Om Mahmood, smiling, promises to return in a few days.

As soon as they are alone, Om Hassan whispers to her daughter that there will be a *zar* that night.

"But, mother, I'm not possessed!" exclaims Zanouba, surprised.

"No, my child, that's not it! It's a celebration on the day of your arrival to honor the spirits and to protect you and your child!"

"Are you sure? You know Abd el Meguid doesn't even want to hear the word *zar!*" says Zanouba.

"Oh, it's a silent *zar*," says Om Hassan, cleverly, "I'm replacing the drums with cushions. Not even the mice will know!"

"What about my father?" asks Zanouba.

"He's going to his brother's in Benha and he won't be back until tomorrow," Om Hassan says, reassuringly.

After dinner Om Hassan and Sitt Habiba send the servants away and prepare the room for the ceremony. They spread white sheets on the ground, stack the cushions and light the charcoal heaped in mounds in two *mangals*. They fill a brass mortar with almonds and place red, green, black, and white candles in corners of the room. Om Hassan fetches a goat from the courtyard, decorates it with colored ribbons, and tethers it to the foot of Zanouba's bed.

"We have nothing to do but wait for the *codia*s who will conduct the *zar*," says Om Hassan, sighing with relief. Zanouba is already reclining on her bed. "Who are these women, mother? Where do they come from?"

"They fled the Sudan to escape the domination of Tayeh, the Mahdi. Haven't I ever told you about the village of Abd el Nabih, outside of Cairo? That's where they settled with their families. The men run coffee shops where

they serve food from their country, dance, and sell *booza*—
you know, wheat beer. People go there to watch them. All
the women of that village are *codias*."

At midnight four black women arrive on donkeys.
Without wasting time, they light the candles, throw incense
on the live coals, and kill the goat. They smear Zanouba's
clothes and sheeting to be used for her delivery, as well as
the baby's clothes. They butcher the goat and cut the meat
into one pound pieces which they divide equally among
four baskets which they place on their heads. To conclude
the ritual, they carry the meat out of the house.

Om Hassan, while preparing for their return, explains
to Zanouba that the *codias* will scatter the meat all over the
neighborhood, in front of houses and shops, and around
mosques.

"But why?" asks Zanouba, puzzled.

"They're for the dogs and cats. Spirits take on the form
of animals who come out at night. If you honor them with
a gift of food, they will thank you by giving you what you
ask for," Om Hassan tells her.

"But what if the animals don't eat the meat?" asks
Zanouba.

"Poor people like the water bearers and the milkmen
making their rounds at dawn will be happy to find it," answers Sitt Habiba.

"But will the *djinns* be angry, Sitti?" asks Zanouba.

"No, no, child, they're far more compassionate than hu-
mans, and they're always in sympathy with the less fortu-
nate," replies her grandmother.

"And what about the almonds?" asks Zanouba.

"They're for the spirit children, the birds. That's what
the mortar and pestle are for. We pound the almonds and
make them into little balls, and toss them over the garden
wall," says Sitt Habiba.

As Zanouba ponders the world of the *djinns*, the black
women return. They fan the fires to revive them, adding

incense. The live coals glow like bright fruit in each of the shallow braziers, set on sturdy cylinders which raise them up a foot or so. The incense nuggets crackle and melt, filling the room with a thin, translucent smoke, and the perfume of frankincense.

Slowly, as if moving in a netherworld of their own, the *codia*s sway from side to side then sit cross-legged in a circle. They begin to drum on the cushions used instead of tambourines. They tap with the palms of their hands, finger tips and elbows, occasionally hitting the cushions against their heads or knees. The silent drumming grows ever more frenetic, gathering momentum. The women, reaching a trancelike state, rise from their seats. Two cover their faces with sheer, white veils, hanging long and loose over white dresses. The other two are dressed in green, red, and black. They shake their hair, vigorously tossing their heads backward and forward and from side to side. Long strands whip the air around them as they spin and gyrate. Swinging their arms wildly, they sweep the floor with fingertips that seem to have no will of their own. Finally, they roll around on the floor before the three exhausted onlookers. All at once, panting from their frenzied ecstasy, they stop and sit. Eyes closed, immobile, they move their lips.

"The god of the spirits has spoken. He has accepted the offering. He is pleased with this home. He will name the awaited child."

Sitting on her bed, Zanouba growns deathly pale. She trembles, huddled together with her mother and grandmother, also speechless with terror. One of the *codia*s, worried about Zanouba, tries to comfort her.

"There's nothing to be afraid of, little sister. You should rejoice and thank God. The *djinn*s are favorably disposed towards you and have agreed to help you."

"So, we will know the name of the child? If it's a boy or a girl?"

"Patience. The king of the *djinn*s will choose a moment

to speak when no one other than ourselves is awake. Even then, we'll have to be vigilant to catch the name," says one of the *codia*s.

The room is silent. Zanouba watches the waning candles and shudders every time a flame flickers, wondering if a *djinn* is passing, here, right beside her. She imagines grimacing faces in every darkened corner, growing ever more tense with anticipation.

"Dear God, when will this be over?" she wonders, wincing at the sticky, dark smattering of blood around her.

Finally she closes her eyes, hearing her blood thumping, her head throbbing, her heart beating. In her belly, she feels the baby quiver. Boy or girl? Soon she will know. Only yesterday, had someone told her that a *djinn* would disclose her child's name, she would have thought they were teasing. But in the strange atmosphere of the room, dizzy with the heady perfume of the incense, spellbound by the silent dance and mute drumming, she is persuaded that an invisible presence will speak. Boy? Girl? How she wishes she already knew!

Zanouba fears that if the child is a girl her husband will no longer even look at her. She pictures herself banished, along with her dreaded child, her cursed daughter, to some far corner of the house.

"I will be like all the others. It will be worse . . . But, if it is a boy what rejoicing will take place!" Zanouba thinks. She can just see it! The baby will hardly have had time to open his eyes before being declared king of the household. And, she will be the honored mother, bearing the name of her son, mother of so and so . . .

"Om Mahmood, for example . . . How beautiful the sound of such a name!" she thinks.

"To be the mother of a son . . ." she muses. She will live through him, because of him. She will become visible. How glorious!

She tries to remember all the signs she has received.

"Can it be that they're all a bunch of old wives' tales," she wonders. Reconsidering, she whispers, "But one never knows . . ."

She has been told to monitor the baby's movements: girls butt their heads against their mother's bellies; boys kick with their feet. Boys move from right to left, while girls move from left to right. But how can she tell whether it is a little head or a little foot thumping? Zanouba has been mindful, but the child moves every which way.

Then there are dreams. She eats an apple every night in order to have good ones, and she reads a few verses from the Qur'an before closing her eyes. She has been told she would dream of a sheikh, and she does. The man is old with a grey, pointed beard and bright eyes. Every night he comes toward her, handing her a different object each time. The women tell her to remember the gender of the object he gives her, as a clue for the gender of the child.

"If it has a masculine name, then it's a good omen," says Narguiss when she comes to visit. Hence, on nights when the sheikh had given her a Qur'an, a ring, or a stick, she rejoices. It must be a boy! If, however, the gift is a box, a rose, or a set of prayer beads, her spirits sink. At first she wept bitterly, but then decided such signs should not be taken too seriously.

She says to herself, "How can you trust them when they're so inconsistent!"

The candles are almost gone. Dawn must be near. Om Hassan and the four *codia*s have not budged, listening in the dense silence. Sitt Habiba is snoring softly, asleep on her chair.

"How much longer?" wonders Zanouba, exhausted.

All at once the *codia*s motion them to listen. They strain to hear, faces pressed forward anxiously.

Gradually, Zanouba makes out a faint murmur. One syllable at a time, the *codia* reveals a name: "Fa Ri Da."

At the sound of a girl's name, Sitt Habiba starts, fully

awake. Om Hassan stares at the *codia* in disbelief. Zanouba sobs.

"A girl? What a calamity!" Om Hassan and Sitt Habiba cry in unison.

Upon hearing their companion, the other *codia*s give her an exasperated look.

"It's Farid, sister, Farid that the spirit whispered!" one corrects.

"Yes, Farid, Farid," concurrs another.

"It was Farid, sister, not Farida. I know I heard Farid," insists the fourth Codia.

"Well, yes, perhaps . . . Well, maybe . . . Yes, it might have been Farid," prevaricates the first Codia.

Everyone sighs with relief.

Farid—"the Unique"—a boy!

"This child will be born alive since his name has been spoken, but he will be unique, an only child," says one of the Codias.

"He will have neither brother nor sister," says another. After a pause, she adds, "He must sleep on the skin of the goat slaughtered tonight his first year and later if he is ever sick. Make a talisman of seven of the animal's hairs for him to wear around his neck. That will insure that he will always have the protection of the king of the spirit world."

"God is merciful and generous. May he grant your son a long and happy life," concludes one of the *codia*s, looking at Zanouba.

They all repeat in chorus, "In Sha' Allah, In Sha' Allah, God willing!"

"Farid," thinks Zanouba, still feeling apprehensive. "A son!" She wishes she could be certain. Why isn't she? Hasn't the king of the spirit world spoken? A sliver of doubt is driving a wedge between her and happiness. "The first *codia* did say Farida, didn't she?" ponders Zanouba. She wonders if the other women have lied. "They're said to be shrewd and cunning. Maybe they changed the name to please me.

Or for fear of losing their reward . . ." The uncertainty makes her uneasy. "How can they really know? Only God is all knowing . . ." She wonders, "Will my child bring joy or sorrow? It won't be long now. Why not believe that the *codia*s are right, that the precautions we have taken will bear fruit? Why doubt that our prayers will be answered? Why assume that God would disappoint Abd el Meguid's hopes and plunge our two families into mourning?"

Zanouba shakes herself to shed her ugly doubts. Gently, she strokes her belly and thinks, "Why not Farid?"

22 · BIRTH

In the *Salamlek,* Abd el Meguid is playing backgammon with a neighbor while two of his friends look on, puffing quietly on a water pipe and sipping steaming, sweet cinnamon tea. In the cold twilight a gentle rain taps against the windows. A servant lights a lamp in one corner of the room and places candles on two small tables near the players. A soft glow caresses their faces as they silently ponder the final moves of the game. A servant brings a freshly stoked water pipe, fans the coals in the *mangal* and, as they redden, throws a handful of incense on top. Smoke rises in fragrant curls, marrying the scents of honey-cured tobacco and musk.

Abd el Meguid throws the dice with a confident flick of his right hand. They land upon the board, clicking. This final move declares him the winner.

Smiling to his opponent, he says, "You're lucky you didn't bet your sheep on this game! You would have lost a beautiful herd!"

"God willing, I will be able to offer you half a dozen of these sheep to celebrate the birth of your son, Abd el Meguid," answers his friend, convivially.

One of the visitors adds, "And I'll send a dozen tins of the best butter fresh from my farm."

"I pledge a celebration," says a third visitor. "I'll invite Youssef el Mandalaawy, whom God has gifted with the most beautiful voice in the world, to sing in your son's honor."

Abd el Meguid, touched, says, "Thank you, dear friends for your kind sentiments. But, I beseech you to remember that the child might be a girl."

A servant ushers in a messenger from Abd el Fattah's household, who informs Abd el Meguid that his wife has just gone into labor. Abd el Meguid rises instantly, excuses himself, and rushes to Gaulisar's harem. He finds the women of his family huddled around the *mangal,* roasting chestnuts. He takes Om Mahmood aside and tells her the news. Soon every woman in the harem is quivering with anticipation.

Abd el Meguid and Om Mahmood soon are on a train to Cairo. In a darkened compartment they sit facing each other, thoughtful, listening to a winter rain splashing against the windows.

Om Mahmood speaks first, "It is a good omen that the birth is on a rainy night, my son. A child born under the sign of the rain will be rich." He replies: "And, everyone knows that without water the earth would be barren and man would be impoverished. However, the child will be rich only if God wills it," Abd el Meguid sighs. "I don't dare hope too much. Zanouba has already lost a child and the rest are girls. May God bless and protect them! He works in mysterious ways, mother! All we can do is commend ourselves unto him."

"That's true, my son, but you know full well that Zanouba's miscarriage was no accident. The child she lost was indeed a boy. This one could be too, God willing."

"May God's will be done, mother. But remember my first wife, Nafissa. Her pregnancy seemed normal, but

when she went into labor her belly was only full of water
. . . There was no child. My poor Nafissa died of grief!"

"My child, why think of that past sadness now?" exclaims Om Mahmood.

"I've waited so long, mother, and my heart has been
broken by each new disappointment. I've lost hope," replies
Abd el Meguid.

"Tonight we must hope, Abd el Meguid," says Om
Mahmood firmly.

"Do you remember Faika, mother?" asks Abd el Meguid.

"Faika was not evil, my son. Her motives were good
even though what she did was wrong. She knew how much
you wanted a son and she was willing to do anything to
make you think you had one. She wanted so much to make
you happy!"

"But this child did not have a single drop of my blood,
mother! Had we not discovered her ruse this stranger would
today be my heir! I don't suspect Zanouba. But Om Hassan is
cunning. She wouldn't hesitate to substitute a boy for a girl.
She could do it without Zanouba being any the wiser . . ."

"Don't fret so, my son. If the child is not born by the
time we get to Abd el Fattah's house, rest assured I will not
leave your wife's side for a minute," declares Om Mahmood. "Everything will be all right, my son. God willing,
you will have a son."

"May Almighty God answer your prayers, mother,"
says Abd el Meguid, calmed by his mother's reassurances.

Abd el Meguid and Om Mahmood finally reach the station at Kubri el Laimoon. It is still raining and they run for
shelter, sending a porter to fetch a carriage. Interspersed
with the rain drops on the overhang, they hear bits and
pieces of a song wafting from the direction of the river.

"What's this?" asks Om Mahmood, perplexed. "Can
there be a wedding in such weather, so near the train
station?"

Abd el Meguid says, "It's from the Casino Bosphore

across the street. That's the voice of Abd el Hay, a famous new singer. I'm told he performs there regularly."

"I've heard women sing for men in such cafés, my son. Can that be?"

"Yes, mother. In fact, they also feature a singer named Tawheeda at the Bosphore. Everyone raves about her."

"Can any shoeshine boy from the street go in?" asks Om Mahmood, bewildered.

"If they have the money to buy a ticket, there's nothing to stop them, of course. But mostly these places are for the rich."

"Have they no sense of shame?" asks Om Mahmood, indignantly. "Don't they have homes and families? Such women will bring the wrath of God down upon our kind, my son! Don't these rich men have Mandaras where singers can be hired to perform for them and their friends?"

"Oh, mother, many people no longer have houses at all today, but live in buildings that house many families," answers Abd el Meguid.

"You mean to say, these newfangled apartments where people live under one roof? Where the same door is the front door and the door to the living room and the kitchen? This is the beginning of the end, my son! We're doomed if Muslims start living like foreigners!" exclaims Om Mahmood.

Climbing into a hackney, Om Mahmood continues her complaints. Abd el Meguid agrees with her. However, he cannot restrain an amused if affectionate little smile at the extent of his mother's pique. She, on the other hand, has exaggerated her responses in an effort to distract him. Before he knows it they arrive at Abd el Fattah's house.

Abd el Fattah is pacing in the courtyard. They hear Zanouba's plaintive cries coming from the harem on the second floor. "We're just in time!" declares Om Mahmood.

Anxiety written on his face, Abd el Fattah informs them that the midwife is with Zanouba but that nothing has happened yet. He invites Om Mahmood to go up, and she rushes to her daughter-in-law's room as quickly as her old legs will carry her. Zanouba is sitting up in bed, her face distorted with pain, her eyes dilated. Beside her, the birthing chair stands ready, decorated with multicolored paper flowers. The midwife is a quiet, imposing old woman, waiting patiently for the moment when her services will be needed. She already has plenty to do just answering Om Hassan's incessant questions, the most frequent being: "Do you think it will be boy?"

"Patience is the key to deliverance, my sister. Only God is all knowing," repeats the wise woman.

To placate Om Hassan, however, she adds, "Certain signs indicate a boy. He sits high in his mother's belly. He kicks a lot. I've delivered a lot of boys these last few weeks . . ."

Upon hearing these words, Om Hassan sighs with relief.

"I've been sure all along that it would be a boy!" she declares triumphantly, and goes downstairs to tell the men that the midwife has assured her it will be a boy. When she returns, she sits down with her cheek resting in the palm of her hand, and closes her eyes. But, only a moment later, she knits her brows, stands up, and sighs, "Allah preserve us! I hope it's not a girl! I have a terrible feeling it is a girl! Do you think it's going to be a girl?" she asks again. The midwife, tired of answering, shrugs her shoulders. Om Hassan frets. She dashes in and out first bringing hard boiled eggs, then slivers of raw onion. She presses her daughter to eat. Eggs and onions, she tells her, are well-known to facilitate labor. Zanouba is too weary to argue and just shakes her head. She is relieved when the midwife intervenes, insisting that she needs nothing. Her contractions are normal, coming at regular intervals. She is doing well.

Om Mahmood approaches and takes Zanouba's hand in hers. She whispers, "Push, push, my child! Push and you'll soon be delivered."

Zanouba does as she is told, but, exhausted at the end of each contraction, she begins to doze. Om Mahmood taps her on the hand and pinches her, "Wake up my daughter! Don't interrupt your efforts or we'll have to pull the child out with forceps. Push, my child, push!"

Through her pain, like a duet, Zanouba hears her mother-in-law's tireless prompting and her mother's refrain, "Keep saying to yourself 'I want a boy, I want a boy.' Keep saying it!" Zanouba, however, wailing loudly, has reached a point where all she wants is to be rescued from the gut-wrenching pain of childbirth. As the dawn call to prayer sounds from the nearby mosque, the midwife declares that the end is near. She helps Zanouba into the birthing chair and tucks cushions on either side to support her. Moments later, Zanouba emits a heartrending cry and pushes her first child into the world. The midwife catches the baby, quickly swaddles it in a shawl, and cuts the cord. Om Hassan and Om Mahmood jostle one another to get to it, but neither dares uncover it nor even question the midwife busily attending the young mother. They look anxiously at the little wrinkled face, eyes still tightly closed. The baby whimpers and wails.

Is it Farid or Farida?

Finally, the midwife turns to the two grandmothers. Her face is sad. She whispers the names of Khadiga and Aisha, the Prophet's two wives. The message is clear.

Om Hassan sobs. Om Mahmood leaves the room without a word.

Downstairs the *mandara* is bathed in a thin, grey early morning light. Abd el Meguid is saying his prayers. His hopes, so close to being realized, have become a source of intense agony. Although he believes himself to be ready to accept the inevitable, he cannot appease the fear of another daughter being added to the many he already has. He stands, palms facing up in a gesture of offering to his divine master. From the corner of his eye he glimpses his mother. She hesitates, her tall, slender figure framed in the shallow recess of the archway leading to the harem stairs.

He knows.

Without turning his head, he continues his adoration, his movements flowing. He gets down on his knees once, twice, three times, having knelt twice already, to complete the five *rakaa*s. He fixes his gaze on a spot on the wall ahead of him, steadying himself, and touches his forehead to the ground, lingering. Feelings of pain wash over him in waves. Thrice he gets up and thrice he prostrates himself, his lips moving, repeating the holy words, trying to overcome his despair.

When he feels strong enough to face her, he turns to his mother, waiting beside Abd el Fattah. She aches to see her son so gaunt. His cheekbones protrude and his complexion has grown sallow as a result of worry and frustrated hopes.

"It's a girl, my son."

"May God's will be done, mother. His designs are impenetrable." Turning to Abd el Fattah, Abd el Meguid says, barely audibly, "Come, Abd el Fattah, let's go up and see the child."

The house is strangely quiet: No voices, no laughter, no joy cries.

When Zanouba sees her husband, she sobs. Abd el Meguid gently takes her hand. His words are affectionate, consoling, but his voice is strained, betraying anger, sadness, and disappointment. Zanouba, ashamed, hides her face in her hands and weeps. On the bed beside her, the baby lets out inarticulate cries. The first sips of air this little being takes, her first efforts at life, are fraught with pain.

Abd el Meguid leans over and gazes at his daughter. In a delicate gesture he gently lifts the gauzy handkerchief covering her little head. For a long moment he contemplates the tiny red face, the wrinkled brow divided by a strand of hair on which a black ball of wax has been suspended to ward off the evil eye—the *fassoukh*. Under his fatherly gaze the baby calms down. A tear, which only Zanouba notices, makes its way down Abd el Meguid's wrinkled cheek and is lost in the greying strands of his beard. His expression softens and a smile plays upon his lips. Zanouba is sure that the angel who comes to console the fathers of daughters has just touched Abd el Meguid. She whispers, "May God be praised! The angel has descended!" Abd el Meguid smiles again and says, "Thank God you are safely delivered, my child." Then, with another delicate gesture he replaces the handkerchief on the child's head.

"Since this is, no doubt, the last child I will ever have, we must celebrate her arrival!" The *seboo,* the festivities for his daughter's seventh day of life, will be magnificent, announces Abd el Meguid. And, turning to Abd el Fattah, he says: "Give me a list of your relatives and friends so I can ask them to join us. In three days I will send a dish of *kishk* to each household and invite them to attend. Om Mahmood will kill our fattest chickens to make the stock. She has mixed the flour and milk for the starter and formed it into balls. In anticipation, these have already been fermenting in the sun for forty days."

"Allah be praised," responds Abd el Fattah, "Your middle name is Generosity, Abd el Meguid!"

Looking resolutely at Zanouba, Abd el Meguid declares: "I want to let everyone know that this child is welcome among us!"

All present listen in silence. All know his pain. Lost is the hope he has nurtured for a son who would piously perform the last rites for him, lay him in his grave, and proudly take his place as patriarch. They respect Abd el Meguid for the dignity and grace with which he comports himself.

Abd el Meguid ponders his destiny: God has decreed that no barber would ever darken his door to circumcise a son born to him. "A little girl's head scarf will be added to all the others, and that will be that," he thinks.

Zanouba has buried her face in her hands, hiding her grief. She has been instructed not to weep—a new mother risks going blind if her tears flow before the fortieth day of her child's life, when she can return to her husband's home.

Several of the women standing beside her bed intone a song lamenting the advent of daughters—their mothers are to be pitied whereas the mothers of sons are praised. Zanouba pictures herself returning to Matariyya with her daughter in her arms, shamefaced and joyless. She restrains a sob, but the words of the dispiriting song haunt her:

> Tell me sister: What was the fruit of the union
> between the queen of roses and the king of lions?
> A daughter, alas! A daughter!
> Had the rose given birth to a son
> she would have been honored and fed daily the
> succulent flesh of pigeons.
> But, she, poor one, whose offering was a mere girl,
> even hard-boiled eggs were more than she deserved.
> Happy is the mother of a son for in her heart
> childbirth's pain is anon replaced with joy.
> But for her, poor one, for her who gives birth to a
> daughter, shame is her reward.

Despite her efforts, Zanouba's eyes brim with tears.

23 · THE SEBOO

A week has gone by since the birth of little Farida. With Abd el Meguid's consent, she received that name after all.

The room where Zanouba delivered is kept darkened. With the shutters closed, not a ray of sunshine comes to play upon the brilliant white walls and bedsheets. At sunset, seven candles are lighted and the candelabra is placed on the night table. The flames quiver, their reflection glinting in the polished brass balls decorating the head of the bed where Zanouba and little Farida sleep.

For six days everyone has kept up a pretense of joyful activity, but Zanouba's room has been an oasis of silence. Even Om Hassan has attenuated her voice and her footsteps. She comes in quietly to change the baby's diapers. Or, she tiptoes into the room bringing her daughter the infusion of *helba*—fenugreek—given to new mothers for strength and to stimulate lactation. Daily, she offers Zanouba and her visitors bread dipped in honey, as is the custom during the week after a baby's birth, to insure that her passage through life will be sweet.

In the morning, women come to visit wearing their best: Om Mahmood, Gaulisar, Narguiss, other relatives and neighbors. They remove their jewelry at the door, knowing that adornment attracts the eye of the envious and causes mother's milk to dry. Their conversation is hushed. They sip steaming caraway tea, sweetened with honey. Om Hassan follows with bowls of the traditional *moghaat* always offered to a new mother and her visitors. Everyone savors the thick, resinous pudding which Sitt Habiba has made herself, generously topped with crushed almonds and hazelnuts. Each one gives advice particularly on how to thwart the evil eye. "Be wary of compliments, my child," says an old neighbor, "they can provoke misfortune." Instead, they all comment on how small Farida is, how poorly she eats, how fussy she seems to be, how sallow her complexion is . . .

Protective talismans surround the baby: a few verses from a Qur'an, a page from the life of the Prophet, some goat hairs from the animal sacrificed to the *djinn*s on the night of the silent *zar,* others plucked from the hide of a female black cat, a white dog, the wings of a bat, a sliver of gazelle horn, and even the prized tooth of a dead man, given to Om Hassan by one of the Sudanese *codia*s.

The women curtail their visits in order not to tire the new mother. After they depart, silence settles over the room once again. The hours seem endless, spent in the familiar company of guardian angels believed to hover over a new mother and child. Farida sleeps peacefully beside Zanouba.

On the seventh day the period of confinement ends. It is the day of the *seboo.*

At ten o'clock in the morning Om Hassan throws open the shutters, allowing golden rays of sun to flood the room. Farida, her eyes unused to the light, begins to whimper, then to cry. Zanouba herself blinks, trying to adjust to the sudden change. Gently, she turns and smiles tenderly at her daughter.

On a special table prepared for the ceremony Om Hassan has set out what is needed for the ritual. In a deep, brass dish half filled with water, some fava beans have sprouted. These tender, green shoots will insure the child a long life. In a shallow bowl, surrounding a porous, clay *olla*—a drinking bottle filled with fresh water—are fifty gold coins which will make her rich. The wide mouth of the *olla* is sealed with the head of a doll wearing a little girl's scarf on which the women have pinned every one of their brooches. Around the long, narrow neck of the bottle they have hung much of the family's jewelry—necklaces, ear and ankle rings, bracelets. The unglazed grey-green clay beneath is almost invisible.

Plates of beans, rice, lentils, alfalfa, fenugreek, and barley are an offering to the spirits. To insure that the child will grow and flourish, two long candles burn slowly, in a large pot filled with clean, sifted sand. Beside Zanouba's bed is an enormous dish piled high with mounds of nuts and raisins, dates and sweets as well as carob pods to suck. Om Hassan contemplates the display. She wishes the water bottle had been topped with a *tarboosh* instead of a girl's headscarf. But, God in his infinite wisdom has willed it otherwise. She sighs, resigned.

Zanouba is sitting on her bed bolstered by pillows. Her mother is helping her put on a new white dress and a head scarf embroidered with fine gold thread. Her two long, black braids dangle down her back. On her shoulders Om Hassan places a gauzy white scarf, then turns her attention to dressing the baby. Farida, fussing and crying, is swaddled in her grandmother's voluminous black shawl, laid down on the bed, and covered with Zanouba's white wedding veil.

The midwife arrives first, followed by Om Mahmood, Narguiss, Gaulisar and all the other guests. Neighbors, relatives, and servants mingle joyfully, congratulating the new mother and her mother. Each lifts the baby's veil to get a look at little Farida and places a gift of gold beside her: a bracelet, a necklace, earrings, a hand of Fatma, attached to a tiny gold pin to ward off the evil eye . . . And, no one forgets to reward the midwife. Each guest drops a silver coin into a dish filled with water, honoring her for her efforts.

As everyone gathers in Zanouba's small room, crowding together and gossiping, voices grow louder, some almost shrill. Each guest is handed a lighted candle. A moment later the ceremony begins. Then the midwife picks up the baby and, holding her over one shoulder, leads the women in procession through the house. On the palm of her left hand she balances a dish full of grains and salt crystals. With her right hand she scatters the mixture, chanting, "Oh, salt of our home, protect our children!"

Solemnly they all proceed to the courtyard, singing:

> Baby, baby, walk nice and straight.
> May your feet grow strong, may your feet grow steady.
> With every step you take, take care not to falter.
> Take care not to fall.
>   Angels who have watched over baby's birth,
> embrace and protect her, this child is your sister,
> this child is your own.
>   Give her today a tongue sweet as sugar.

Give her a face as fair as the moon.
And, if God wills it, vigilant ones,
give her a brother, as her father's right hand.

The women stroll casually behind the midwife and repeat each verse as she sings it. Candle wax drips on dresses, carpets and floors. No one minds. Singing, the procession goes full circle, finally reentering Zanouba's room.

Glory be to the Prophet!
May the one who denies his powers
be struck blind by a grain of salt!
To this child the name Wealth must be given.
How black are her eyes and how piercing her gaze.
May God shield her from the eye of the envious,
and spare her eyes from infirmity.
Allah! Allah! Grant this child long life,
a life as long as that of our oldest member.

The women chant "Allah! Allah!" They encircle the midwife. A servant brings a sturdy flat sieve, with high sides, normally used to sift flour. The midwife places the baby in it then, squatting on the floor, tosses her up and down as if she were a handful of grain. On her tiny trampoline, the startled Farida shrieks. But a little crying doesn't matter, since this brief shock will preserve her from stomach ailments for the rest of her life! However, only by looking at the contracted features of the baby can the company see she is crying. The clamor in the room is deafening. In one corner, a servant rhythmically pounds a mortar into an empty brass pestle, a ritual to strengthen the baby's ears, accustom her to noise and keep her from becoming a nervous child.

Once this is over, the midwife replaces the sieve, the wailing Farida still in it, back on the floor. In chorus, the women intone a litany intended to enlighten the baby.

"Be respectful to your father, obedient to your mother,

submissive to your husband, docile toward your mother-in-law," they chant several times.

The baby grows quiet, exhausted by its own efforts. The midwife places a carefully wrapped bundle beside her: Farida's umbilical cord and the knife used to cut it, additional precautions to insure that her mother's milk will be abundant.

Zanouba is helped out of bed by her mother and the midwife, for the first time during the entire ceremony. Although she is still shaky, she is instructed to go out of the room and return seven times to guarantee that her child will live at least seven times ten years. Next, Zanouba is helped across the sieve containing the sleeping Farida. She goes back and forth seven times to make sure that no curse will blight her chances of conceiving again. Zanouba, weary, is helped back to bed just as the little Farida begins to cry again. As Zanouba prepares to nurse her baby, the company trickles out, leaving the two alone. To quiet her daughter, she puts her warm nipple against the little mouth, watching tenderly as her milk begins to flow.

In the next room, two or three women have begun a song in praise of the mothers of daughters.

> When they told me it was a girl,
>   my heart rejoiced.
> God has sent me a friend,
>   a busy friend who washes and sews,
>   a friend who cooks and makes sweets for her mother.
> When my daughter marries, she will give me a boy.
> He will love his grandmother even more than his mother
>   loved her own mother.
> When they told me it was a girl,
>   my heart rejoiced.
> The mother of sons has troubles of her own.
> Her eyes are not free of tears.
> She must be attentive to her mother-in-law's every need.
> In my own daughter's son, I will have a son with none

of the heartaches of the mothers of sons.
Happy, happy are the mothers of girls!
Anxious, anxious are the mothers of boys!

Zanouba shakes her head as she listens. Why this pretense? Why try to console her with words? A girl is nothing
but a girl no matter what they say. Why has God not
granted her a son? She would have been so proud to show
him off to her husband!

She considers her beloved Abd el Meguid. He hasn't
been back to see her since Farida's birth. Will he remain
away for the whole forty days? She senses the depth of his
discouragement because she knows him so well now. Will it
keep him from her? Will he keep his anguish to himself?
Zanouba, seeing him in her mind's eye, cannot repress a
muffled sob. Her chest heaves, pulling the nipple from the
nursing baby. Farida cries. Zanouba looks sadly at her
daughter. She whispers, "Oh, little grain of a woman, will
you ever know what grief your birth caused? Poor little
creature! To you the world is still no more than a drop of
milk running down your throat!" She replaces the nipple in
the baby's mouth, and soon forgets her. Farida suckles,
pressing her little fist against her mother's breast.

Zanouba is lost in thought. She soon forgets the room
where she is. She forgets the women singing outside her
door.

An image of Abd el Meguid haunts her. She sees him
kneeling in prayer, his hands stretched heavenward. His
beard is completely white. His lips are trembling. His face is
marked by sorrow. And his eyes which so lovingly embraced the child she was when he married her, are sad, so
sad that it breaks her heart.

Zanouba remembers the kind old husband she loves.
Her eyes fill with tears, which fall silently upon the child,
quietly nursing.